Heart to Heart

PENELOPE FREED

Heart to Heart

Editing by Caitlin Fitzgerald, Lasairiona McMaster, and Corrine Basmaison
Cover design by Vanilla Lily Designs
Interior design by Stephanie Anderson, Alt 19 Creative

ISBN: 978-1-7364893-3-8

For T, B & D

For teaching me how to love,
how to be brave,
and to embrace the things that make me who I am,
dorky bits and all.

CHAPTER ONE

Trevor

MY FEET pound against the sidewalk. My pace matching the unforgiving beat of the music blasting in my ears. *The squeak of her crutches against the urgent care floor as she walked away.*

Angry lyrics can't drown out Hannah's voice in my head.

That wasn't your decision to make, Trevor.

I suck in oxygen, blow it back out. I wish I could exhale the weight of my guilt with it.

I'm done here.

Loki's tongue lolls out of his mouth as he keeps pace beside me. At least *he* won't leave me. Wind whips across my face as I pour more speed into my burning thighs. But I can't outrun the absolute betrayal on Hannah's face when she realized what I'd done.

"On your left," I call out as we pass my neighbor running in the same direction as us. Even that doesn't get the usual smile from me.

We're done.

I slow as I turn the corner onto my street, admitting to myself no magic number of miles I run will ease the sharp pain in my chest at the thought of her. My heart is broken and it's my own damn fault.

I attempt to control my breathing, knowing I'll be back out here in the morning for another three-miler, the burning in my chest having nothing to do with my running and everything to do with Hannah. Running myself into oblivion is the only relief I've found from the broken record of my thoughts. I could spend the whole day outside, pounding my feet against whatever pavement I can find. Instead, I settle for my usual 5k loop, following the route my dad and I mapped out, back when I was in middle school and Loki and I needed a way to release all of our pent up energy.

"We're home!" I call out as Loki pushes the door open with his nose. "Peggy?" Unclipping his leash and hanging it on the hook by the door, I call out for my little sister.

"That's not my name, dummy!" She pokes her nose out of her room, already dressed in her dance clothes. "Loki!" He trots over to her, shoving his nose in her stomach to say hello. "Ack!" We've never figured out exactly what kind of mix Loki is, but he's huge. Over the years we've guessed there's some Labrador, maybe some Mastiff, Ridgeback, or even Greyhound. All I know for certain is he's black and brown, comes up almost to my waist, and is too smart for his own good. Hence the name.

"Technically, it could be," I goad Mags. "Peggy is a well-known nickname for the name Margaret." My little sister also has the take-no-shit attitude of one Peggy Carter, which is why I started calling her that.

Mags just huffs at me, flipping her curly brown hair over her shoulder. "I know, but I hate it. Why can't you just call me Mags or Maggie like everyone else?"

"What would be the fun in being just like everyone else?" I scratch Loki's head as he wanders past me, aiming for his water bowl. Catching a whiff of myself, I wrinkle my nose. "I'm going to take a shower, don't do anything stupid."

"Pfft, I'm not the one who's been out for two runs today." Mags/Peggy eyes me thoughtfully. "I think the better question is, are *you* okay?" Shrugging, I don't say anything, the momentary distraction of the run and teasing my sister gone in a blink, bringing back the weight of my actions last weekend and the ache in my chest from missing Hannah. "I would hug you, but..." Maggie's wrinkled nose says more than words.

"Yeah, yeah. I'm going." I sigh. "Let me know when you're ready to go, okay?"

"I will. My class starts at four."

With a thumbs up, I head down the short hallway between my room and Maggie's, Loki at my heels. We've shared a bathroom for as long as I can remember, our bedrooms on one side of the bungalow-style house, my parents on the other side of the central living space. It's just a big square and we're always getting in each other's way, but since this was my grandparents and great-grandparents house before it was ours, there's no use complaining about it. The only thing that's been updated since the fifties are the ramp out front, the kitchen appliances, and the one-room studio apartment my parents built in the backyard a few years ago that we rent out to local college students.

Plugging my phone in to charge, I can't help checking to see if there are any texts from Hannah. I know there won't be, but it's a habit from the last six months, always waiting to hear from the girl I'm madly in love with. A blank screen is all I get, same as the last five days. I haven't heard a peep from her since she walked—can you call it walking if someone is on crutches?—away from me on Saturday night, leaving my broken heart on the floor of the urgent care waiting room.

Waiting for the water to heat up, I scrub my hands through my hair, staring at myself in the mirror. The question of how to fix this, how to fix us, repeats in my head. When I called the front office at her ballet school to see if they had a therapist on staff who could check her ankle before the performance the next day, I just wanted to make sure she was okay. Admittedly, I was also in an internet-deep-dive-induced panic after spending too much time searching up symptoms. After everything my family has been through in the last few years, can you blame me? Visions of my dad in the hospital kept haunting my dreams. On top of that, she was lying to me about how much pain she was in. It never occurred to me that she would see it as a betrayal.

I spend my shower talking myself into being patient. Giving her space is the goal, no matter how hard it is. But I'm not going to sit here and do nothing forever. I did text Lisa to make sure they made it to California okay, but since then I haven't heard from any of them, not even Tyler. I've been reduced to Instagram stalking, just like before. But she hasn't blocked me, so I'm assuming that means the possibility of forgiveness. If she truly hated my guts she would have, right? I cling to the hope that we'll get through this. Somehow.

No longer smelling like a swamp monster, I flop back on my bed, scrolling through my camera roll. I torture myself with picture after picture of the two of us, smiling, laughing, and kissing. The bliss of the last six weeks while Hannah was here in Seattle, preserved for whenever I need to remind myself of how happy we were before I screwed it all up.

"How much longer do I let you be miserable before I need to stage an intervention?" Maggie says, crawling up onto my bed, plucking my phone from my grasp.

"Give that back." I go to grab it from her sneaky little paws, but she dances back out of my reach. "Maggie, give it back," I growl, when she clutches my phone behind her back. I could pick her up and take it, but I prefer not to manhandle her. The scar on my upper arm is a permanent reminder that she's scrappier than she looks.

"Nuh-uh. You've been the worst all week. Is this about Hannah? She's pretty. What did you do? You were gone soooooooooo long and you never tell me anything! Did she break up with you? Is that why you're so grumpy?" Pretty sure Mags didn't stop to take a breath once.

I reach behind her and snatch my phone back while she inhales before jumping back out of reach. "No intervention required. I'm fine." I'm not fine, but my eleven-year-old sister doesn't need to know that. "I'm not grumpy, I'm just tired," I add. Which is only a half-lie. I am tired, but I'm also grumpy and I know it. Between Hannah leaving, knowing school and cross-country season starts soon, and the daily barrage of emails I get from every college in America—the stress of senior year is already overwhelming, and it hasn't started yet.

"Whatever. I'm ready to go." Maggie walks backwards out my door, waiting for me to follow.

"It's only three o'clock." I sit on the edge of my bed, phone clasped in my hands, hanging between my knees.

Maggie waves a credit card in the air. "Mom promised we could get a snack on the way." Grinning, she walks out of sight. "Come on Grumpasaurus!"

Dragging my hands down my cheeks, I look up when something wet touches my knee. "You wanna come for a ride, buddy?" Loki spins in a circle, his feet scrabbling against the wood floor as he rushes to the door. By the time I have my keys, phone, and wallet, Loki is by the door getting ear scratches from Maggie. Even sitting, he comes up to her chest.

I unlock the van doors and Maggie lets Loki into the backseat. He hops up on the bench seat in the back and flops on his side. Maggie climbs into the front seat next to me, tossing her dance bag onto the floor beneath her feet.

"Ready?"

"Yup! Can we get smoothies?" Maggie asks, kicking her feet.

"Why not?"

Maggie lets me drive in silence for a while, scrolling through her phone while I stew in my own brain. I miss Hannah with every beat of my pathetic heart. I'm pulling into the parking lot when Maggie makes a funny "eep!" before glaring at me.

"What?" I ask, eyes scanning for a parking spot.

"You didn't tell me Hannah won the Grand Prix." I park the van before I turn to answer, rolling down our windows before turning off the engine. "Trev! I'm serious, why didn't you tell me?"

Loki hops onto my seat the second I slide out of the van, sticking his big face out the open window as soon as I close the door and move away. "You just figured this out? Some secret agent you are Peggy," I tease, instead of giving her a straight answer.

Unfortunately, my voice cracks a little on the last word, my throat closing up from talking about the girl I miss so much. "But to answer your question, yes. She won the regional Grand Prix in California and was in the top fifteen in the Finals. Happy now?" I hold open the door for her and we step inside the smoothie shop, the scent of fresh fruit tickling my nose.

Maggie huffs and stares up at the menu. "I can't believe you didn't tell me." She crosses her slim arms over her chest. I stifle a laugh at the muttered words. Since Maggie's eleventh birthday back in June, she's been getting nosier and nosier. Puberty hasn't reared its ugly head, but it will soon. I'm just hoping I'll be away at college when the worst of it hits.

Instead of laughing at her, I drape my arm around her shoulder. "It doesn't matter now. She broke up with me before she left. Besides, she lives in California, it was always going to be hard." I hide behind the excuse I've been telling myself for the last five days. Not that it mattered to me in the last six months, but right now it's keeping me from falling apart.

"Yeah, but she lives by Aunt Rachel and Uncle Tom, right?" I nod. "So, we go see them all the time." She points out the obvious like I haven't thought the exact same thing a thousand times since January. Like I didn't beg to go to California for Spring Break this year, or back in June.

Instead of pointing out to Mags that the reason I couldn't go in June was because of her birthday and dance recital, I push her in front of me so she can order her smoothie. I have them add extra protein powder to mine. I did run twice today and coach will kill me if I don't keep on top of my nutrition this year. Not with a podium at State and college recruitment on the line.

Mags cranes her neck to look up at me, before she speaks again. "I'll let you be sad this week, but that's it. You suck when you're grumpy."

I just shake my head. "I know Peggy, I know."

I LET MAGGIE'S chatter with our parents wash over me at dinner, lost in my thoughts until Dad addresses me directly. "So, two more weeks until school starts." Dad pushes his plate away from him, while the rest of us finish eating. "Any big plans before you start senior year?"

"Well," I start, hoping that this time it works. "Actually, I want to go visit Tyler. He…uh…invited me to come stay with them the other day." He didn't, but there's been a standing invitation from him ever since Hannah and I started dating. I'm pretty sure that was Olivia's doing, but I'll take any help I can get right now. Hannah is still ignoring my phone calls and texts, I need to go see her in person if I'm going to fix this.

"Is that so?" Dad eyes me for a second before glancing at my mom. "What do you think, Sweetheart?"

I hold my breath, hoping they'll say yes. I might just go anyway, even if they say no, but since my eighteenth birthday isn't for another few months, technically, I shouldn't. Mom gives me a long look. "And how do you propose you get there?" Ha! Prepared for this exact question I pull my phone out of my pocket so I can show her what I've researched.

"I've been saving my tutoring money for a while, and flights are pretty cheap right now." I never had a plan for that money, I just started saving it because I couldn't think of anything else to spend it on. A flight to try and win back my girl is definitely worth it.

"I don't know, it's kind of last minute..." Mom says, scrolling through the flight options I gave her. She glances at my dad, worry flashing across her face.

"Please, Mom? This is the last chance I'll have to go down there before all the craziness of senior year starts. I was hoping for a chance to relax." When she doesn't say anything I go for the Hail Mary. "I could take a look at UCLA while I'm there." I was hoping to win them over without throwing out the vague promise of looking at my dad's alma mater, but desperate times call for desperate measures, right?

"Who's going to take care of Loki?" Dad asks.

"What do you say Peggy? Will you take care of Loki for me? You did pretty good when I was gone for running camp." I add, buttering her up. When she hesitates I send her a smile, hoping it will win her over.

Mags crosses her arms over her chest, dinner forgotten. "This weekend is the auditions for PSB's Nutcracker, maybe I don't have time. What's in it for me? And for how long?"

Ignoring the comment about PSB, I'd forgotten that Mags was planning to audition this year, I scrunch my face and pretend to think. I drag it out, hoping she'll offer up a suggestion of what she wants before I commit to anything. "Will you take me and Abby to the movies? *And* buy us popcorn and candy?" Before I can open my mouth to agree, Mags yells, "And a slushie, too!" With a furtive glance at Mom, who never lets her get both, Maggie sits back in her chair and waits for my answer.

"As long as Mom says that's okay. Name the time and the place, Agent Carter, and you've got yourself a date."

That problem solved, I turn back to my parents, ready to pull out the puppy dog eyes. "Please?"

Mom takes her time before answering, cutting a piece of chicken and popping it in her mouth before looking at my dad again. I hold my breath while I wait for her to swallow. The dramatics giving me hope she'll say yes.

"Does going to California have anything to do with Hannah?" she asks. They didn't meet Hannah at the mock meet at the end of my camp, they only came on Saturday morning since my dad had appointments. I've talked about her often enough that they put two and two together, especially last week when my camp was done but I was still driving over there to have dinner with Hannah every night.

"It has everything to do with her," I admit. "I gotta go win my girl back."

"Well then, in that case," Dad says, smiling at me. "Let's get you to California."

I should have led with that, the softie.

CHAPTER TWO

Hannah

DO NOT throw your crutches.

Do not throw your crutches.

Do not throw your crutches.

My mantra comes to a halt as the end of one of my stupid crutches catches on the doorjamb, almost sending me flying through the door to Mike's physical therapy clinic. I hate these things so much. They hurt my arms, my skin is rubbed raw from them and I can't open a freaking door without knocking myself over. I grit my teeth against the constant frustration bubbling in my chest. Combined with everything else I'm worried about, some days being civil is all I can manage.

"Hannah!" Mike calls my name as he crosses the lobby. "How are you feeling? Having any pain?" I follow him through the door to the treatment room, grateful when he holds it open for me.

"A little achy at night but I've been staying off it, just like I promised."

"We've been keeping an eye on her," Olivia says following me to the table Mike points to, taking the crutches from me so I can boost myself onto the flat surface. Since it's my right ankle that's fractured, I'm not allowed to drive. My mom was going to take time off work to bring me, but with all the uncertainty of me moving to Seattle in a few weeks, she's trying to take as little time off as possible. When Olivia volunteered to drive, I jumped at the chance to take that worry off my mom's plate. Lisa also offered, but to be honest, I have a hard time hanging out with her right now and I'm sure the feeling is mutual.

"Do you have the x-rays?" Mike asks, coming to stand next to the table. Olivia hands them over so he can look at them. I'm crossing as many fingers and toes as I can that these x-rays show how seriously I've been following directions. All my dreams hang in the balance. I know a fracture is supposed to heal cleanly but there are no guarantees, no matter how brave a face I put on for everyone else. If anyone can get me in good enough shape to start training full-time at the Pacific Sound Ballet School in three weeks, it's Mike. He worked a miracle on Ms. Parker, he can work one on me too, right?

Mike spends a long moment studying the x-rays before blowing out a breath. "Well, since it's only been a week, we won't see much change, but I'm glad to have these. Normally, I wouldn't have had you get them again so soon, but I know you're anxious to get back to dancing." He hands the film back to Olivia before undoing the straps on my boot so he can look at my ankle. "For now, we're just going to go over the things you can and can't do, and I'll show you some exercises you can do at home, okay?"

We spend about thirty minutes going through his list. No dance (obviously), as little walking as possible for at least two more weeks, no swimming for one more week. I'm allowed to do yoga sitting up and non-weight-bearing exercise. "You're sure you don't have any pain?" Mike asks for the third time as I slide off the table, my boot firmly strapped back on.

"I promise, no pain as long as I'm careful." And for once I'm being honest. I spent all summer lying about how much pain I was in, which is what led to this mess in the first place. Determined to perform in the end-of-summer-intensive workshop at PSB, I'd kept quiet about my ankle until it was too late.

"Great, let's keep it that way. I'll see you in a few days." Mike waves us out the door.

What we now know was a stress fracture had developed in my fibula over the summer. When I didn't stop dancing on it, it turned into a full-blown crack in the bone. I'd felt it pop as I was dancing on stage in the final workshop performance, only by very good luck had I made it to the end of my last dance before it happened.

Lisa is still pissed at me for hiding it from her.

Well, she's also pissed because I got invited to go back and train at PSB full-time and she didn't. Not that I think she's mad at *me*, I think she's just sad and disappointed for herself since it's been both of our dreams for years.

"Are we going back to your place? Or do you want to go to Katy's? Everyone is over there." Olivia pulls open the door to her car.

"You can just drop me off at home," I mumble. I can't help glancing at my phone. For two days after we left Seattle, Trevor bombarded my phone with texts and phone calls, begging me to talk to him, to let him explain. I'd ignored them all, too hurt by his betrayal to face him. "I'm tired," I add when Olivia doesn't say anything.

It's been a week since I left Seattle, a week since I told him we're done. My heart hurts just as much now as it did when I left him in the urgent care lobby, glassy eyed and shocked. I couldn't bear to see the hurt on his face, so I'd done the cowardly thing and left without looking back. I hate myself for it, but what's done is done.

"Has he called?" Olivia asks, seeing my phone in my hand.

"Not today. He tried calling once yesterday." The texts stopped on Wednesday, the number of phone calls dropping steadily since then. I'm so angry at Trevor but I miss him so much I want to scream. Everything is just *wrong* all the time now. I got so used to him being there for me, whether we were separated by a thousand miles or housed in the same building, he was my rock. And then he took that away when he betrayed me.

Now I'm all alone and it's my own fault.

Olivia shoots me a glance from the corner of her eye. "Maybe I should just force you to come to Katy's house, make you stop avoiding us." I grimace at her words. I have definitely been avoiding everyone. "You know..." she trails off, drumming her hands on the steering wheel instead of answering.

"Know what?" My heart picks up, what does Olivia need to tell me? "Is something wrong? Is it Lisa?"

"Calm down, it's not Lisa. And no, nothing is wrong..." I exhale, relieved, but my nerves stay on edge. "Look, I just think it sucks that you keep avoiding us. You're leaving soon, we should be hanging out as much as possible."

That isn't what I was expecting, and I have a sneaking suspicion that wasn't what Olivia was originally planning to say, but I let it go. She has a point, but I can't help wanting to avoid the sadness in Lisa's eyes whenever she looks at me. Avoiding everyone has been pretty easy since I'm not supposed to be doing anything except resting my ankle.

In the week I've been home I've made a serious dent in the list of movies Trevor was horrified I'd never seen. Every time I finish one, the urge to text him what I think overwhelms me. But then I remember how he almost ruined my chance to train full-time and the urge passes. Or else I cry. It's been a toss-up.

I've also been spending a lot of time with my parents, trying to figure out what happens next, how to send an almost seventeen-year-old to another state to live on her own. To say I'm intimidated by the idea is an understatement. Really, between my broken heart, my broken ankle, fear of leaving my parents and my friends, I've cried so much in the last five days I'm pretty much perpetually dehydrated.

The conversation shifts as Olivia drives us to Katy's house, looks like I don't get a choice in the matter anymore. I suppose I can't avoid my friends forever. Olivia and Katy would never let me get away with it, even if Lisa might. I'm surprised they've let me get away with it for this long.

I flip my phone over in my hand as she drives, wishing it would buzz. I miss Trevor's thousand little texts. Do I even deserve them anymore?

When it does buzz, Olivia's buzzes at the same time, killing any hope that it's Trevor. We started a new group chat including her on the drive home from Seattle. Honestly, it's hard to remember why we excluded her from the old one in the first place.

KATY: Are you on your way? What did Mike say? Are you allowed to swim yet?

Since Olivia is driving I answer for both of us.

ME: I've been kidnapped, Olivia is forcing me to come hang out. Mike says it looks okay, but it's too soon to tell anything. No swimming for another week. Boot has to stay on unless I'm showering or sleeping.
KATY: Good job Olivia. No more avoiding us Banana, we get you for another 3 weeks, I demand you spend as much of it with us as possible.
KATY: Besides, we only have 3 days to plan your birthday!

Another topic I've been avoiding. My seventeenth birthday is on Tuesday. I'd been looking forward to it all summer, Trevor coming up with more and more ridiculous ways to celebrate it. But right now, it doesn't feel like there's anything worth celebrating.

"QUIT RE-READING your texts, we're planning your birthday party." Katy pushes my phone down as she walks past me, forcing me to pay attention to the conversation around me, but the words linger in my mind.

TREVOR: Please just talk to me, let me explain.
TREVOR: I miss you, Twinkle Toes. Can we talk?
TREVOR: How can I make this up to you? I'll do anything.

Does it count as missing him that I want him to be here, but also want to strangle him? Without Trevor I'm adrift, not sure what to do with myself all day. No boyfriend or dance has left me aimless, rudderless. Just drifting along trying to make it through the days until *something* happens again. Anything, really.

"No more sad faces." Olivia leans against Tyler, her legs swung over the side of the loveseat to my right. "It's your seventeenth birthday party, *and* you're about to move to Seattle, we have to do something big."

"Pool party?" Lisa looks around the Quinn's house from the armchair where she's sitting, Hunter on the floor between her legs. Maybe I'm the only one who notices that she never meets my eyes. Or maybe I'm just imagining things. Whether it's on purpose or not, it still has me shrinking back into the couch cushions.

"That's boring, we're always here," Jack complains.

I jump in, hoping to smooth over the hurt on Lisa's face. "I wouldn't want to impose…"

"I was going to suggest bowling, but I don't know if you'd be able to manage." Hunter waves in my direction, his eyes never leaving the TV, even as he presses a quick kiss to Lisa's knee.

"Disneyland?" Jack offers from his spot on the floor. "No!" The momentary distraction cost him his lead in Mario Kart, Tyler's chuckle letting me know who took it. Olivia takes her hand off her controller just long enough to high-five her boyfriend before concentrating on the game.

"Dummy, Hannah can't walk that much." Katy hits Jack upside the head as she passes him on her way back, JJ following in her wake, arms full of water bottles.

"Ow! We could get her a wheelchair, then we'd be able to get on all the rides easier."

"I see, just using me for my ability to get you on all the rides," I tease back from my spot on the couch, cracking a smile for the first time since Olivia and I arrived.

Jack throws a grin over his shoulder at me. "Can you blame me?"

Katy lifts my foot from the couch cushion before sitting next to me, laying it back down on her lap as JJ sits next to her. "What about a bonfire at the beach?" JJ hands out water bottles. "We could make a whole day of it."

"I don't know, I feel like walking on the sand isn't the smartest…" I hesitate, unscrewing the cap and taking a sip of water.

Reaching back to pat me on the leg, Jack grins. "Bet that wheelchair and Disneyland is sounding better and better, right?" Debate about what to do for my birthday continues, the logistics of the beach versus a day at Disney being hashed out without any input from me.

I let the conversation wash over me, only answering direct questions. Jack and Olivia each trying to drum up support for their activity of choice. Is it weird that Jack seems to have taken on the job of looking out for me? But I suppose it makes a kind of sense. Everyone else has a partner, ready-made back up, Jack and I are the only ones here without a significant other. Not that Jack couldn't have his pick of the girls at school, but for the three weeks I have left before moving to Seattle, I'm grateful that when everyone else pairs off I won't be as obvious a third—seventh—wheel, like I was at the beginning of the summer.

I miss Trevor.

My phone buzzes in my pocket and I whip it out, for one happy moment thinking that it's going to be Trevor. My heart sinks at the unknown number, until I read the message.

> **UNKNOWN:** Hey love, guess who got themselves a fancy new American phone?

There's just one person I know who would be texting me about getting an American phone.

> **ME:** Roberto Bolle?
> **ME:** No, wait, this must be Ivan Vasiliev.
> **ME:** Or maybe Kimin Kim?

I save his contact info while I wait for his reply.

> **MARTIN:** Haha, very funny. A real crack up. How's the ankle? Any news?
> **ME:** PT says it's too soon to know. Still not allowed to do anything.

I send him a quick snap of my booted foot resting on Katy's lap. I flip the camera and send him another snap of my sad face. Katy catches me and raises an eyebrow. "Martin," I mouth at her.

> **MARTIN:** I take it you still haven't made up with Trevor? You wouldn't look so depressed if you had.

I tune out my friends and let my fingers type. Somehow, it's easier to talk to Martin over text than to articulate how I'm feeling to my friends. Maybe because I keep wavering between wanting to be with them as much as possible, and wanting to get the leaving over with so I can stop worrying about it. But now I don't even know when I'm going to Seattle. Everything happened so fast at the end of the intensive, but because of my stupid ankle, it's all up in the air. The waiting is torture.

> **ME:** No. Not yet. I don't know what to do. I'm still angry. But I'm sad, too. Name an emotion and I'm feeling it. Am I being ridiculous?
> **MARTIN:** I think you should at least let him explain. You didn't even give him a chance. I'm not saying what he did was right, but he deserves a fair shake.

Martin's words simmer in my mind as I look around the room. Olivia has said more than once that I'm being ridiculous and should just forgive him already. But of course she's going to say that, Tyler and Trevor are cousins. Katy thinks I'm being over-dramatic, but she wasn't there. She doesn't understand what the intensive was like, what the pressure is like. I wish I knew what Lisa was thinking.

I miss her almost as much as I miss Trevor.

"Hannah?"

I drag my eyes away from my phone to find everyone looking at me. "What?"

"Um, it's your birthday, don't you have an opinion?" JJ asks from her end of the couch.

Oh. Right. My birthday. "Not Disneyland. Other than that, I don't care." I shrug. It's true. Without Trevor here, nothing sounds like fun. He was the one who made everything fun, always coming up with plans. I go back to my conversation with Martin. Sometimes I think he's the only one who understands what I'm going through. Except for the breaking up part—he and Sammy are still happily together.

> **ME:** How's the apartment hunting going? Did you and Sammy find a place yet?

Yeah, that's a whole other thing I'm worried about that my friends just don't understand. PSB doesn't have any kind of dorms or school affiliation so my parents and I have been trying to figure out how I'm going to finish school and where I'm going to live.

You know, ordinary, normal, high school stuff.

> **MARTIN:** So…about that.
> **MARTIN:** Things here are…a bit tense?
> **ME:** What happened????
> **MARTIN:** Sammy's visa got denied. He's going home on Monday.
> **MARTIN:** To NZ.
> **ME:** What?!?!? OMG, what are you going to do? Is there someone else you can get a place with? What about that friend of Rebecca's? The place you were subletting during YIPG?
> **MARTIN:** No space for me, already tried. I'm working on it.
> **MARTIN:** As for Sammy, wish me luck. Let's just say he isn't taking it well.

I get a snap of Martin pulling a face to go with his last message. Why is everything falling apart for us? Is this what we get for trying to be more than normal teenagers?

"Hey Hannah? Are you ready to go?" Lisa lays a hand on my shoulder. "I have to take Ray to swim camp—I can give you a ride home if you want?"

"Oh, yeah." I'm surprised to see Hunter still on the floor, engrossed in the game he's playing with the guys. Lisa hasn't offered to hang out alone with me since we got back from PSB last week. "That would be great, thanks." I swing my legs down off Katy's lap and say my goodbyes while Lisa holds my crutches for me.

Neither of us says anything until we're in the car, my crutches tucked awkwardly between my legs, poking me in the chin. It's Lisa who breaks the silence first. "I'm not mad at you for going to Seattle."

"But you *are* mad at me?" I ask, noticing her pointed explanation.

"I'm hurt that you lied to me about your ankle, I'm mad that you didn't tell me you got invited to go back for the fall and I'm furious that you were going to spend your last three weeks here avoiding us. Avoiding *me*. We should be hanging out as much as possible before you leave." Lisa's tone gets sharper with each word, slicing through my self-absorbed funk.

I swallow hard, I guess we're hashing this out now whether I want to or not. "I'm sorry I didn't tell you my ankle wasn't getting better. I was afraid you'd tell someone, and they'd make me stop dancing." Lisa just raises an eyebrow at me. "I know! It wasn't my finest moment. I know it wasn't smart to keep dancing on it. But I'm going to be fine."

"Fine? You have a freaking fractured ankle Hannah! How is that *fine*?" Lisa explodes at me. "You could have seriously damaged your body—you still don't know how it's going to heal. What part of that situation seems fine? I thought you were smarter than that." Lisa shakes her head, disappointment written all over her face as she turns onto my street. "Geez. You know you're lucky you didn't need surgery, right?"

"Mr. Mike and Dr. Lee both said they think it will heal, Lisa. Even if you think I'm an idiot, I assume you trust their opinions?" I huff. "Besides, if I'd stopped dancing when it started hurting, I wouldn't have gotten offered a spot in the fall. I don't care what you think, I don't regret not telling anyone. I did what I had to do."

Lisa parks in front of my house but locks the door when I go to get out, trapping me. "I never said you were an idiot. I thought we were best friends, that we told each other everything."

"Like you told us about Hunter?" I throw back, not caring that it's a low blow.

"Nope, you don't get to bring that back up, it's old news and we're over it. Besides, that secret wasn't hurting anyone. This is about you not trusting me to help you when you needed it. That's not what best friends do. If you couldn't trust me, you should have at least trusted Trevor. That boy has never wanted anything but good things for you, and you know it. You were too stubborn to see that what you needed was someone to tell you to stop for a second and look at what you were doing to yourself. I think the real reason you're so mad at Trevor is that he knew your body better than you and did something about it—you needed to stop dancing before you broke yourself. And he was right."

She takes a deep breath. "And I know this is stupid, but I'm mad that we won't get to be in Nutcracker together this year. This was supposed to be the year we got to do Dewdrop and Snow Queen together, maybe even Sugar Plum. I know it's lame, but I was excited about it. It just sucks that we won't get the chance now."

Lisa's reminder of everything I'm going to be missing out on back home while I'm off in Seattle hurts more than she intended. How could she know that I've been fighting the urge to stay here where everything is safe?

Tugging at the door, Lisa's words echoing in my head, I manage to get myself out of the car. Lisa doesn't offer to help, just stares out the windshield, gripping the steering wheel with white knuckled hands. Before I can close the door behind me, she blows out a breath. "Hannah?"

"What?" I snap, struggling to get my crutches under my arm on the sloped driveway.

"You're not allowed to avoid us. We only have three weeks before you leave. School starts in a week and a half, we can fight about everything else later."

CHAPTER THREE

Trevor

*P*ACING BACK and forth, scorching heat drifts up from
the concrete into my face, the strap of my heavy duffle bag
already chafing against my skin in the California heat. I
don't have a billion dollars worth of advanced technology to turn
into a fireworks display to win my girl back, like Tony Stark.
What was I thinking? That I'd just show up in California and
everything would be fine?

Well, yeah.

What about her friends? Whose side will they be on? Am
I going to have to win them over? Olivia seems like the best
place to start—she was Hannah's best friend, but surely she'll
be on Tyler's side. I assume that Tyler is going to be on my side.
Cousins, right?

I'm hoping Lisa won't be hard to win over, she was the one
who texted me that they made it home. Is it terrible that I'm
hoping her own anger over Hannah lying to both of us is going
to work in my favor? After spending six weeks hanging out with

her at PSB, I'm counting on Lisa to be on my side. But I don't want to depend on it either. Hannah is leaving her to come be with me, that's gotta sting, right?

Well, she's not leaving California to be *with me*, specifically, but it's the same city so that counts. Besides, I'm hoping that the solution I'm offering to one of her problems wins me big points with everyone. Especially her parents. Oh god, her parents. They're either going to love or hate my idea and I have no idea which.

The noise of planes taking off and landing mixes with the babble of people talking, buses and cars driving by. The sharp smell of dust, car exhaust, and dry heat dries out my nose, leaving my skin dirty and itchy.

"Yo! Trev!" A black SUV pulls up in front of me, Tyler's thick bicep leaning on the open window. Damn, I always forget how built he is in real life. I'm not scrawny, but my wiry runner's build seems like it in comparison to Tyler and his friends.

I toss my bag in the trunk before sliding into the front seat next to him. "Hey, thanks for picking me up, I owe you."

Tyler just laughs. "Don't worry, picking you up earned me major brownie points with the girls." Grinning, he pulls out into the LAX traffic, navigating the sea of cars with ease. We spend the hour-long drive chatting about school and college plans. Junior year for Tyler is almost as stressful as senior year is for me. I avoid the topic of Hannah for now, not wanting my cousin to think it's my sole reason for being here. It is, but I need to remind myself that there's more to life than my girl, even if she's the only thing I can think about most of the time.

It's when we pull up to my aunt and uncle's house that the nerves hit me. "Does she know?" I blurt out, my inner Peter Parker unable to keep it inside any longer.

"Who? Hannah?"

I can't tell if he's messing with me. "No, asshole, I meant Olivia." I give it a beat. "Of course, I meant Hannah. Love you man, but I didn't beg my parents to let me fly down here just to see your ugly face." Tyler laughs at me as he parks in their driveway. Growling under my breath, I pull my duffle out and follow him into the house.

"Trevor!" Aunt Rachel grabs me in a hug, bending me almost in half to plant a kiss on my forehead. "I hear you're here to win back a girl?" Groaning, my cheeks flair bright red with embarrassment at Tyler and Uncle Tom's chuckles. "Oh hush you two. You'd do the same thing and you know it."

"I wouldn't screw it up with my girl in the first place," Tyler gloats.

"Don't get cocky." I glower. "I know an embarrassing story or two I could tell Olivia."

Uncle Tom chokes on a laugh but ducks out of the way of Aunt Rachel's smack to his arm. "I'll let Aaron know you made it, unless you already did?" My dad is Uncle Tom's younger brother, they've been close for as long as I can remember which is why Tyler and I are so close, despite growing up in different states. When my dad was in the hospital, Uncle Tom stayed with us for a few weeks, helping my mom deal with everything.

"I did text them." I grab my duffle bag. "Do you guys mind if I shower real quick?"

Aunt Rachel nods her head toward the stairs. "Sure thing sweetie, you're in the usual room. We didn't think you'd be planning to spend the week with us old farts, don't worry about us. You boys enjoy your time."

Tyler leads the way up the stairs, not that I need help, I've been staying in the same guest room here my whole life. "So, quick question—did you want to get started on the groveling right away or...?" He walks backwards up the stairs, grinning.

"Shower first, groveling second." I have a whole plan laid out in my head, I'm just praying it works. "Think you can find a way to get Hannah out of the house?"

"I got this. You go clean up."

After my shower, Tyler leads the way outside. When I throw a questioning look as we pass his car, he grins. "Jack's house is that one with the red front door on the end of the street. I always walk, it would be weird if I didn't."

"Are they there?" I ask, making sure I'm following the plan. We head down the street toward the Quinn's house, my heart racing and my stomach clenching with each step. I force myself to breathe slow and steady, doing what I can to stay focused and calm. Now is not the time to panic.

"Yeah, I saw Lisa and Olivia's cars out front. Olivia said she was picking Hannah up on her way over. She's one-hundred percent Team Trannah, by the way. I don't know about anyone else, but you've got the two of us on your side."

"Trannah? That's a terrible couple name." I grimace. "Hannor?" I can't argue with the face Tyler pulls. "Yeah, they're both terrible."

Tyler slaps me on the back, nearly sending me tumbling down the steps leading up to the front door. "You ready?" Without bothering to knock, he opens the front door.

"Yup. Let's do this." I have a girl to win back.

MAY HAVE overestimated my ability to channel Tony Stark this time. Hannah's looking at me like there's no way in hell I'm going to charm my way out of this one.

"What are you? How? What?" I'm pretty sure if it wasn't for the enormous black boot on her foot, she would have run inside the moment she laid eyes on me. The crutches hiding under the lounge chair she's laying on are probably working in my favor too. Everyone else is scattered around the backyard—in and out of the pool that takes up most of the space back here.

"Hi." Six sets of eyes stare at me as I wipe my hands on my shorts. This was much easier in my head. Without an audience. I glance around at everyone else. Tyler has Olivia gathered up in his arms, in the middle of saying hello, but she throws a grin at me over her shoulder. Lisa is eyeing me warily from her perch on the edge of the pool, her legs dangling in the water. Hunter is in the water next to her, his elbows hooked over the edge of the pool.

Katy and JJ are in the water, floating in the middle of the pool. Well, they were until I showed up. Now they're treading water, sizing me up. Maybe surprising everyone wasn't the best beginning to my plan.

I clear my throat, nerves clogging it. "Uh, surprise?" I add a little jazz hand action to my words, praying someone laughs. I don't bother to check, I only have eyes for the girl I came here for.

My beautiful Hannah doesn't say anything, her wide blue eyes turning glassy but never leaving mine. I take another step toward her, unsure what she's thinking. Tyler and Oliva won't stop me, but I can't guess how anyone else feels about me being here. Splashing behind me and the slap of wet feet on cement is the only warning I get before a heavy hand on my shoulder stops me. Hannah flinches and turns away before I gather my thoughts enough to see which twin has his hand on my shoulder.

Not surprising, it's Hunter, Lisa at his side. "Hey man, good to see you. You wanna come help me with something for a second?" Lisa scoots around him to perch on the edge of Hannah's lounge chair, giving him a long look before turning to Hannah.

The hand on my shoulder pulls me away from the girls. I could push him off, but I'm not here to cause a scene. Instead, I follow Hunter and Jack, who has joined us, to the house. Sending one last look over my shoulder, Hannah is already surrounded by the other girls, hands flying as they argue in harsh whispers. Jack and Hunter lead me around the side of the house to what must be the garage. Pushing the door open, Hunter leads the way, dripping water on the cement floor inside.

"So," Hunter starts, letting Jack and Tyler make their way over to the fridge in the corner. "I assume you're here to grovel in person, since she won't take your phone calls?"

"Um, yeah?" I answer, not sure whose side he's on. "You guys know I didn't mean to hurt her, right?" If I can get the guys on my side that will make all of this much easier.

Jack laughs, pulling soda cans and water bottles out of the fridge, handing some to Tyler to carry, my cousin must have snuck in behind me. "Yeah we know. Don't worry, we didn't bring you here to slice off your balls or anything." I exhale loudly at his words, earning another laugh from all three of them.

"Your face, Trev!" Tyler laughs, bumping elbows with Jack since both their hands are full. "I told you man, we got your back."

"I'm not gonna lie, I'm really glad you didn't tell me you have a Hulk." I tip my chin in Jack's direction. He's built enough to play the part.

The guys look at each other in confusion for a second, my reference not registering with them for one long embarrassing minute before Jack chuckles. "Oh my god. It's such a waste that you don't live here, that would be an awesome Halloween costume and you would make a perfect Loki—you look like him. I could totally rock a pair of ripped purple pants. Although Mom would kill me if I got green paint all over the house."

Tyler grins and turns his back to us, looking over his shoulder. "What do you think? America's ass?" Hunter pulls something out of his pocket and flicks it off Tyler's butt. The ringing of the penny hitting the cement floor echoes in the empty garage.

"It's okay, I guess." Hunter winks at Tyler who laughs right back. I wish I had a group of guys like this at home. Derek and Matt are my closest friends, but I don't hang out with them much outside of school—I've always had too many other things to take care of. "Listen, Trevor. We," he points to the guys and himself, "are on your side. It's the girls you gotta watch out for. Lisa is ready to be won over, she's too busy dealing with her own issues to be mad at you."

"Katy and JJ are mad at you for Hannah's sake, but I'm pretty sure they can be bought." Jack adds, handing me the drinks in his hands so he can rummage through the plastic bin full of individual chip bags beside me. How much food does this family keep in their house? Now that I'm not fearing for my life, or the lives of my future children, I take a second to look around the garage.

Shelves line the walls on two sides. One side holds an assortment of the random tools and paint cans you'd expect to find in a house. But the shelves on my side of the garage look like someone picked up one of everything at the local Costco. Hunter notices me eyeing the shelves and grins. "We have an older brother. My mom cleans out Costco once a month."

Tyler leads the way out the door, jerking his head to indicate I should follow. "My mom goes with her and splits the bill. She says it's because I eat half of it." The guys all laugh at the old joke. "Take those to the girls." He pushes me in front of them with a grin.

The moment I round the corner of the house and see the girls, the grin drops off my face. Hannah is still sitting on the lounge chair, Olivia and Lisa perched on either side of her. Katy and JJ are standing at the end, towels wrapped around their shoulders as they talk to her. I can't tell if the arrangement is meant to keep me out or keep Hannah in. Either way, if I'm going to get to my girl, I'm going to have to fight my way through the protective shield they've formed around her.

"Um, here you go," I swallow hard before I offer up the drinks in my arms, having no idea who wanted what. How did the guys even know what to grab? I never heard them ask. Katy plucks a soda out of my hand, JJ pulling the water bottle tucked in my elbow free. Lisa reaches over for the water bottle in my other hand. One of the sodas starts to fall but Olivia reaches out a hand to catch it before it hits the chair.

"Nice catch." I transfer the lone water bottle in my possession from hand to hand. None of the girls move and Hannah hasn't looked at me yet. I have no idea what to do now. My plan to beg for forgiveness crumbles in the face of this protective flock standing between us. "Hannah…" I choke off at her sharp intake of breath when I say her name.

No one says anything, but my Spidey senses are telling me that the girls are doing that silent communication thing us guys will never understand. Not knowing where to look, I keep my eyes down, watching the water bottle I toss from hand to hand, Hannah's legs and that damn boot the only part of her I can see.

"Good luck," someone whispers in my ear, squeezing my shoulder. I think it's Katy, but I can't be sure. The girls retreat, making space for me to approach. When Olivia pulls Hannah's crutches out from under the lounge chair I panic. I thought she was on my side?

"I'm just going to take these with me," Olivia says, a hint of mischief in her tone. "We'll be over there." She nods her head to the other side of the pool.

"Olivia! Give those back!" Hannah sits up, trying to grab the end of the crutches before Olivia can walk away with them, but somehow, Lisa is in the way—was that on purpose—and she misses. With a groan, she lays back in the chair, an arm thrown over her face.

It's only been a week since I've seen her, but it feels like longer. With the girls gone, I drink in the sight of her long, slim legs, the muscle tone evident even when she's lounging. Her pale, creamy skin is tempting, memories of running my fingers over it assaulting me. I'm thirsty for her like a man trapped in the desert, terrified she's a mirage.

She's wearing a pair of jean shorts, a plain green shirt and some fancy earrings I've never seen before. With the exception of the earrings, it's almost exactly what she wore on our first date in Seattle. I know it's not on purpose, but memories of that night stab at my heart, reminding me of her stubbornness, the way Hannah can be blind to anything but her own hurt. Then I catch a hint of red on the skin of her upper arms, probably from the crutches, and all I want is to soothe the skin, kiss away the pain.

Her thick red hair is loose for once, tumbling over her shoulders. My fingers itch to claim a lock, twirling it like I have a hundred times before. I'd be lying if I didn't also want to tug on it, not enough to hurt, but to remind her of the pain she left me in. Instead, I hand over the water bottle and lower myself to sit next to her, taking the spot Olivia left for me.

Since all my plans blew up the second I met her eyes, I don't know what I'm expecting. I know my girl—I know she's shy and anxious, but I also know she has a core of steel underneath all that. The boot on her ankle is proof enough that she's tough as nails beneath the pretty package. So, when she pulls her arm away from her face I have no idea what to brace for.

I should have known there would be fire in her eyes.

CHAPTER FOUR

Hannah

I SHOULD HAVE known better when Olivia informed me she was coming to pick me up. My phone buzzing against my nightstand had scared the crap out of me, I was so engrossed in my movie. Who knew *Bend It Like Beckham* was so good?

> **OLIVIA:** Get dressed. I'm picking you up in 10.
> **OLIVIA:** Wear something cute.
> **ME:** I was watching a movie.
> **OLIVIA:** You can finish off the list Trevor made you later. 9 minutes.
> **OLIVIA:** Clock's ticking....

What did I need to dress up for? I can't *do* anything, and we were just going to Katy's. Our conversation in the car earlier comes roaring back to me, everything making sense now.

The second I'd slid into her front seat she'd spoken. "Um. Trevor is in town."

I froze, the click of my seatbelt the only sound while I fought to catch my breath. "What?"

"He flew in this morning, he's staying with Tyler, obviously." Olivia shot me another glance. I'm not ready to see Trevor. I'm desperate to see him, but I don't know what to say.

I moved to climb out of the car but Oliva had it in gear and was backing out of my driveway before I could do more than unbuckle my seatbelt, trapping me. "Olivia…I can't. I don't know what to say."

Olivia didn't say anything for a minute, but I knew that face. Olivia's "Tough Love" face. I wasn't going to like what she was about to say.

"Hannah Banana O'Brian, you're an idiot."

That was not what I was expecting. "What?"

"If you don't talk to that boy, you're going to regret it. He's crazy about you and he's doing everything he can to show you how sorry he is."

I'd twisted in my seat to face her, careful not to knock my boot against the center console. "He could have cost me everything," I told her for the millionth time. Why can't anyone understand why I'm so upset about this? "What if they'd pulled me from the show? What if they didn't want to deal with any of my drama? I was already on thin ice with my injury before. The last thing I needed was him interfering."

"Girl, you are losing your mind." Olivia had snapped back at me. "First of all, you were never on 'thin ice' and you know it. How many other people at the intensive had issues? You can't tell me you were the only one who had some kind of injury. Besides,

I heard what Mike said, he thinks the stress fracture started in New York. The injury was inevitable."

None of that was news. I'd already heard it from my mom, Ms. Parker, Lisa, Katy. Everyone keeps pointing out that I over-reacted. Deep down, in a scared little corner of my heart, I agree. I was angry that night in Seattle. I was hurting—literally and figuratively—and I lashed out at Trevor. Logically, I know he was trying to protect me, that he thought he was helping.

I cleared my throat before answering. "I know." My voice so quiet I'm not sure if Olivia even heard me.

"Then why are you being so stubborn about this?"

My shoulders lifted to my ears, brushing the earrings I'd put on this morning in a fit of boredom. "I don't know what to say. I feel terrible," I'd admitted.

"Well, how about you start by not avoiding him anymore?"

How was I to know that when Olivia said Trevor was in town I'd see him not fifteen minutes later? Watching him follow Tyler into the Quinns' backyard sent my heart racing. All I wanted to do was throw myself in his arms and forget about the giant decisions looming over me. But I was still so angry at him.

How is it possible to be so angry and still want him so much? It doesn't seem possible to feel two such opposing emotions at the same time. The way his voice caught on my name, before my friends abandoned me, cracked my heart open. I threw my arm over my eyes, so I didn't have to see the look on his face as he lowered himself to sit next to me. The way those brown eyes begged me for forgiveness without saying a word. It's easier to stay mad when I'm not looking.

Keeping my eyes covered, I remind myself of all the reasons I'm in the right, that I deserve to be angry. Calling the front office of PSB to tell them I was hiding an injury was the worst kind of betrayal. Right? Does it matter that it was true? And because I hadn't stopped dancing, I'd aggravated a stress fracture into a full blown fracture to my fibula? Scrunching up my nose and pulling in a deep breath, I hold onto my anger and drop my arm.

The devastation on Trevor's face almost makes me falter but I stay strong. "I'm still mad at you." I say it out loud to remind myself of how I'm supposed to feel.

"I get that, T. I'm sorry. I really am. Looking back on it, I realize it wasn't the greatest idea I've ever had." I use my hands to push myself up, sitting up straighter. The back of my stupid boot catches, pulling against the slats of the lounge chair, the pressure on my ankle painful for a second before I can get it free.

Trevor doesn't miss my wince of pain, it's obvious from the way his hand shoots out towards me but stops short of touching me. Instead, he balls his hand up in a fist and drops it to his side. He angles his body to face me, one leg bent and resting on the chair. "Please, just listen to me for a second, Hannah. I can't take back what happened. And I don't know if I'd change anything if I could pull an Endgame and go back for a do-over." I open my mouth to protest, but Trevor keeps talking, not letting me argue. "I care about you. All I could see was that you were hurting. I could tell you were in pain, even if you wouldn't admit it. Watching the girl I—" He stops himself, eyes wide. Shocked, I silently beg him to finish that sentence. The girl he what? Trevor closes his eyes for a second, his Adam's apple bobbing as he swallows hard before opening them again.

"Watching you pretend to be fine, pretend that every step you took didn't hurt? Hannah…it was killing me. I couldn't take away your pain, but I could make sure that someone smarter than either of us knew there was a problem. That's what those PTs are for. It's their job to make sure that us athletes are physically okay to compete, dance, whatever. So no, I wouldn't take it back. But I regret not talking to you about it, for not trying harder to convince you to tell them yourself."

Trevor's hand steals up to twirl a lock of my hair around his finger, his eyes glued to it, mesmerized, or maybe just giving me a moment to process his words. My lungs work overtime, trying to take a full breath, but I can't—Trevor's words have stolen it right from my lungs. I thought I'd done such a good job of hiding the pain. That he didn't know and acted anyway, disregarding my words.

"How can I be so mad at you and miss you so much all at once?" The whispered words are out of my mouth before I can stop them. A glimmer of hope burns in his eyes as he looks up, tearing them away from the lock of hair he's claimed. Tears well up in my eyes and I don't bother to fight them. I fall into the warm comfort of his arms and let myself cry for the first time since it happened, the tightly wound bands around my chest finally loosening enough to let them out.

"Hannah!" Katy's voice echoes across the pool. I forgot that we had an audience. Heat burns my cheeks. "Thumbs up if you're okay, thumbs down if you need a rescue?" Without lifting my face from Trevor's chest, I give her a thumbs up behind his back. "Just checking!" she calls.

I'm going to miss my friends when I'm gone.

A gentle hand strokes the top of my head, smoothing my hair back. "Hannah?" Trevor's worried tone pulls me back to the present. "Are we okay?"

I sniff, pulling back so I can look at him. I hate the cautious edge to his smile, as if he's ready for me to rip it out from under him at any moment. "Yeah, I guess we're okay. I think I understand why you did it. I still don't like it, but I can see where you were coming from, I guess."

Tentatively, Trevor runs the back of his fingers down my cheek, his smile growing when I don't pull away. "That's all I ask." We're interrupted from the moment by Olivia plopping down on the chair by my feet.

"Okay lovebirds, enough of the sappy stuff. We have birthday party planning to do."

CHAPTER FIVE

Hannah

"THAT SEAGULL is eyeing your chips," I point out to Tyler from my spot in the shade. It's a little cooler down here at the beach, but only by a few degrees. Lisa insisted we bring the Quinns' big pop up canopy so I wouldn't be stuck sitting in the blazing sun. Even knowing I'll be parked underneath it all day, I'm slathered in the highest SPF sunscreen I could find. The last thing I need is to add a sunburn to all my other problems.

But I'm not thinking about them today. It's my seventeenth birthday and I'm spending the day at the beach with my friends. Olivia wanted to go to Santa Monica, but I insisted we go to one of the beaches closer to home. When I pointed out that using my crutches on the pier wouldn't be very easy, Trevor and Lisa backed me up. I was already worried about the logistics of getting onto the beach without hurting my ankle, but everyone told me not to worry about it.

"Nah, he wouldn't dare." Tyler eyes the seagull, its red beady eyes unblinking.

"I don't know, I wouldn't trust it. That thing looks evil." I laugh back, mentally high-fiving myself for bantering with him. Who would have thought that a year ago the boy I'd been crushing on for years, but who never knew I existed, would be a friend? Life is weird.

"Need anything?" Trevor asks, snatching the bag of chips away from the greedy-eyed seagull. Katy, her brothers, and JJ got here before us and set everything up so that when I arrived with Tyler, Trevor, and Olivia, Trevor could carry me straight to the chair they'd set up for me in the shade.

"Can I have a water?" I don't bother asking for anything else, the heat making me a little grumpy.

I hate to complain when they've gone to so much trouble to set up a fun day for me, but while the sun is out and the heat is scorching, it appears the water is proving more tempting than the pleasure of my company. I'm pretty sure they've assigned each other shifts so that I'm not left alone. The only person who's stayed with me all afternoon is Trevor. Not that I can blame anyone else. But it *is* my party. I'm entitled to be a little put out. Right?

Trevor hands me a cold water bottle, dropping a kiss on top of my head before he sits on the towel next to me. "Here you go." I need to get out of this funk. Tyler takes off to join everyone else down at the water's edge. Are they doing it on purpose so we can be alone? But why would they do that when all I've heard from them all week is that I'm leaving in two weeks and they want to spend as much time with me as possible? I can't keep up anymore.

"So, have you and your parents worked out your plans for Seattle?" Trevor asks. He's trying so hard to be nonchalant about it, but he can't hide the tiny hint of excitement in his words.

"We're still working out the school and living situation." I settle back in my chair, flicking sand off my arm. "I've dreamed of going away to a professional school for years, but I never thought about all the details that went with it. It's so much more complicated than I imagined. I don't want my parents to have to quit their jobs and move with me. I'm almost eighteen, if I was a normal kid, I'd be thinking about moving away to college in a year anyway, so them moving with me seems dumb. But, I'm still a minor so they worry about me being on my own if something happens."

I skip over the long nights of crying and the fact that my mom has snuck into my room to cuddle with me almost every night since I got home. We always knew this was coming, but the reality of leaving them, of growing up overnight, is harder than I ever imagined.

"My dad cancelled all of his travel for the next two weeks so we can be together." Now that I've started talking I can't stop. My friends are all so busy trying to put on a brave face for me that I haven't been able to talk to any of them about this. Trevor is the one person who's not going to have to miss me when I leave, so he gets to endure my word vomit. Besides, isn't that what a boyfriend is for?

"Once I'm moved in, I'll get to see my dad more than my mom, since he travels up that way pretty often and he promised to come see me whenever he can. And I'll be home for some holidays, but..." I shrug. "It's harder to leave them than I thought it would be. I'm not ready to be an adult yet."

Trevor clears his throat and I look down at him. "You know, you can always come hang out with my family whenever you want. In fact." He swallows hard, looking nervous. What is that about? "If you haven't figured out where you're going to live, I have a suggestion."

"What's that?" I know he can't mean to come stay at his house, that would be... too weird. Besides, he told me once they have a three-bedroom house. What would I do, share a room with his little sister?

"Did I ever tell you about the little studio apartment we have? The detached one that we rent out to a student every year?"

"No, but now you have."

"Well, the girl we had staying there last year transferred schools and is moving to Colorado next week. I asked my parents to hold off on finding a new renter until I could talk to you."

My heart stutters in my chest. Live with Trevor? Well, not *with* him, but in his backyard? "Oh, um. Wow..." I don't know what to say.

"Think about it Han, it would be perfect. We could see each other all the time, even if your schedule is crazy busy. My parents will love you and my little sister is already obsessed with you—she's been following you on Instagram for ages and keeps begging me to introduce you."

I let him keep talking while I mull the idea over. On the one hand, I would feel better knowing that there were adults I know nearby, in case of emergency. I know my parents would be happy about that. Would they be happy that my boyfriend was so close? I don't know.

"You'd have your own space, and privacy. You know, in case your parents don't like the idea of you living with your boyfriend.

It's a completely separate building from my house, has its own entrance and everything."

A seed of a thought plants itself in the back of my brain—what happens if things don't work out between us and I'm *right there*. I'm about to start a whole new life, what if we can't work things out? I'd still have to see him every single day.

"I know you said you hadn't figured out the school thing yet, but that would solve your problem. If you're living there, we could go to school together. We could even carpool if you wanted. It would be perfect, Hannah."

School? He wants us to go to school together? This is too much. I need to think, I need to talk to my parents.

"Wow, you've, uh, thought this one through." I stall, picking my words carefully. I do not want to fight with him about this, we just got back together. "I have to talk to my parents about it." Taking a sip from my water bottle so I don't have to say more, I stare out at the ocean, Trevor's voice washing over me.

Truthfully, my mom and I decided last night that I would enroll in an online high school. We've been doing research since I came home and found one that will let me combine my last two years of high school into one, so I can take my GED and graduate at the end of this year. Knowing how hard it was for Ms. Parker to juggle finishing school with her first year in the company at CBC, I want to make sure I'm ready for whatever happens next in my life.

Does it mean I'll miss out on all those supposed normal high school experiences? Yeah. But I've never cared about them anyway. The single sporting event I've been to is the track meet Lisa and Katy dragged me to last year and things like Homecoming and Prom pale in comparison to the chance to be a professional ballet dancer.

I could go my entire life without receiving a promposal and be perfectly happy. In fact, if anyone ever did one for me, I would throw up from embarrassment on the spot. Even watching YouTube videos of them has my stomach roiling with second-hand embarrassment.

"You could come with me to the games, and it would be so cool to have you come to my meets. Although, I get it if they interfere with your schedule. Do you have your schedule at PSB yet? Are they going to let you start in September?"

"Slow down, Tiger!" I laugh, forcing myself to let go of all the questions I don't have answers to. "I don't know anything right now. Can we just enjoy the day?"

Instead of answering, Trevor gives me a long look, then takes my water bottle from me, digging it into the sand next to him.

"What are you—" I don't get to finish my thought before he's on his feet and tugging me out of my chair.

"Sorry, I'll be quiet now. Just tell me to shut up when I get carried away." His grin is so adorable, I can't help leaning forward to kiss him, my hands splayed across his chest for balance. I've spent so much of the last week with everyone at the Quinns' pool that I didn't think twice about the fact that we're all in our bathing suits. Now that my hands are firmly against the warm skin of Trevor's chest and his hands are resting on my hips, awareness blooms through me making my heart beat a little faster.

"You don't have to be quiet, just quit asking me questions I don't have answers to," I tease, doing my best not to sound as breathless as I feel.

Trevor leans down and presses another kiss to my lips, before scooping me up in his arms. "Want to go down to the water?"

I eye the crashing waves. "I don't know if it's a good idea…"

"You want to stay here in your chair all afternoon? Just come down for a little bit. I promise to keep you safe." Trevor puts me down, thumping his fist on his chest. "You have my shield, m'lady." He finishes by kneeling in front of me. Of course he sends a cocky smirk up at me from the sand at my feet.

Laughing, I rest my hands on his shoulders for balance, his hands stealing up to hold my thighs. "Oh my God, you're such a dork!" Bracing my hands against his shoulders, I lean down and press a kiss to the top of his head. "But you're my dork and that's all that matters. Fine, I'll go down to the water for a bit."

Trevor looks up at me with a grin. "You know it. Hop on my back, it'll be easier for me to carry you." He turns around so I can loop my arms over his shoulders, then he scoops his arms under my thighs, lifting me onto his back. His skin is hot and sticky against mine, little grains of sand rubbing in rough patches, but I ignore it and focus on enjoying the safety of Trevor's arms.

Picking his way across the hot sand, Trevor takes us right up to the water's edge, stopping once he gets to the packed wet sand. Everyone else is in the water, diving and splashing in the breakers. Katy is the first to spot us, body surfing her way back to shore and popping up out of the water a few feet away.

"Decided to come up for air, have you?" The knowing grin she tosses my way sets my already warm skin on fire.

"Katy!" I hiss over Trevor's shoulder, ducking my head. He just laughs and turns his head to plant a kiss on my nose.

"Oxygen is overrated," Trevor whispers in my ear. "And what about you and JJ, huh?" His gravelly voice carries over the water. "I was worried I was going to have to call the lifeguard for one of you. Although you both look pretty skilled at CPR."

Katy's outraged cry ends in a gurgle when JJ pulls her under water, her splashing progress hidden by the sound of the crashing waves. "You okay?" Trevor checks on me quietly.

"Yeah, I'm okay. Are *you* okay to keep carrying me? I can't be that light." Thinking back to my struggles with pas de deux over the summer and how my partner, Noah, struggled with some of the lifts in the Black Swan pas de deux we'd been cast in. Not that I'm self-conscious about my weight, I'm built pretty slim, but surely he must need to put me down?

"I got you, T. I'm not letting you go."

WRAPPED IN a blanket, I curl up as best I can against Trevor's side, the fire in front of me hot on my face. I gave up not getting sand in my boot hours ago, it's awkward and heavy no matter what I do. The marshmallow Trevor's roasting for me dances above the licking flames as he turns it one-handed. His other arm is draped across my shoulders, pulling me close.

There is something magic about sitting around a fire with all my favorite people. A mix of rightness and sadness fills me as I look around. Olivia is feeding Tyler a bite of her s'more, giggling when he gets a string of marshmallow goo stuck to his chin. The way she leans in and licks it off, not caring about what the rest of us think? Classic Olivia. Lisa and Hunter are comparing the quality of their roasted marshmallows to see whose is more evenly browned. The good-natured competition between them is exactly what I'm going to miss. What am I going to do in Seattle without Lisa to push me?

JJ and Katy are busy eating just the chocolate and graham crackers, but I don't miss the way JJ gives Katy an extra piece of her chocolate, or the way Katy slides an extra graham cracker onto JJ's pile. When JJ leans in to kiss a piece of chocolate off Katy's cheek, I have to look away before I cry. How can I leave these people?

I haven't left yet and I'm already homesick.

"I'm going to miss you guys, you know that?" I blurt out. "I know I don't say it enough, but I'm really going to miss you." Trevor squeezes me against his side and kisses the top of my head.

"What do you think we've been trying to tell you since you got back, dummy?" Katy says. "We're going to miss you too! But you'll be home for Thanksgiving and Christmas, right?"

I shrug. "I assume so? I haven't heard anything otherwise. That's assuming this—" I pick up my ankle and show off my hardware "—is healed and I'm dancing again."

Lisa swallows a sticky bite of her s'more before she speaks. "Have you figured out school yet? You're on your own, right? PSB doesn't have its own academics."

Trevor speaks up when I hesitate. "We were just talking about it earlier. There's a studio apartment at the back of my parents' house, I think Hannah should come live there. Then she could go to Shoreline with me."

Whoah. I never agreed to his plan. Everyone else starts chiming in with what a great idea it is without letting me get a word in.

"Oh my god, you guys can carpool to school every day!" Olivia grins.

"Aunt Ellen and Uncle Aaron are okay with that? Nice!" Tyler reaches over and high-fives Trevor.

The chatter keeps going without me while I silently nibble at my s'more. Lisa is the only one who notices I'm not saying anything. She gives me a puzzled look from across the fire but I just shrug. I don't want to hurt Trevor's feelings by rejecting his idea in front of everyone else, even if the more I think about it, the more questions bubble up in my mind, piling on top of the other million questions I don't have answers to either.

My stomach turns sour and I toss the last bite of my s'more in the fire, no longer hungry. The weight of the decisions I've been putting off crashes down on me. A burden resting on my chest making it harder and harder to breathe. My racing heart sets my stomach clenching. I can't breathe. I need air, need space. This stupid boot makes it impossible to get up by myself. My eyes flick from person to person around the fire, their voices a dull roar in my ears.

How can they all sit there, casually talking about these things that are going to change my life forever? It's not their life, not their dream. *I* haven't decided what I want to do yet, what gives them the right to act like it's so easy? What gives Trevor the right to plan my life out for me? I know we just made up, and he came all the way here to see me, but right now? Trevor is the last person I want to hang out with. I need to get away from the never-ending questions and pressure.

Pushing up onto my knees, I struggle to get to my feet. "Hang on. Let me help you." Trevor starts to shoot up from the sand next to me, but I was using him for balance and the sudden movement pushes me backwards. I land on my back, my right heel thumping against the ground, sending a searing jolt of pain up through my ankle.

"Ah!" Biting my lips hard, I close my eyes against the pain, trying to keep the tears building behind my eyelids from escaping.

"Hannah! Are you okay? I'm so sorry, I didn't realize you were holding onto me." Trevor's hands are running over my shoulder, my leg, the panic in his voice building the longer I stay silent. Keeping my eyes closed, I hold up a hand and shake my head, waiting for the pain to subside before I speak.

"I'm okay." Trevor's hands are still roaming over my body. "Stop it, Trevor. I'm fine." I shrug him off, maybe a little harder than intended. Paired with my sharp words, I don't have to look at him to see I've hurt his feelings. Someone grabs my hands, someone female, and I'm pulled to my feet. JJ hooks an arm around my waist, Katy stepping in on the other side of me.

"You look ready to go home." Katy says in a quiet voice. "Want us to take you?"

Silently, I nod my head, holding on to JJ while Katy throws my stuff in a bag. Trevor keeps opening his mouth like he's going to speak, but no words come out. Knowing I can't leave him like this, no matter how upset I am, I wave him over. Once he's close enough, I let go of JJ and grab his arm, ignoring the rest of my friend's stares. "I'm sorry. I'm just tired and overwhelmed by everything. I'll text you in the morning, okay?"

I pull his head down to press a quick kiss to his sad face.

"Can I carry you to the car at least?" Trevor grabs my hand before I can turn back to JJ.

"Sure." I let him sweep me up in his arms and carry me to JJ's car.

"You'll text me in the morning? Promise?" Trevor tucks a strand of hair behind my ear, worry written all over his face.

"I promise. I'm not mad. I'm just overwhelmed." I squeeze his hand with mine before climbing in the backseat.

I was mostly telling the truth.

CHAPTER SIX

Trevor

*S*PRAWLED ON the bed in the guest room, my hair almost dry after my shower, I've read her text a dozen times, trying to figure out how to respond.

> **HANNAH:** Good morning. Sorry about last night, feeling better now.

I woke up a couple hours ago and stared at the sunrise through the window until I couldn't take it any longer. I snuck out of the house and took myself for a long run to kill time while I waited to hear from Hannah. The steady pounding of my feet on the concrete, paired with the babble of my favorite podcast hosts chatting didn't take away the pain, but at least it's a good excuse for not being able to draw in a full breath. Besides my own stupidity. The combination settled my brain and dulled the sharp edge of the ache in my heart.

Running into Katy and JJ on my way back helped too. "Trevor!" Katy called out from her lunge on the grass while JJ stretched her quads. "You okay?"

I'd pulled my earbuds out and slowed to a stop, dropping into a hamstring stretch on the Quinns' front lawn. "Sort of. Didn't sleep very well, to tell you the truth." I'd shrugged and switched legs. "Is Hannah okay?"

I still don't understand what went wrong yesterday.

JJ was the one who answered, oddly enough. "Honestly? I think she had a mini panic attack or something. She didn't say much on the drive home, just stared out the window, twisting her fingers."

"Yeah. I think she's more overwhelmed by everything than she's admitting. I would be." Katy shrugged, standing up to join JJ. "I suggest you go easy on the planning for a few days. Maybe that will help." I'd waved them off as they took off on their own run, walking the rest of the way home.

I hadn't meant to overwhelm Hannah, I only wanted to help. But I couldn't stop the image of her face, grimaced in pain after she fell on the sand, from haunting me as I chewed up mile after mile. It mixes in my mind's eye with her face backstage after the show—the fear flashing from the depths of those blue eyes, the quiver of her lips as she fought back tears. Even worse was the carefully blank mask she hid behind both that awful night at the urgent care and again last night. It's that mask that scares me the most. What is she hiding behind it?

"Yo." Tyler swings into the room. "Last day here, man. What do you want to do?" Tyler's hair is damp from his own shower. He went to the gym with Jack and Hunter while I was out running. "Is she speaking to you yet?"

"She sent me a text just now, but I haven't responded. What do you have planned? It's your last day of summer vacation."

"Ugh, don't remind me. I am not ready for junior year." Crossing his arms, Tyler leans against the doorjamb, looking every inch the high school football star he is. Can you blame me for spending a couple of months earlier this year hating his guts? Those months when I wasn't sure if Hannah still had a crush on him were torture.

"I'll text Olivia and see what she wants to do." Tyler shrugs.

"Remind me to thank Olivia," I say, as he types on his phone.

"Why?"

"If she hadn't been a bitch and set me up with Hannah back in January, I never would have met her." I shrug, finishing the rest of the thought in my brain, guarding the secret I haven't dared say out loud. I really do need to thank Olivia for introducing me to the love of my life, even if she did it for a weird kind of revenge.

I dodge Tyler's half-hearted swing, letting him graze my shoulder. "Don't call Liv a bitch." But I know he's not mad from the grin on his face. "The girls are planning to go back-to-school shopping after Hannah's physical therapy appointment. Hey, there's that new Marvel movie out, have you seen it yet?"

"Of course, I've seen it, but I'll watch it again. A movie seems like a good idea, then Hannah doesn't have to walk around. Actually, I have an idea." I unlock my phone and type out a response to Hannah, indecision gone.

> **ME:** Good morning beautiful. Don't worry about last night, I get it.
> **ME:** I heard a rumor of back-to-school shopping happening after your PT appointment? If you don't want to go

shopping, I'd be happy to take you to PT. Maybe we could
get coffee after?

ME: It's my last day here, I'd love to see you as much as I
can before I have to go home.

"Hey, can I borrow your car?" I ask, realizing I should have
figured that out before I offered to take Hannah to PT.

"Sure. I'll hitch a ride with Jack. Where are you going?"

"I just offered to take Hannah to her PT appointment then
coffee after. I have a feeling she might not want to go shopping
for a school she's not going to be at. We can meet up with you
guys after."

"Sounds good."

My phone buzzes and I glance down to see Hannah's response.
It's not Hannah.

MOM: Hey sweetie, just checking on you. How'd it go
with your girl? Dad says he'd give his left leg to know. His
words, not mine.

She adds a gif of Fozzie bear shaking his head. My dad and
his terrible jokes. I don't have time to respond before the text I
actually wanted comes in.

HANNAH: That would work. My appointment is at 11:30.
Do you have a car?

ME: I'm borrowing Tyler's. He suggested a movie with
everyone, is that ok with you?

HANNAH: A movie sounds good. My arms are so sore from the crutches, anything that isn't walking around is good with me.
ME: I had a feeling. Too bad you don't have an adamantium skeleton. That would have come in handy now.
HANNAH: Have a what?

I give her a brief overview of Wolverine while getting ready to pick her up.

"I'll text you when we're done," I tell Tyler a few minutes later when he hands over the keys to his SUV.

"Yup." He claps a huge hand on my shoulder, nearly knocking me over. I'm not scrawny, I'm really not. It's just in comparison to my cousin and his friends that I feel more like Shaggy from Scooby-Doo than the Asgardian trickster-god I prefer to compare myself to. "Good luck!"

Why do I feel like I'm going to need it?

CHAPTER SEVEN

Hannah

*E*YEING THE crutches in Mike's hand, I'm ready to promise anything if it means I don't have to use them anymore. "Short distances only. Got it? And try to walk as normally as you can in the boot so you don't end up with a secondary issue." Mike looks at me expectantly and I nod.

"Got it. Use the crutches if I'm going farther, short distances are okay without it, walk normally. Be careful." With the rest of my life in flux, Mike's rules offer me something solid to hold onto. Besides, I'm determined to make sure my injury heals as fast as possible. "So, say we were going to a movie tonight." I point in the direction of the lobby where Trevor is sitting on his phone. "I should use the crutches to get inside, but I don't have to use them to find my seat?"

"Right." Mike nods, his careful fingers feeling around my ankle and calf. "Any pain?"

I shake my head. "It's been much better, except last night when I fell, that hurt." I'm embarrassed to admit that I was at the beach, but I swore to myself I would be one hundred percent honest with Mike. "We were at the beach for my birthday," I add.

"That would explain the sand in the boot."

I duck my head at Mike's words, but he doesn't scold me, just grins. "Sorry? I promise I didn't walk around, Trevor carried me pretty much everywhere, it was just one time when I lost my balance," I babble, needing Mike to know I'm taking my injury seriously. He's been in touch with Dr. Lee, the PSB therapist and I don't want him to tell her that I'm messing around and not focused on healing.

"Did you have fun? And happy birthday, by the way. Seventeen, right? That's a big one."

"I guess." I fight back the urge to spill my thoughts out to Mike. Instead, I bite my lips and watch as he gently manipulates my ankle. "And thank you. It sounds so grown up, but I don't feel like one," I can't help saying. I look around the clinic, my eyes drifting over the equipment dotted around the space.

"I guess it sounds pretty grown up, but you're still just a kid. You don't have to have all the answers yet, you know. Just try to think two steps ahead before you make any big decisions. That's the only advice I have for you." Mike winks at me from his stool, fitting his hand to the ball of my foot and pressing up, slowly. "I generally leave the pep talks to Leslie."

The mention of my beloved teacher's name is both a weight on my chest and a shot of confidence. I'm going to miss her, our private lessons, her great pep talks and hugs. But if she could do this even younger than me, I can do it too. I trust that she's prepared me for this, given me the skills I'll need to thrive in my new dance home. Of course, knowing she'll be a text away helps.

"You did alright." I grin and hold my hand out to Mike to high five.

We spend some time doing non weight-bearing exercises and some careful work on strengthening the upper half of my right leg without disturbing my ankle. I'm not allowed to do these ones on my own and I won't, even if it's tempting. I made a promise and I'm determined to stick to it.

"You all done?" Trevor asks, tucking his phone in his pocket as I emerge from the back.

"Yup." I navigate across the lobby on my crutches, for once not catching the ends on anything.

"Trevor, right?" Mike follows me through the doorway, holding his hand out to shake Trevor's. Trevor flinches as they shake hands, I have no idea why. "Hey Hannah?" Mike looks at me. "Think you can get yourself in the car on your own? I'd like to chat to Trevor for a second."

Trevor's eyes go wide, and he flashes me a worried look.

"I think I can manage." I hold my hand out for the keys. "Good luck?"

Chuckling to myself, I maneuver out the door.

Trevor climbs in a few minutes later, sliding into the driver's seat with a heavy sigh.

"You okay?" I ask, looking up from my phone, my half-typed message to Martin will have to wait. Is he a little pale or is that a trick of the light? I hide my grin. Mr. Mike gave Tyler some kind of 'guy talk' speech over the summer. According to Olivia, whatever Mike said scared Tyler so much he hadn't done more than peck her on the cheek for days afterwards.

"Uh, yup. All good. No problem, just a little chat between guys." I'm so tempted to point out the way his voice squeaks, but

I refrain. "Is it weird that everyone is starting school without you tomorrow?"

I pick at an imaginary bit of lint on my shirt, pushing Martin's offer to the back of my mind. "Kind of. We figured out what I'm going to do for school." My voice cracks a little on the words. Guess it's a good thing I didn't tease.

"Yeah?" Trevor holds out his phone to me. "Can you do the map?"

I take his phone, typing in the movie theater we decided on. After angling his phone in the cup holder, I tuck my hands under my thighs. I don't know what he's going to say when I tell him what my parents and I decided, but I know he's going to be disappointed.

"T?" Trevor's worried voice has me cringing. "You didn't answer my question."

I take a deep breath and spill it all out. "Well…see, since we don't know where I'm going to live yet, we couldn't enroll in any of the public schools—"

"But I thought—" Trevor starts to interrupt me but I plow on.

"Also, I don't know what's going to happen with my dance career, but there's always the possibility that I could get offered an apprenticeship with the company after a year. Or maybe even one at a different company. I've talked to Ms. Parker about it a lot and she always says how hard her first few years in the company were because she was trying to juggle school and being a professional. So, I decided to enroll in an online school and do my junior and senior years at the same time so I can graduate early. Then I don't have to worry about juggling everything." After unloading all my word vomit, I drop back in my seat, staring at him as he takes it all in.

"Oh." Trevor's throat works as he swallows, glancing at the map before getting into the left lane to turn at the next light. The clicking of the turn indicator is the only sound in the car. I squirm in my seat, regretting telling him, but knowing I couldn't have answered him any other way.

He doesn't speak again until the light changes. "I guess that makes sense. I just thought…" He clears his throat and tries again, the determined cheerfulness in his voice obvious, but I'm going to go with it. It's his last day here, I do not want to spend it fighting. "Never mind. You and your parents have to do what you think is best. It's not like I won't get to see you, right? No more having a thousand miles between us."

"Right."

We turn into the mall parking lot and hunt for a parking space, an uneasy silence hovering between us. It's crowded for a Wednesday afternoon, but since it's the last day of summer vacation, for everyone except me, I suppose there's a lot of last-minute shopping to be done. Most of *my* back-to-school shopping was done at the dancewear store in town.

"Yeah," I agree. "I'm excited to be in the same city as you. I wish I had an idea what my schedule is going to look like, but I'm sure we can make it work." Climbing out of the car, I lean against my door while Trevor pulls my crutches out of the backseat.

"You good?" he asks, cradling my cheek. I lean into his hand for a second, reminding myself of how nice it feels. I know all his plans left me feeling smothered, but he's just excited that I'll be in Seattle. It's still my life, my dream.

Leaning down, he kisses me softly on the lips. All the hurt and irritation I've been holding onto melt away under his kiss. I lean into it, bracing my weight against the crutches. Deepening the kiss, a tiny, breathless noise escapes me. As if it was the encouragement he needed, Trevor leans in, backing me against the side of Tyler's SUV.

My back rests against the hot metal of the door, crutches forgotten, as Trevor uses both hands to angle my face and kiss me thoroughly. I close my eyes against the bright sunshine as he kisses along my jaw, his tongue and lips caressing my skin. When my knees melt, he steps in closer, holding me up with his body. I don't know if it's the sun or his lips that have my skin burning, all I know is I don't want to stop.

"Hannah," Trevor whispers, his breath tickling my skin as he kisses his way up my neck to my ear. "We really should go…"

"In a minute," I whisper back, reaching for him, my hands clutching at his waist. The clatter of my crutches falling to the pavement startles us both. Trevor jumps back and I slump back against the car door. Now that I'm coming to my senses, the metal is hot. Really, really hot. So hot it's burning my skin.

"Ow!" I hiss and limp a little step away from the car door.

"Are you okay? Is it your ankle?" Trevor asks, worry lacing his tone as he stoops to rescue my crutches from the sidewalk.

"I'm fine. The car door was hot. I hadn't…noticed. Um. Before." Suddenly shy, I fumble over my words until Trevor hands me back my crutches with a wink.

"I'd offer to kiss it better, but everyone else is already there and waiting for us." Taking my phone and slipping it into his pocket since I don't have one, Trevor steps aside so I can swing myself out on my crutches.

"Did you ever talk to your parents about staying in our studio apartment?" Trevor asks as I hop up the curb. Everyone else is waiting for us in front of the theater, Olivia waves as I brush my hair out of my face.

"Um, we talked about it a little. They're not sure yet. They're still deciding if my mom is going to move up with me." The white lie slips out easily. There was discussion of my mom moving up to Seattle with me, but she didn't feel right walking away from her job on such short notice, and we know my dad will be able to visit me often. One of his company's big contracts is with Boeing, so he's in Seattle at least every other month. Joining a pre-professional school is something we've been preparing for. At least now I'm old enough that me going won't uproot my entire family.

What I don't tell Trevor is that my mom is pushing me to take him up on his offer. She loves the idea of having someone to look out for me up there. I think my dad would like the idea more if Trevor and I weren't dating. I'm the one who's pushing back. I have a gut feeling that it would be a bad idea. Neither of us knows what it's like to be together when life is "normal," whatever normal is. What if my ballet life and his running life are incompatible? I can't help picturing all the texts Trevor sends me in a day as times he would "pop over" or want my undivided attention. What we have works because he understands when I'm busy with dance. Will he still be that understanding if I'm *right there*?

But as of now we haven't found a better option. Although Martin's message about his change of plans, and his offer, may change everything.

"Hey!" Katy bounces over, pulling JJ by the hand. "We have your tickets already, let's go." I let everyone go ahead while I rest my arms for a moment. Lisa hangs back keeping pace with me.

"How'd it go?" she asks.

"Good. I'm allowed to start doing a little bit here and there. If I don't have the crutches I'm not supposed to limp, it's going to be hard."

Lisa nods and I get moving towards the theater. Trevor is waiting for us, holding the heavy door open. "Does Mike think you're going to be able to start in a few weeks?" That's the big question, the question that makes all this planning so hard. If we knew I was heading up to Seattle to start dancing at the beginning of September, it would be easier to find a place for me to live. But if it's not healing quickly enough, what's the point in moving up there now?

"He won't tell me until after the x-ray next week." I manage an odd half-shrug without dropping my walking sticks of death and follow her through the door.

The movie is fun, Trevor's whispered commentary in my ear reminding me of all the nights we've spent watching movies together over our laptops, his voice in my ear the same way. The addition of his arm around my shoulder puts this a step above watching it together over long-distance. Although I have to admit, watching while snuggled under my covers is way more comfortable than the ice-cold movie theater with the armrest digging into my side.

"Ugh, I am not ready for school to start tomorrow. I'm so jealous of you Hannah," Olivia says as we emerge from the dark theater.

"Why are you jealous? I'm going to be stuck at home doing school all by myself. I don't love school, but at least we could always hang out at lunch and stuff." I'm not looking forward to doing school all by myself, I hope it's worth it in the end.

"Yeah, it's going to be so weird not meeting you for lunch at our bench," Lisa says. She's tucked under Hunter's arm, like usual. I'm pretty sure he isn't going to be letting her go any time soon.

Olivia looks back over her shoulder. "Aren't you going to come eat with us? I assumed you would since…" she waves at the two of them.

"I hadn't thought about it," Lisa says slowly. I know she's nervous to eat lunch with the popular crowd that Hunter and the rest of them hang out with at school.

Hunter drops a kiss to the top of her head. "I don't care where we eat as long as I get to see you. And if anyone gives you a hard time, you let me know."

The conversation continues on without me, just like my friends will keep living their lives here once I'm gone. The thought tugs at my heart. I suppose it goes both ways, we'll be living our lives and missing out on all the little day-to-day things that I've taken for granted all these years.

I won't know when Katy figures out the perfect Halloween costume, they won't know when I finally land a quadruple pirouette to the left. I'll miss out on Olivia's plans for Homecoming, they'll miss out on my pas de deux woes. We'll all be dancing in Nutcrackers, but not the same one.

As if he can sense the sad thoughts filling my mind, Trevor slips his arm around my waist, taking the crutches from me and handing them off to someone on my left. "Come here, T. That sad face calls for some sugar." Bending down to press a quick kiss to my lips, he scoops me up in his arms before I can protest.

"Lead the way, someone. My girlfriend needs either ice cream, cookies, or chocolate."

Olivia is the one who dances out in front. "Oh my god Trevor, swoon! The hero carrying his lady to safety." Everyone laughs at that.

"You going to carry Hannah over the threshold like that at Aunt Ellen and Uncle Aaron's place? At least the ramp will make it easier." Tyler calls, scooping Olivia over his shoulder, like I've seen him do a dozen times before. Olivia just laughs and props her chin on her hands, her elbows digging into his back. "Hope you like lasagna, Hannah. Aunt Ellen makes it for dinner every Saturday night."

I don't know what it is about Tyler's words, but they set alarm bells off in my head, banging and clanging so loud I can't ignore them. "Put me down," I hiss at Trevor.

"What? Why?" The way his forehead wrinkles like a concerned puppy almost sweeps away my anger, but I hang onto it by a thread.

"Trevor, I can't live at your parents' house. I just can't." I wiggle again, forcing him to put me down. I can't have this conversation being carried like a baby.

"But, I thought we decided already..." The confused puppy face doesn't go away, just gets sadder.

"No, *you* decided Trevor." Tears prick at my eyes in frustration. I hate that we have an audience right now, but maybe this means I won't have everyone ganging up on me to find out what happened later. Small mercies, I guess.

"Hannah... I—"

I interrupt before he can finish that thought. "It's just," I take a deep breath, pushing down the nerves that have my stomach clenching. "You showed up with all these plans. They're not bad plans," I add, "but they're not *my* plans. This is *my* dream, Trevor, you have to let me make my own decisions."

He reaches for my hand, twining his fingers with mine, but keeps his eyes cast down, not meeting my eye. "I'm sorry. I didn't realize…" He swallows, giving my hand a quick squeeze. I hate that I've made him sad. The weight on my chest is as much for my own frustration that he's not listening to me, as the fact that he's hurting and it's my fault. I'm a mess of contradictory feelings. "I saw a solution to the problem and assumed you would be as excited about it as I was."

I squeeze his hand back, hoping he'll look at me. "I'm excited to be in Seattle with you, I really am. But I'm worried that living with you—" He opens his mouth to protest and I grin. "I know it's not really living with you, but you know what I mean. I'm worried that it's too much, too soon. We're seventeen, Trevor. We have so much life to live, so many things to do and see. And I'm about to leave everything I know." I catch Lisa waving out of the corner of my eye, pointing to the Starbucks just ahead, indicating they're going inside. I lift my hand in acknowledgement, glad they're not leaving, but also thankful for the privacy.

"But shouldn't that be an even better reason to have something or someone familiar nearby? I'll be there for you when everything else is new and scary. I *want* to be there for you, Hannah. I—" He cuts himself off and looks away. "I wasn't trying to pressure you into anything, I just wanted to help. Do you know how many people have told me to keep an eye on you, take care of you?"

Why is this so hard?

Instead of letting the thoughts tumble around inside my head, I let them out, contradictory or not. I can't keep this inside any longer. I don't care that I sound ridiculous, flip flopping from excited to nervous to angry to happy with every word.

"Part of me wants to live there so badly. I'm so scared about moving, Trevor. I have so many questions and no answers. What if I can't keep up? What if my ankle doesn't heal and I keep having issues? What if I get so homesick I can't stand it? Will I be able to cut it? Living so close to you, knowing you'd be right there *is* a comforting thought." I keep going, not giving him time to say anything. "Honestly? My mom likes the idea. Well, she likes the idea of me not being completely on my own. Neither of my parents is *super* thrilled about the idea of me being alone in an apartment in your backyard. My dad is a little…um…worried about my boyfriend being so accessible."

Trevor grins at that and I can't help grinning back. I'd be lying if I said the thought hadn't crossed my mind. In a vague sort of way. Although Olivia has brought it up more than once.

The brief moment we share fades as I look into his eyes and brace myself for the next words I need to say. I have to be brave, right? Trevor's not going to like this, but I have to be honest. "And what if…" I let my words hang in the air, the weight of them making everything go still. I swallow and try again. "What if we don't work out?" I whisper, eyes on his shoes, unable to say the words any louder, hating that I said them at all.

Trevor doesn't say anything. The silence between us stretches on for long, painful minutes. Finally, I can't take it anymore and I look up, dreading what I'm going to see.

Those brown eyes of his are so sad, I almost lose it right then and there. I want to take it back, take it all back. Cover his face in kisses and promise that I'll love him forever and that *of course* we're never going to break up. Wait.

Did I just say I'll love him forever?

I love him?

Holy cow. I love him.

Trevor doesn't give me a chance to wrap my brain around the thought before he speaks. "Do you?" He swallows. "Are you saying what I think you're saying?"

"What? No, no. I'm not breaking up with you." I stumble over the words they try to escape so fast. "I'm just saying, I don't know what I'm saying. It's just...we're still young, Trevor. How can we know what's going to happen in the future? I don't even know what I'm going to be doing next week, let alone in six months." The sadness doesn't leave his eyes, no matter how reassuring I try to make my words. "I'm sorry, I'm so sorry, I didn't mean it like that. I just..."

With a heavy sigh, Trevor pulls me against his chest, the arms I've come to love so much wrapping around me. The sense of safety I only get when he holds me creeps back in. Sliding my arms around his waist, I hold him tight, letting myself relax against him. Breathing my anxiety out and the citrus and soap scent of him in. "I don't want to fight," I mumble against his shirt, the fabric sticking to my lip.

"What was that?" Trevor's words tickle the hair on top of my head.

I pull back just far enough to look up at his face. "I'm sorry, I didn't mean that like it sounded. I'm so worried and scared about everything that making plans freaks me out right now. I know you're trying to help. And I appreciate it. I do." I can't push up on my toes like I normally would to emphasize my words with a kiss, so I dive back into his chest again, squeezing tight.

Trevor pulls back. For a moment, I'm worried he's about to push me away, so I keep my face down, not looking him in the eye. "Hey." He slips a finger under my chin, lifting my face to meet his eyes. "I'm sorry too. I didn't mean to bulldoze you like that. I shouldn't have assumed your doubts were you wanting to throw everything we have away. I just got you back and I guess I'm still a little nervous that you'll come to your senses and realize you could do much better than me."

He leans down to press a gentle kiss to the tip of my nose. "Trust me, I am very aware that you are out of my league. And if I'm being honest, there was a little part of me that was excited about getting to show you off at school, to introduce you to my friends. My family. I want them to know how amazing you are. I know you're just being cautious, it's who you are. My brave but cautious Hannah." This time he kisses me on the temple. "My badass girl." He kisses the other temple and I hum a happy little noise. "My tough as nails ballerina." A kiss to one cheek. "My little ball-buster." He kisses me on the other cheek before I swat at his chest.

"Stop!" I laugh, but he steps back, out of my reach. Without my crutches I can't pursue him, but I do take a few slow steps in his direction. "We're good right?"

Instead of answering, Trevor scoops me back up in his arms and strides off to where our friends are sitting outside the Starbucks, my crutches sticking up in the air like a beacon. "Yeah, T. We're good."

I let him carry me without protest this time. But I can't get rid of the worry that's wormed its way into my heart.

CHAPTER EIGHT

Trevor

MOM: did you get checked in for your flight ok?

ME: sitting at the gate right now

I SEND HER a picture of the gate. Not a selfie. One look at my face right now would have my mom threatening to rewrite the laws of time so she could be here in California before my flight takes off. But there's no way to pull a Doctor Strange and rewrite a version of my life where everything didn't go to absolute shit last night.

MOM: I'll be there to pick you up from the airport. Mags too. Will you text me when you land?

ME: I promise. Any chance you can bring Loki? You know how much he loves a car ride.

I leave out the fact that I could really use my dog right now. Someone who I know will love me, no matter what idiotic thing I say or do.

I shouldn't have said what I said about Martin last night, shouldn't have made her feel like she had to choose. I knew it was the wrong thing to say the second it came out, but there's no way to take it back now. I don't think there's any way to come back from it, either. Hannah and I are done for good.

I thought my heart was broken a week ago? That was just a crack. This? This empty feeling inside me? Knowing that the one girl I would do anything for hates my guts right now and never wants to see me again? This is a thousand times worse.

As much as I want to blame Martin, I know who's really to blame.

It started when Tyler and Olivia kept teasing Hannah about the possibilities of living at my place. The innuendos that I could stay the night whenever we wanted, that Hannah's parents wouldn't be there, forgetting that mine would be just a few feet away. In fact, my parent's window faces the door of the apartment—something I tried to point out. Hannah's face was getting pinker and pinker by the minute. If I'd been smarter, I would have listened to the voice in my head yelling, "Abort mission!" à la the alternate opening to Iron Man 2, but since the other voice inside my head wanted Hannah to see the advantages of living there, I kept silent.

Eventually, Hannah exploded with an angry, "This! This is why I can't live with you!" indicating the friends who were giving her a hard time. Grabbing her crutches, she swung off, getting an impressive distance before I gathered my thoughts enough to join her.

"Hey, T. Slow down a second," I'd called out, jogging to catch up with her. "They were just teasing. You know they didn't mean it, right?"

She'd swung to face me. "Don't. Don't defend them. I have enough on my plate, I do not need to add the complication of… *that* to my life."

"Excuse me?" The words had popped out before I had a chance to think. "I'm not sure how I should feel about that statement." I'd tried to backtrack, but the damage had been done, on both sides apparently. I know I'm not built like my cousin or the Quinn brothers, but I didn't think I was repulsive. Hannah certainly hadn't been turned off earlier in the day. My pride and my feelings took a hit and I couldn't stop the words I said next.

"Is that what this is all about? You don't want to be pressured into sleeping with me? Is the idea of being with me that terrible? Or do you think so little of me that I would pressure you into something you didn't want to do?"

Every time I'd seen Hannah angry or upset before she got twitchy, fidgeting with the hem of her shirt, or a strand of hair, pulling back into herself. I knew my girl had a core of steel underneath all that anxiety, but I'd never truly seen it until now. This Hannah wasn't my soft and delicate ballerina. This was a fierce warrior who just happened to fight with her art instead of weapons. But words are cutting enough.

She went deathly still. The kind of still that had alarm bells going off in my head, alarm bells that sounded an awful lot like "Ohshitohshitohshitohshit."

"It's. Not. About. You." She'd punctuated each word with a finger stabbed into my chest. "How many times do I need to explain this? This is the first, most important, step towards my dream. A dream I have had since I was a little kid. Before I met you. A dream I had before I met Lisa or Katy. I have laid in my bed every night, staring at the signed picture of Julie King on my wall, wishing and hoping that one day I could be like her. I have worked my butt off in classes with Ms. Parker every day, wanting nothing more than to be like her."

Her beautiful blue eyes flashed and I took a step back, apologies battering to escape me. But my pride stopped me. That damn feeling of never being the one who got picked, whether it was comparing myself to Tyler or the guys at school, I've always secretly felt like the runt of the litter.

There's a reason I have framed artwork of Hawkeye on my wall next to some of Loki—I pretend to compare myself to Loki, to the brash, confident trickster. I pretend that looking like him is enough to make me feel like him too, that I deserve to be treated like I'm someone important. But it's an act. In reality, I'm the useless Avenger, the ordinary guy trying to keep up with literal gods and superheroes. Before I can blurt out the words building inside me, Hannah keeps talking.

"I meant what I said earlier, Trevor. I'm terrified of everything that's about to change. You don't get it, no one is expecting you to make grown-up decisions *right now*. I am barely keeping it together, I can't take care of your feelings too. Maybe it's selfish, maybe I'm back to being the old self-absorbed Hannah, but if this is what it's going to be like…" she trails off eyes going glassy.

"Well, excuse me for taking it personally that you're turning down my offer. An offer I made because I wanted you to be *safe*. Because I wanted you to feel like you had family to take care of you, even if it's not your own. You say it's not about me, and I'm trying not to feel that way, I really am." I had to stop and take a shuddering breath, my heart thumping painfully inside my chest, screaming at me to shut up, to stop talking, we're making it worse. But I couldn't stop. "But it sure feels like a kick to the teeth every time I make a suggestion and you turn it down. I'm trying to help. Let me fucking *help* you."

Steve Rogers would be so disappointed in me. Hannah flinched at my language, but didn't back down. Nope, not my girl. "I can't keep fighting with you, Trevor. You can't keep trying to manage my life for me. I don't need a babysitter or a knight in shining armor to fight my battles for me."

"It didn't seem to me like you were taking very good care of yourself at the intensive. If you'd just listened to me, you wouldn't be on crutches right now." I'd waved a hand at her booted foot, ignoring the death-glare I got in return. Not my smartest move, I can see that now. "I understand the school thing, but—"

Hannah had cut me off with an exasperated shout. "You're not listening to me! I am asking you to trust me to make my own decisions. I'm not asking you to agree with them. Trevor, I can't live with you. I just can't, it's too much pressure. I'm going to live with Martin."

"What the fuck?" The words popped out before I could stop them. "Martin? You're picking Martin over me? You've known him for a fucking week, Hannah."

"That's not true and you know it. I spent more time with him in person than I had with you before we started dating," she threw back in my face.

I have no excuse for what I said next. None. If I could take back every word from that night, if I could hop in a T.A.R.D.I.S. and start the day over, time travel paradoxes be damned, I would. "I can't believe this. You're so afraid of committing to us, to being with me for more than just the summer, more than just over the phone, that you're going to live with a fucking stranger just to avoid me? Are you ever going to choose me first? Or am I always going to come second to ballet?"

"Don't do this," Hannah whispered, tears filling her eyes and spilling down her cheeks. "Don't make me choose between you and ballet."

It was her tears that snapped me out of the emotional spiral my wounded pride sent me down. "I'm not…I'm sorry. I didn't mean it like…" I'd fumbled for words, to say what she needed to hear so I could keep her. "I'm not asking you to choose."

"Then why does it feel like you're fighting me on every choice I make? I need you to support my decisions, not second-guess them. I'm trying to choose what's best for me in the long-term. Hopefully, that's also what's best for us. But Trevor—" She swallowed hard and that was the moment I knew I'd lost the battle. That maybe it was too late. That my love for her wasn't going to be enough. "Don't ask me to make my decisions about you. I won't. I've had this dream for as long as I can remember, and I'll have it whether you're in my life or not. Don't make me choose. You won't win."

Neither of us had noticed our friends creeping closer. Lisa, Katy, and Olivia move to stand behind Hannah. It wasn't until the last words filled the air between us that Lisa stepped forward and placed a hand on Hannah's shoulder. "Come on," she'd said, her quiet voice echoing in the silent aftermath of our argument. "Let's go before you both say something you regret."

Like I wasn't already regretting every damn word I'd said.

Driving home from the movie theater with the guys, showering and packing up my bag was all a blur. Even this morning, saying goodbye to Tyler as he left to pick up Olivia for their first day of school, was hazy. It was only when Aunt Rachel pulled up to the curb at LAX that everything snapped back into focus.

"Can I make a suggestion, honey?" she'd said as I pulled my bag out of the trunk. "Give her some space. I know you love her. But you can't smother her into choosing you. She has a point too. You guys are still kids. Now is the time to make selfish decisions, so you can grow into the best versions of yourself. If you're meant to be, you'll find a way." She'd pulled me in for a hug and I'd barely been able to stop myself from sobbing against her shoulder.

"You two are going to be okay. I have a gut feeling," she'd whispered in my ear.

"Aunt Rachel, you never even met her." I'd tried to joke, but it fell flat.

"I've seen that girl around for years, and I've always admired her determination to pursue her dreams. I keep track of who my boy hangs out with, honey. I definitely prefer Hannah's crowd to the bitchy cheerleaders Olivia used to be friends with. If she can make my Tyler a better man just by being friends with his girlfriend, then she's worth the wait. I have high hopes for you." With that, she'd pulled me down to kiss my forehead and let me go.

As the speakers overhead announce that boarding for my flight is beginning, I do my best to hang onto Aunt Rachel's words. Is Hannah worth waiting for? Absolutely. She's the Peggy to my Steve—I'd sacrifice anything to save the world for her. I won't force her to choose between me and her dream, and I won't pressure her to make the choices that I want her to make. I'm going to trust her, trust that one day she'll love me as much as I love her and then it won't be a choice at all.

But waiting is going to be hell.

CHAPTER NINE

Hannah

KATY: I still think they wouldn't care.

ME: I can't drive so it doesn't matter.

LISA: If we went off-campus for lunch we could meet you there, then no rules would be broken.

ME: Still can't drive

OLIVIA: Party pooper.

*M*Y LAUGH echoes in the empty house at Olivia's addition to the conversation. I'm still in my pajamas and haven't gotten out of bed except to pee and brush my teeth, even though it's already past eleven. I'm sure Mom tried to wake me up when she left for work this morning, but I must have fallen right back to sleep because the next thing I knew it was ten in the morning.

Waking up to a silent house isn't new, but knowing that all my friends are at school and I'm lying in bed with nothing to do is strange. I don't even have the satisfaction of a sick day, when you get to miss school but know you'll see everyone again the next day. This is my life now—stuck in one place while everyone else lives life without me.

The fork in the road taking my life in a different direction to everyone I know is barreling down on me and I'm not sure I'm ready for it.

My phone buzzes, snapping me out of the whirlpool of my thoughts. It's a private text from Olivia.

> **OLIVIA:** Thought you'd want to know Trevor made it home. Tyler just let me know. You doing okay?

No, no I'm not okay. Why do I keep accidentally breaking up with him? I did it again last night in a haze of fear, frustration, and overwhelming pressure. I regretted it the instant the words came out of my mouth, but how many more times can I hope he'll forgive me? Every time I get angry or scared, I push him away and I don't know why.

Maybe that girl at the intensive was right, he deserves a girlfriend who wants the same things he does, not a self-absorbed mess like me. Letting my mind dwell on it has iron bands snaking around my chest, cutting off my ability to breathe. I bite my lips to keep from crying, even though there's no one to see, I can't let myself break down over it again. I cried enough last night.

Instead, I blink hard to clear my eyes and respond to Olivia.

> **ME:** Thanks. Not really, but I appreciate you checking in on me. When does cheer start?
> **OLIVIA:** I see you avoiding the conversation. I'll let it go for now. Cheer starts today, wish me luck!

Heart to Heart

ME: Go get 'em Captain!

OLIVIA: Co-Captain, but thanks. Gotta go, bell just rang.

If cheer starts today, then Olivia is wearing her uniform for the first day of school. I wonder what everyone else is wearing. I glance down at my own tank top and flannel shorts, avoiding the boot on my ankle. I'm sure they're more put together than me at any rate.

Alright, enough wallowing Hannah, time to do *something* productive. I push myself out of bed and roll the yoga ball that's taken up residence under my desk into a clear space in my room. Flipping through the playlists on my phone, I pick out one that's upbeat, but not too cheerful, and start doing all the exercises that Mike gave me. No way am I getting to Seattle out of shape, even if I can't dance yet, there's plenty of other things I *can* do.

An hour later, I finish up my two hundredth crunch and flop back on my floor. Technically, crunches weren't on the list of things Mike said I could do, but I have my feet propped up on the yoga ball so fingers crossed he won't object. I'll double check with him on Friday at my next PT appointment. Promise.

With the entire afternoon looming ahead of me and nothing to do, I gingerly make my way downstairs, grateful I don't have to use the crutches inside the house anymore. Opening the fridge, I survey my options for lunch. My stomach growls after the workout I just did and the leftover chicken parmesan I spy is tempting. But since I'm not actually dancing right now, I grab one of the ready-made salads I insisted my mom buy instead.

But I do grab a handful of Oreos from the cookie jar for balance.

With nothing better to do, I flop onto the couch and start flipping through Netflix praying something catches my eye.

I'm halfway through my third Christmas movie, don't judge, when my front door opens.

"Hello!" Katy's voice calls through the house. "Where you at?" Another voice murmurs too low for me to make it out, until Katy's voice answers at full volume. "We all know where the spare key is, don't be dumb, babe."

Chuckling to myself at their argument, I wave my hand above the back of the couch so Katy and JJ can see me. "I'm in here."

Katy drops their backpacks by the door. "So, lucky duck, what'd you do all day? Besides watch…" She eyes the paused movie. "Christmas movies? You know it's August, right?"

I push myself up on the couch to make space for her and JJ to sit. "No judgement allowed. I'm not the one who watches Halloween movies for Easter." Dropping my head back on the arm of the couch I sigh. "I'm so bored. How was school? Do you have any classes together?" Desperate to know all the details, I pester Katy and JJ with details of their day.

"Okay, enough." Katy laughs after giving me a run down on every one of her classes. "We came over for two reasons."

"Not just to hang out with me?" I fake pout.

"Well, the two reasons involve hanging out with you so stick that bottom lip back in." Katy pokes at my face until I break out in a laugh. Man, I missed her this summer. "First, my personal trainer and I came to see if you had already done your exercises from Mike or if you wanted some company while you did them." She leans up to plant a kiss on JJ's cheek. "And second, we came to figure out how we can sneak you on campus so you can have lunch with us until you leave."

At the mention of me leaving, my stomach hollows out. "Oh. Um. Yeah, I already did my exercises. But I can do them again with you if you want?" I offer, not wanting them to leave.

"You shouldn't overdo it though. We just figured we'd ask." JJ surprises me by answering. "Lisa was sure you would have already done them, but Katy wanted to come over anyway."

"Where is Lisa?" I ask, peering at the door like she's going to walk in.

"She and Hunter are studying for some test. I dunno, it's one of their AP classes." Katy says, her shrug and air quotes getting a grin from me. Does my heart break a little at the thought that I don't have anyone to "study" with, air quotes or otherwise? Maybe. But I'm determined not to think about Trevor right now.

"Hey," Katy pulls me from my sad thoughts. "So more importantly, how are we going to sneak you on campus for lunch? When can you drive again? When does your new school start?"

"Um, new school starts on Monday." Same day as Trevor. "And I don't know about driving. I have an appointment with Mike on Friday, so I'll ask."

"Lisa thought that might be the case. We discussed this at lunch," she adds at my confused look. "She was going to go ask the librarian at school if you could come work there during the day. JJ can pick you up and one of us can drop you off after school."

I look at JJ, not sure why she got volunteered to pick me up. "I live two streets over," she explains.

"Um. Sure, I guess. If it's ok with the school. It would be nice not to be stuck here all by myself all day." Even sitting in the school library, weird smell notwithstanding, sounds better than staring at the walls of my house all alone. Maybe it will be easier not to think about Trevor and what an idiot I am all the time if I'm surrounded by people.

"Okay. Lisa is going to ask tomorrow." Katy nods like everything is settled. "Are you going to come to class next week? And the Nutcracker auditions on Saturday? I mean, obviously you aren't auditioning, but are you going to come watch or something?"

When I don't answer, Katy's cheeks turn pink. "It just feels too weird for you *not* to be there. I don't know. I should stop talking."

I sigh. I've been avoiding thinking about how I'm going to miss out on our Nutcracker this year. It's always been the highlight of the winter for me, it doesn't feel like Christmas until I'm performing Nutcracker. "Maybe? I'll have to talk to Ms. Parker. But I'm planning to come to class and do floor barre as long as I get the okay from Mike," I add.

"Cool. We can work out some of us coming to pick you up, if you can't drive yet."

Katy and JJ hang out for another hour or so, watching the rest of my cheesy Christmas movie with me before heading off. Watching them holding hands as they walk out the door makes me miss Trevor all over again. I'm such an idiot.

But part of me isn't sorry. I need to make decisions for myself right now, not based on whatever fledgling relationship we have. Had. All the months we spent dancing around our feelings for each other make it hard to remember that we were only officially together for about two months. And we were in the same state for six weeks. I'm not heartless to think that's not long enough to be making plans around each other's lives. Right?

I drag myself back upstairs to my room for nothing more than a change of scenery, my phone buzzing a few times as I slowly climb the stairs.

Sitting on my yoga ball, I arch back over it so my head is resting on the floor, my good foot bracing against the end of bed, my booted foot propped up on the bed so I don't step on it. I twist my shoulders, enjoying the stretch in my spine after sitting on the couch all afternoon. My phone buzzes again so I open it up, reading it from my upside down position.

> **MARTIN:** Hey gorgeous, I just emailed you a couple of leads on some places I found out here. Are you bringing a car? That might change some of our options.
> **ME:** My parents are giving me my mom's old car. I'll look with my mom when she gets home from work. Can I just tell you how glad I am that you're coming to Seattle instead of NYC? I realize it's selfish of me, but it's the truth.
> **MARTIN:** I get it love. If I can't have my Sammy, I suppose you'll do.

Laughing, I roll sideways off the ball, catching myself on my hands and good foot. Pulling out my laptop, I settle on my bed before opening Martin's email. We pass the rest of the afternoon looking at various apartments and places for rent. Martin makes an excellent distraction from missing Trevor.

"Hannah?" Mom's voice drifts up the stairs, hours later.

"I'm up here!" I call back.

"Hey sweetie," she says a moment later, poking her head in my doorway. "You hungry for dinner now or do you want to wait a bit?"

"I'm good for now. Martin and I have been looking at places, want me to email you the best ones so far?"

It sounds so weird to be talking about renting an apartment with my mom. I hate how grown up I sound. I'm pretty sure she does too, based on the sad look in her eyes.

"Sure, baby. I'll look after I've changed." She starts to walk away before turning back. "I know I was all for you staying at the Stanley's place, but the idea of you living with Martin is growing on me."

The text I'd gotten from Martin yesterday afternoon, while I was waiting for Trevor to come back after my PT appointment, changed everything. There's a chance I wouldn't have been so adamant about not living in the studio apartment at Trevor's house if I hadn't had Martin's offer on my mind.

When his boyfriend Sammy couldn't get a Visa to stay in the United States, Martin put in a call to PSB. I hadn't known it at the time, but he had hoped to go to PSB originally, but switched to CBC when Sammy got offered a spot at the Alvin Ailey school so they could be together in New York. Without Sammy, Martin had no reason to be in New York. Besides, Seattle is a much more affordable place to live on your own. Me being there too was just an added bonus. So, the plan as of last night, when I tearfully arrived home, is for Martin and I to get a place together in Seattle. He's eighteen already, I won't be living alone, my dad doesn't have to have a panic attack that I'm living in my boyfriend's backyard, and I'll have a roommate who will have the same schedule as me.

What more could I ask for?

CHAPTER TEN

Trevor

THIS IS not how I pictured the first day of school—exactly the same as every other first day of school. It's my senior year, isn't the first day supposed to be better than normal? It's definitely not supposed to be worse, my last texts with Hannah echoing in my head.

> **ME:** This is really what you want?
> **HANNAH:** No.
> **HANNAH:** But this is what I need to do.
> **ME:** I'll give you space, but I'm not giving up on us.

I took Loki for our usual run this morning, just like always. Said bye to Mom as she rushed out the door to get to work on time. Pounded on the bathroom door for Mags to hurry up. Told Loki to keep an eye on a sleeping Dad, and hustled to the van to drop Mags off on my way to school. Just like any other school day.

"Trev!" Derek calls as I pass him in the hallway, chatting with our other friend Matt. "What were you up to all summer, man?"

"Hey, Derek, hey Matt. Just busy you know." I shrugged, wishing once more I had Hannah here with me. It's not that I wanted to show off the fact that I had this amazingly gorgeous girlfriend. Okay, I did want to show off how amazing she is, but not because I need to prove anything to these guys. They've been my friends for years, but with everything I've had going on in the last few years, my family has been a bigger priority than my friends. The fact these are the guys I'd call my closest friends and yet I haven't spoken to them or seen them since the last day of school in June is proof enough of that.

I just wanted my senior year to be a little more normal, a little more typical All-American than the last few years have been.

"Hey, did you ever get anywhere with that girl you were hung up on?" Matt asks, peeling the wrapper off a protein bar and taking a huge bite. Dude eats more than anyone I've ever known, where the beanpole puts it, I have no idea. "The ballerina?"

I swallow hard, damnit, I was hoping to make it at least to lunch before they asked. "Sort of."

Derek laughs. "What the fuck does 'sort of' mean?" He slaps me on the back like it's the funniest joke I've ever told, forcing me to stumble forward a step.

"We were dating most of the summer." I shrug, hoping they'll drop it.

"Were? As in no more? Oh damn, what happened?"

"We got in a fight when I was down there last week. I don't know where we stand at the moment, but it's not looking good."

"Can't you just buy her chocolate or flowers or something?" Matt asks. "Although, I guess sending it to California could be tricky..."

"She's actually moving up here in two weeks. Maybe." I explain the situation but the bell rings for class before I can finish.

Matt takes off for the other end of the building, being late to band is apparently a big deal, while Derek and I head toward our English class. "Senior year man, you ready for this? We gonna go one-two this weekend?" Derek asks as we walk.

"Sure, I guess." Our cross-country meet this weekend is the last thing on my mind, although a few days ago I was looking forward to Hannah being there at the finish line to cheer me on.

Talking about Hannah has me thinking about how different her day is to mine. She starts her online school today, her junior and senior years combined so that she can graduate early and pursue her dream.

The thing that stuck with me the most from our argument last week is how much she's willing to sacrifice for her dream. The moment she asked me not to make her choose between me and ballet I knew without a doubt, she'd choose ballet over me. I knew it in theory, but I'd never dared to test it, to see if she would really do it. Maybe somewhere deep inside I hoped she'd pick me. I can't even fault her for it.

I've never wanted anything as passionately as she wants to be a dancer. Well, anything I had control over at any rate. She's moving a thousand miles away from her family and her friends, just for a chance to pursue her dream. If she'd been offered a place in New York City instead of here in Seattle, she would have gone there without a second thought.

Part of me hates that I don't factor into her decisions at all. Part of me admires it. It's one of the things I love about her, and one of the things I hate most.

I just wish she'd let me help.

School passes in a blur, with me wondering what Hannah's doing the whole day. Is she home alone? Did she meet anyone in any of her online classes? How is her ankle? Did she keep it elevated enough today?

"Stanley! Quit daydreaming and get it in gear!" Coach McKinley's booming voice snaps me from my thoughts as I wander out onto the track, lagging behind my teammates.

"Sorry, sir!" I shout back before jogging to catch up to the rest of the cross-country team and joining in the warm up. I join the rest of the varsity and junior varsity teams sitting on the grass in the center of the track, while Coach explains the route we're going to run to the newbies. Stretching in preparation for the three-mile run ahead of us, it's not until someone clears their throat in the silence that I notice everyone looking at me. "What?"

"Dude," Derek's voice is awed. "How are you doing that?"

I let go of my ankles and look around. Matt's eyes are bugging out of his face, none of the other junior and senior guys sitting near me, all of us with our legs straight out in front of us, are touching their toes. Some of the girls are, but that's normal.

"Uh, Hannah showed me some tricks." I shrug. It's a tiny white lie. She didn't show me tricks, she just made me stretch with her every night when we were hanging out in the dorms. I never thought twice about it since her whole gang of dancer friends were always stretching in some way. They just sit like that. All the time. I don't think they realize they're doing it. It's weirdly comfortable for them, to lay around on the floor like a bunch of overgrown cats. It took some getting used to over the summer. "And at the training camp I went to, we stretched a lot," I add, lamely.

"Let's see if that flexibility translates to some faster times this year, huh?" Coach McKinley booms from behind me, startling me. "Senior year—you ready, Stanley?"

I scramble to my feet, brushing bits of grass and dirt from my legs. "Yes, sir." Mentally, I'm not. I'm so not ready.

"We're gonna get you up on that podium at State, right?"

"That's the plan, sir." Fingers crossed. That's the goal. Last year I missed getting on the podium at State by mere tenths of a second. This year is going to be different. I swallow down my apprehension and nod my head. Hannah's not the only one of us with goals. Scholarships and the chance to run for a college team are in my sights, if I can stay focused.

"You run this morning already?" he asks, eyes assessing mine.

"Yes, sir. An easy three." I nod. "Just like we discussed."

Coach nods his head before making a note on his clipboard. "Good. Sure I can't change your mind about being co-captain this year? You know I'd love to have you," Coach asks with a smile, his hand heavy on my shoulder. "How's your dad, by the way?"

I shake my head. "Sorry sir, I'm not changing my mind. Family is doing okay, thanks."

Coach gives my shoulder a firm squeeze. "Let me know if you need anything?"

"I will." Thankfully, he steps away after that, off to go pep-talk someone else.

Derek pitches his voice low before asking, "Trying to convince you to take the co-captain position again?"

"Yup."

"You should, you know. It would look good on your college applications and you know you'd be awesome at it. Everyone loves you." I hate Matt's reminder of the looming pressure I've been avoiding all summer.

"I can't, you know that. Besides, I think Jason and Michelle need it on their applications more than I do." I nod toward the pair of runners being swarmed by a pack of nervous freshmen and sophomores. Just then, Coach climbs on his bike and blows his whistle, signaling it's time to go.

Grinning, I take off, the route familiar after the last three years running it, or a variation of it, three days a week. One advantage of not being a captain? No need to extricate myself from a pack of bumbling newbies to start running. Derek and Matt keep pace with me as we head down the hill, away from the school. The familiar feel of my legs pumping beneath me, my buddies keeping pace beside me, Coach shouting directions to the newbies behind me and the open road in front of me, combine in a soothing meditation.

Running has always been like this for me, a chance to clear my mind, let go of the swirling thoughts that only seem to settle when I'm out here. The steady rhythm of my legs hitting the sidewalk helps me follow each thought from start to finish, untangling them one by one. It's why cross-country has always been my favorite, track events are too short, and the stadiums are too noisy for me to get into this zone, the place in my head where things are calm.

"Watch your pace, Stanley!" Coach's voice floats up from behind me. "Keep it steady!" I grin but maintain the pace I'm at, even as Matt drops back. Throwing a thumbs up in the air so he knows I heard him, I don't slow down. Risking a glance at my watch, a cheap knock-off brand fitness tracker but it gets the job done, confirms that I'm maintaining my new base pace. I've kept this pace up on longer runs most of the summer. Derek keeps pace with me for another mile, but he can't keep it going for the last mile, dropping back with a curse at my back. Grinning to myself, I run the last mile on my own, the noise in my brain quiet as I focus on putting one foot in front of the other.

I wave to the pair of sophomores sitting at the stadium entrance on my return, so they record my time. My quads are burning, and my heart is thumping nice and steady. This right here, the way my whole body hums with heat and life when I finish a run, that's my favorite part. Pausing my tracker, I check my time, pleased at the five-minute mile average blinking up at me. Not bad. Not as fast as I ran over the summer, but a faster start than last year. No need to blow my legs out this early in the season.

Derek and the other guys trail in not far behind me while I walk it off, shaking my arms and legs out, swinging my arms in circles while I pace. Hannah would tell me now is the perfect time to stretch, but I'm not prepared to do the whole series we worked out together over the summer in front of the guys, mostly because I don't want to have to talk about who taught it to me.

Thinking of my girl sends a painful squeeze through my pumping heart. I know Aunt Rachel said to give her space, but I don't know how much longer I can take it. I need to know if she's okay, if she's made plans yet.

If I factor into those plans at all.

"I swear to God, if you say 'on your left' to me even once this year, I will beat you." Derek laughs, dropping into the grass next to me while we wait for the slower runners and Coach to show up. Matt drops down on the grass beside him, flipping us both off but grinning.

"It's okay, there are plenty of newbies, I'll get my kicks elsewhere." The words sound normal but my heart's not in it and Derek knows, judging from the sideways look I get. Fortunately, Coach and the last of the stragglers arrive, saving me from having to talk my way around my feelings.

"Let's go! We're not done yet!" Coach yells over the bullhorn.

"I could do this all day," I mutter under my breath in an attempt to psych myself into staying focused on the workout instead of wondering what Hannah's doing.

By the time Coach is done with us, leaving my body tired but pleasantly worked over, Derek's let it go. Climbing into the front seat of my minivan, I pull my phone out, hoping for something, anything. I swipe away the text from my dad asking me to pick up milk and eggs when I pick up his prescriptions, and reread my last texts from Hannah, the ones she sent me two days ago. The ones that sent me barreling out the door for a late-night four mile run with my heart stomped on and bleeding.

> **HANNAH:** I know I shouldn't do this in a text, but I don't think I'm brave enough to do this any other way. I'm sorry.
> **HANNAH:** I miss you so much.
> **HANNAH:** I hate fighting, or whatever this is, with you. But I need to do this, and I need you to understand that this isn't about you or how I feel about you. This is about me setting my whole future up and I have to set it up right. I'm already starting at a disadvantage with my ankle, I can't risk anything else happening.

HANNAH: I have so many things to try to figure out right now and I need to make good decisions for my future. So right now, I need you to give me space. I need to make the smartest choices I can, not choices based on you or if there's an 'us.' I know you don't want to hear that, but since I know you're smarter than me, I think eventually you'll agree I'm right.

HANNAH: I'm not saying this is for forever. But I'm not going to ask you to wait for me to get my life together, that wouldn't be fair. I won't do that to you.

ME: You're breaking my heart Hannah. I wish I could see your face.

HANNAH: I'm glad you can't, I'm a crying mess right now.

ME: This is really what you want?

HANNAH: No.

HANNAH: But this is what I need to do.

ME: I'll give you space, but I'm not giving up on us.

HANNAH: I can't ask you to wait for me, Trevor. I don't know what my life is going to be like next week, let alone in a month.

The echo of our old conversation, when I'd come dangerously close to confessing my feelings to her the first time, haunts me. Everything was so much simpler back then.

ME: I know you're not asking, I'm offering.

My last message to her is just sitting there on read. I have no idea what she's thinking, what she's doing, or what she needs right now, but she knows where to find me. Until she does,

I'll just have to wait. Even if the waiting is a piece of shrapnel inching its way towards my heart, killing me in slow motion. Until Hannah says it's over for good, I'll build an Arc reactor and keep waiting.

CHAPTER ELEVEN
Hannah

*L*ISA TAKES my yoga mat from me as Mr. Parker pulls me in for one more hug. "Oh sweetie, I'm so proud of you but I'm going to miss you so much!" Her words are muffled against my head as I hold tight to the woman who's taught me so much more than just ballet. "I know I've been pestering you with bits of advice every time I've seen you for the last two weeks, but remember, I'm just a text away. I will always have time for you, no matter what."

Ms. Parker has let me come in and take class on the floor for the last two weeks, once Mike gave his permission. I'm itching to stand up and just *dance* but I know I can't, so I'm pretending that half a class lying flat on my back is enough. My skin itches from doing nothing but I'm reining it in as best I can. The fear of my fractured fibula not healing properly is the only thing keeping me from throwing caution to the wind right now.

I hold tight, the tears that have been threatening me all day running down my cheeks. "I know. I promise to text and let you know how I'm doing. I'm going to miss you so much." We hold onto each other for a few moments longer before Ms. Parker gently pushes me away. Holding me by my shoulders, she looks into my eyes, blinking the tears out of her own before she speaks.

"It's time, sweetie. Go live your big dreams. You'll always have a place here, no matter what happens, but now is the time for you to go be brave and make your mark. When it gets hard, remind yourself why you're doing it—because ballet is part of your soul. But don't forget that you're a person first, a dancer second. Don't let anyone or anything treat you like you're disposable or that you don't matter. You have a right to just as much oxygen in the room as anyone else." She stops to swallow back a few tears, sending a fresh wave of tears cascading down my face. She gives me a watery smile. "Take care of yourself first, okay? Ballet isn't worth anything if it's hurting you. Promise?"

I can't speak so I nod instead.

"Love you sweetheart, I'm so, so proud of you. Thank you for letting me be your teacher, you've given me more than you'll ever know." We squeeze each other tight for a second before Ms. Parker pushes me towards Beans 'N Things, where my friends are waiting for me. "Go. You know where to find me whenever you need me."

The girls are waiting for me inside, Katy and Lisa already at a table while Olivia is ordering the drinks. "Hot chocolate, right?" I nod in response to Olivia's question before making my way over to the table. Katy is already in tears and Lisa looks a bit watery herself. I'm still crying from saying goodbye to Ms. Parker. We're a mess.

"Okay, we have to get it together," Oliva says, pulling out the fourth chair at the table. "You know we're going to miss you.

And you're going to miss us." She pokes Katy and Lisa on the shoulders. "But no more crying tonight. We're going to hang out like old times. And we'll see Hannah again soon, it's not like she's leaving forever. You'll be home for Thanksgiving, right?" Olivia added, looking me in the eye.

"I don't know." I shrug. "I think it depends on if I get asked to be in their Nutcracker, and how my ankle heals. But I'll come home when I can, I promise," I add at Katy's distraught look. I wasn't expecting Katy to be the one to take my leaving the hardest, to be honest.

"You have to stay in touch, okay. Promise?" Katy manages to get out.

"Of course. I'll send snaps and you know Martin will make me take a billion pictures all the time." Mentioning Martin is what snaps us all out of the teary pit we've fallen into. The conversation turns to the apartment Martin and I decided on, my new schedule and speculation on what parts Ms. Parker is going to give them for Nutcracker. It isn't until the manager points out that we've been there for over an hour and a half and they're ready to lock up that we stop talking.

Gathering up all our stuff, we wander outside. My steps are slow, and not just because of my boot. I'm not ready to say goodbye, but it's now or never.

"Go kick ass, chica." Olivia says, squeezing me tight. "I promise to be mostly good and keep an eye on them." Her added whisper almost breaks me, but I sniff hard and give her a smile. What am I going to do without a friend who can read my mind like Olivia? We've had our ups and downs, but at the end of the day, there's never been a day of my life she hasn't been part of.

"I hate that you're leaving me again, but I always knew you were destined for this. And tell Martin I'll come kick his butt if he doesn't look out for you." Katy's blubbery laugh and silly karate chop action arm sends me laughing into Lisa's hug.

"Save a spot for me at the barre, I'll be there soon." Lisa whispers, hugging me hard. I nod, praying her words come true. "You're going to be amazing, I know it."

The flash of headlights in the parking lot, Dad waiting for me, cuts our tears short. After one last hug, I walk away from my friends, loneliness already sweeping in. Dad takes one look at my face and pulls me into his side for the whole drive home, letting me cry on his shoulder.

Tonight was harder than I could have imagined. The last two weeks have been a blur of getting ready to move—every time I think I've got it together, another wave of questions and decisions comes up. Combined with the frustration at not being able to dance and attempting to stay focused in my online classes, despite everyone sneaking into the library at school to see me, it's done an excellent job of distracting me any time I thought about having to say goodbye to everyone I know.

And it's all layered on top of missing Trevor. I keep waffling between being proud of myself for doing this without relying on him being there for me, and wanting to talk to him so badly I made Katy hide his contact info in my phone. I even deleted our text thread, after taking screenshots of the best bits, just in case.

Car packed to the brim, we'd gotten an early start on the road, dropping Dad off at the airport this morning so he could get to his delayed meeting. "Bye pumpkin, be good, okay? I'm so very proud of you. I'll see you in a few weeks okay? I'll take you and

Martin out for dinner. Pick out somewhere fun and we'll try it together, okay?"

Crying, I'd nodded my head and hugged my dad tight. He'd held me for a moment, before kissing the top of my head. "You guys need to get on the road. Love you always." I sniff back my tears as I step back to let my mom say goodbye. Knowing I'll see him again in a few weeks helps.

"I thought the girls were going to come see us off before school?" Mom says, climbing into the driver's seat.

Sleepy, I grip my cup and take a sip of chocolatey, mocha goodness before trying to answer. I watch my dad walk into the terminal, just like I've done a thousand times before. "We said goodbye last night. Honestly? I'm glad they didn't. I don't think I can take any more goodbyes right now."

Mom and I make our way over the Grapevine and descend into the long, empty stretch that is central California, a long day of driving ahead of us. The goal is to get to southern Oregon before we stop for the day. Even though Mike cleared me to drive a few days ago, I'm not supposed to be doing it for too long at a time, so I'll take shorter turns at driving when Mom needs a break.

"Sweetie, if you're not in the mood to talk…" She reaches across the seat to rub my knee, "will you turn my book on?" Nodding, glad she understands I don't want to rehash all my goodbyes out loud just yet, I plug her phone into the car. I tune out the familiar drone of Jim Dale's voice as Harry and Ron argue with Hermione about something or other, and stare out the window at the vast expanse of nothing between here and Sacramento. It doesn't seem real that a month ago we were driving the other direction, my booted foot propped up on a pile of bedding in the backseat, throbbing with each bump in the road.

When am I coming home again? I have no idea. Everyone keeps saying they hope to see me at Christmas and I don't have the heart to tell them that I'm secretly hoping I won't be able to come home. Not because I won't miss them, but because I'm hoping to get asked to dance in PSB's Nutcracker, which has performances all the way until Christmas Eve.

Staring down at my still-booted foot, I send a little prayer to the ballet gods that my ankle keeps healing the way it is. I had my last doctor's appointment two days ago, a fresh x-ray in hand so we could see what kind of progress the fracture is making. After a series of indecipherable "hmmm's," she turned to me with a smile and declared that it was making good-enough progress to let me head up to Seattle.

Mom and I went straight from the doctor's office to Mike's clinic and had a conference call with him and Dr. Lee up at PSB. As much as I was scared to hope for good news, they decided it would be better for me to come up to Seattle and start the term with everyone else and do my last few weeks of recovery with Dr. Lee. That way, as soon as I have the all-clear, I can get started without having to then move and get caught up on meeting my classmates and teachers.

Nothing is worse than being the new kid *and* starting the year late.

"Hey, Mom?" I ask, still staring out the window. This early in September, everything is baked and dried yellow and brown. The lone spots of color are the gas stations and odd buildings along the side of the interstate. I'm sure there are parts of this area that are beautiful, but they aren't wasted on the trucks and cars zipping by at ninety miles an hour.

She leans forward to pause the audiobook. "What's up?"

"I'm doing the right thing, aren't I?" All my worry and fear bubbles up into the vague question.

"That's a pretty big question, sweetie. Are you nervous?" Her hands rest on the steering wheel, her face relaxed. I don't know how my mom manages to be so freaking calm all the time, she never seems to get upset. Even when I was rushed off the stage with my fractured ankle and she was whisked backstage by security, she was calm and collected while I freaked out.

"Nervous feels like a massive understatement." I sigh, leaning back into my seat.

Mom laughs. "That sounds pretty reasonable to me. This is a huge thing. Scarier than going to New York for the finals, and think about how nervous you were for that. But…" She gives my arm a quick squeeze. "You've wanted this since you were little. It's normal to be nervous at the last second, sweetie. It doesn't mean that you're making the wrong decision."

"It's normal to be questioning all of my life choices up to today?"

Keeping her eyes on the road, Mom nods. "Absolutely. This is a life-changing decision, sweetheart. You've been lucky in life not to have had any major upheavals yet. No parents divorcing, no moving, the same teacher, the same friends. Not a lot of people are lucky enough to have that kind of stability in their lives when they're growing up. It's a blessing and a curse."

I mull over her words for a few minutes before answering. I suppose she's right. Just thinking about my friends, I am pretty lucky. Olivia lost her mom so young and then inherited Martha and her siblings without any choice in the matter. Lisa and her family moved from San Francisco when we were nine—it's not nearly as traumatic as Olivia's mom dying but it's still a major change to make in life. Katy and I haven't had any major family stuff happen, but she had been at a different studio before joining ours and had that experience of starting all over. I'm the only one in the group who's never had any practice at making a huge life change like this. It figures I'd make the biggest change of all on the first try.

While I'm thinking, Mom keeps talking. "How many kids are lucky enough to have started with a teacher like Ms. Parker? You didn't need to change studios when you decided to pursue professional training. Lots of kids your age would have left their childhood teacher years ago, gotten a little practice at making big changes like this."

We drive in silence, Mom passing trucks and other cars while I let my mind wander. She's right. I know she's right. Going to PSB is the next step towards my goal of becoming a dancer. Even if it's scary right now, arriving injured and still unable to dance.

"You're as ready as you're ever going to be, sweetie." Mom breaks the quiet, as if she's been following my unspoken train of thought. "Do I want you to stay my baby girl for a few more years? Of course I do. I'm going to miss you terribly and you know I'll text and call way more often than you want. But I have a gut feeling that this is what you need to do, even if it means my baby is growing up a little faster than I'm ready for." Tears prick at my eyes. What am I going to do without my mom there to take care of me?

"Mom?"

"Yeah sweetie?"

"Can I tell you all the things I'm nervous about? Will you talk it through with me?"

"Of course. We have two days in the car, we can talk over your list a hundred times if it'll make you feel better." That makes me laugh, even knowing it's true.

"Okay. I'm sorry if I'm all over the place."

Mom gives me a reassuring pat on the head. "That's not new, sweetie. Just say it as you think it, I speak Hannah pretty fluently."

"Things I know I can do—laundry, driving myself to classes, navigating the city. I'm glad I had a couple of weeks to get into the swing of my new school before now, I feel pretty confident about keeping up and knowing what's expected of me."

My online school is pretty chill, even if I hate that it's all Zoom classes and online assignments. I chose it, so I'm going to deal with it. Yes, the homework load is pretty significant since I'm doing two years at once, but I can handle it. If Lisa can handle her load of schoolwork, I can do this.

"You have the lists of meals and snacks from the dietician?"

"Yup. She gave me her email address so I can check in with her in a few weeks." That had been Ms. Parker and Mike's parting gift to me—they set me up with a friend of Ms. Parker's who's a registered dietitian in New York that specializes in dancers. I got to meet with her last week to go over what kind of foods I should be eating, and how much. After the comments and conversations I heard at the summer intensive, I had a lot of questions, especially about if I could eat carbs. Alyssa had laughed and explained the difference between simple and complex carbohydrates and helped me understand that my body needs both to keep up with the demands of dance. We spent ages on the phone going over all my questions, but when she told me to eat bread and pasta without guilt, I wanted to shake a fist in stupid Becky's face.

I really love garlic bread so that was a huge relief.

"We'll go grocery shopping once we arrive and get you all stocked up on the foods on her list. I think we should look for things that match her list that are fast and easy for you to make. You're not going to want to cook from scratch every night, not after a long day at school and dance."

"Martin can cook too. We talked about taking turns," I remind her.

"I'm so glad you won't be on your own. You and Martin will have to look out for each other." There's a sad look in her eyes as she speaks and I know my mom is thinking about how I won't have Trevor or his family to look out for me, like she was hoping.

I'm sad about it too.

"I know this is just me being your nagging mom, but try not to let your place get too messy. If you just clean one little thing each day and plan to keep the dishes under control, it won't turn into a big chore."

"We already talked about this, Mom. I know. We'll keep it clean, I promise." I'm not the neatest person in the world, but I don't think I'm *that* much of a slob.

Mom just raises an eyebrow and smirks. "I'll bring my rubber gloves next time I come up to visit."

We pass the next couple of hours with my mom giving me a hard time about keeping the place clean and listening to her book. There isn't anything interesting to stop and look at on the way, just endless fields, roasting in the heat. Even if the car didn't tell us the outside temperature is over one hundred degrees, the wavering lines rising from the asphalt would prove it.

When we stop for gas in the middle of nowhere, opening the car door is like opening an oven on full blast, the heat smacking me in the face. Sweat prickles along my spine and under my boot, the cold air conditioning from the car leaving my skin in a flash of goosebumps.

Stepping inside to use the bathroom, grateful again that I don't need my crutches anymore because this floor is gross, I tune out the disgusting bathroom around me by wondering how Trevor is doing. *What* he's doing. How was his first cross-country meet? Did Coach give him a hard time or did his times improve from last year? How's Loki? Washing my hands, I don't bother looking in the dirty mirror in front of me, knowing my messy hair is piled up on top of my head and there are dark circles under my eyes. I don't need the reminder that I'm an emotional mess right now. I have forty-eight hours to wallow in my sadness before it's time to grow up and move on. My new life is waiting for me in Seattle.

Once I finish, I can't help checking my phone as I wander down the aisles, waiting for my mom. How pathetic is it that I keep hoping for a message from the one person I purposefully haven't talked to my mom about? And I know I made Katy hide his contact from me, but it wasn't hard to figure out who "Tom Hiddleston" is supposed to be.

"Excuse me," I murmur, squeezing past a couple standing in front of the cold drinks. No more stalling, it's time to move forward.

"Ready to take a turn?" Mom is waiting for me as I step outside, leaning against the passenger door.

Am I ready? Am I ready for any of this?

"Sure."

CHAPTER TWELVE

Hannah

NAPPING MY hand back, I get the fridge door closed before anything falls out. "Mom, I don't think we bought enough food." I manage to keep the laugh inside for all of two seconds while she eyes me.

"Seriously, Mrs. O," Martin has already adopted my friends' nickname for her, much to my mom's delight, "I don't know where to fit these." Martin shakes the two bags of rice in his hands, bewilderment on his face as he stares at the stuffed pantry cupboards.

"I know, I just can't stand the thought of you two not having enough to eat," Mom says, laughing at herself. "I'll make it all fit, you two go finish unpacking Hannah's stuff."

I follow Martin down the hall to my room. Cute two-bedroom apartment? Check. Close to the University of Washington campus? Check. Yummy coffee shop down the street that Martin's already put in an application to? Check and double check. There's plenty of stores and restaurants within walking distance. Maybe we'll feel less like ballet freaks if we're surrounded by college students all the time.

"Is your mum going to be alright?" Martin asks, lifting a box onto my unmade bed for me. Between him and my mom I haven't been allowed to lift a thing, they just keep bringing me boxes to unpack without me moving much from one spot. I shouldn't be annoyed. I'm not annoyed at them, I'm just annoyed that my injury is forcing me to be so useless.

"Are you worried about leaving her unsupervised in the kitchen?" Laughing, I open the flaps of the box and survey the contents. Various framed photos and bits of decor look back at me. I pull out a tissue-wrapped lump and carefully set it aside before pulling my bedside lamp out of the box, where I can see it every night. "It's retail therapy for her. At least I talked her out of buying us that giant block of cheese. Did you see it? It would have taken us a year to eat it."

Laughing, Martin pulls open the box marked "books" and starts pulling them out and shoving them in the bookcase next to the desk. "My mum would have done the same. Actually, my mum would have bought twice as much food." He stops, laughs, then pulls out the scrapbook the girls made me before I left. "What is this?"

The book is hideous, which is part of the joke. Katy insisted that the cartoon baby elephants on the cover needed tutus, bits of tulle are haphazardly hot glued to the page, along with a string of plastic beads around the edge, one corner already falling off. She'd tried to fix the out-of-proportion faces of the elephants by coloring in parts of it, but really it just made it worse. I'd laughed so hard at the mustache she drew on the one that I'd nearly peed my pants when I opened it. The pages inside are filled with pictures and inside jokes between us. My personal favorite is the collage of our favorite ballet boys, cut and assembled by Olivia from old copies of Dance Spirit magazine, for "when I'm lonely."

Martin and I abandon unpacking while I look through it with him, trying to explain the jokes that make no sense when a muffled crash from the kitchen interrupts us. "You okay, Mom?"

"Yup, all good. Just dropped a box of crackers. As you were!"

"Did we buy crackers? I don't remember crackers?" Martin's whisper sets me off giggling. "Was that what the cheese was for?"

Cracking jokes, we keep unpacking my room, falling back into the easy camaraderie we had in New York, laughing over anything and everything. We're both giddy with excitement now that we're actually here and decorating our new place.

Ours. As scary as it is when I think about being on my own, now that it's happening I'm eager to get started on my new adventure.

"Do you miss them?" I move on to my suitcase and start pulling out clothes to hang up. "Your family, I mean. You haven't been home since May."

"Of course I miss them, but we knew this was going to happen. I miss Sammy more." Martin grabs another stack of books to put away.

"When did he go back to New Zealand?" I maneuver carefully between boxes to hang up an armful of clothes. "Have you heard from him?"

Flipping my copy of *101 Stories of the Great Ballets* over in his hands, the cover bent and dog-eared, Martin slumps. His mood shifts in an instant, the laughter we'd been sharing fading away. "He left the day before I flew out here. Broke up with me on the subway on the way to the airport."

"What?" I abandon my armload of clothes, dropping onto the floor next to him. "Why? You two were so crazy about each other." The weight of how things ended with Trevor comes crashing back, my own mood flipping to match Martin's.

Martin leans his head against my shoulder while I awkwardly pull my booted foot out from under me and prop it on a pile of pillows. His deep sigh almost knocks me over. "He decided that being long-distance was going to be too hard. Especially since neither of us know when I'll be back, or if he'll get a chance to come to the States again."

"I'm so sorry, Martin." I can't think of anything else to say so I hug him hard, hoping it's enough for now.

"I don't blame him. All that uncertainty, not knowing what's coming next. It's scary. I get it. I'm scared too. I just didn't think it would be enough to make him give up on us."

Martin's words are a bullseye straight to my heart. Isn't that what I just did to Trevor? In all the uncertainty of moving up here, I got scared and pushed him away? Only I was far stupider than Sammy. The thousands of miles of ocean between here and New Zealand is a much more reasonable obstacle than my own overwhelmed anxiety. For goodness sake, I just moved *closer* to Trevor, it should be easier, not harder to be together.

Wrapping an arm around my shoulder, Martin squeezes me in a lopsided hug. "As mad as I am at Sammy for giving up on us, I understand it. If I'm being honest, we're both to blame." I wait, sensing there's more to the story. "All of our plans, the plans we made together, got turned on their head. We were supposed to be starting our new life together in New York City. When his visa got denied, well, everything fell apart. He wanted me to come back to New Zealand with him. We fought over it for days while we tried to get the visa fixed."

"What? That's crazy? He wanted you to just give up all your opportunities to be with him?" I hadn't heard this part of the story, my opinion of Sammy rapidly changing. How could anyone ask their partner to give up their dream like that?

Martin chuckles at my outrage. "I know that. Sammy knows that too. But in the moment, he panicked. When he was angry and scared and felt like he was going to lose me anyway, it didn't feel unreasonable."

"How do you know this?"

Martin digs out his phone and unlocks it, showing me a text thread between him and Sammy. I read the thread, Sammy saying everything Martin just told me. "So…are you back together now?"

"No. He's right, staying together when we have no idea how or when we'll be in the same country again is asking too much. I still love him, he still loves me. If life ever works out that we can be together, we'll figure it out when we get there. But for now. No. It would be unfair to both of us."

We sit in miserable silence together for a few moments. The only thing I can think of is the look on Trevor's face when I walked away from him the last time. How can he ever forgive me?

With a groan, I bang my head against the wall behind me. "Martin. Why am I like this?" I spill the whole story of how I kind of broke up with Trevor the last time I saw him, and the last texts we exchanged. How scared and overwhelmed I was, how much I regret it now. I don't bother to hide the tears that leak out my eyes as I talk. I haven't had a chance to talk about Trevor or cry over it with anyone. Crying about missing him when my best friends were already upset about me leaving never felt fair, so I'd kept my tears to myself. As far as my friends know, we broke up because of something he said. Not even Tyler seems to know any different.

Pouring it all out to Martin is such a relief. Even though I'm crying, I manage what feels like the first full breath I've taken in weeks. Once I finish my story, Martin stands up, pulling me to my feet. "Good lord, girl, we're a real pair."

"Am I stupid? It's not that I don't want to be with him, but I couldn't handle all the pressure. It was too much." Looking around the room, this strange room that's supposed to be my new home and feels nothing like it, it's just boxes of crap and bare walls. Minutes ago, I was giddy with excitement over the chance to start fresh. Now I'm sad and scared all over again.

"You're not stupid, yeah? You also weren't totally in the wrong."

"What do you mean? I was a brat about the whole thing. He was trying to help." The more time that passes, all I remember is how Trevor was trying to help and I kept throwing it back in his face, refusing to let him, because I wanted to do it on my own.

Martin grips my shoulders, forcing me to look at him. "Hannah, stop that right now. Yes, he was trying to help. But you need to trust your instincts. If you had a gut feeling it was too much, too soon and that he was trying to make your choices for you, then you did the right thing by standing up for yourself."

"Martin's right, you know." Mom's voice from my doorway startles me. "I know you care about Trevor, but I'm glad you stood up for yourself and didn't make the choice that was easiest and best for *him* over what was best for you."

Sniffing and wiping the tears from my eyes I chuckle, falling into the hug Martin offers. "I got you, love. We're gonna be alright."

"Promise?" My voice is watery, but, deep down in my gut, determination to succeed swirls.

"Come on you two, I want to make sure you're all unpacked before you take me to the airport in the morning." Mom claps her hands together and surveys my room. "Hannah, you finish what you can in here. Martin, there's more stuff in the car to bring inside. Let's go." She grabs Martin by the arm and pulls him through the door.

Bare walls mean a chance to start fresh. A new home means I get to make of it what I want. Trevor or no Trevor, moving to Seattle is about me and my dream, my choice. Haven't I always said that I wanted more than just good grades and a boyfriend? This is my chance to make it happen. To be more. To do more than just be a typical teenager.

I've had my chance to wallow, I've had a good cry, and a hug. I can do this. Falling apart is not an option, not anymore.

CHAPTER THIRTEEN

Trevor

SEPTEMBER

"T**HAT'S MY** boy!" Derek tackles me into the grass moments after he follows me over the finish line. Rolling us over and over, he thumps my back, his laughter booming in my ear. "Did you see that time? That's five seconds off my PR baby!"

Coach extends a hand to pull me to my feet. "Well done, son. Another undefeated weekend. You keep this up and you'll be drowning in offers for the fall." We stand to the side as the rest of the runners cross the finish line.

And even though I shouldn't, I can't help searching the crowd. Maybe this time I'll spot a messy bun of fire-red hair. I should be celebrating my first-place win with my friends, not pinning my hopes on the girl I haven't heard from in over a month.

She isn't here.

Again.

OCTOBER

"DUDE, SHE'S not coming." The couch dips as Matt plops next to me, his head in his hands. Literally.

I knock the wolf-head mask out of his hands as I shove Matt off me. "Dude, you're sitting on my cape. And yes, I know she's not coming." I pull the yellow and black cape out from under him before rubbing my hands up and down the slippery green fabric covering my thighs, ignoring the twist in my gut. Matt didn't mean it like that, I know that. It doesn't make me feel any better though.

It should be an "L" for Loser on my chest instead of an "R" for Robin.

"Are we still moping over this? Come on man, let it go. It's Halloween, try and have some fun."

I don't answer, just stare at my phone, stuck on the photo Hannah just posted to Instagram of her and Martin.

She dressed as Starfire.

Is that a message? Or is she just that cruel?

I don't want to believe she'd do it on purpose to hurt me, but it's like a knife to my chest. Every day I don't hear from her, the knife slides in a little deeper.

The purple mini skirt hugging her hips, her long red hair cascading down her back. I ache to be the one holding her, even as fury at her burns low in my gut. These days, it never stops.

NOVEMBER

*M*AGGIE'S SHRILL cheers reach me over the rest of the crowd as I step up onto the podium. Grinning, I duck my head so the official can loop the medal around my neck. "Yeah, Trevor! Whoo!"

My dad's deep cheer joins hers, my mom's embarrassing cry of "That's my baby!" reaches me a second later. I wave at them in the stands, not letting my eyes wander over the crowd. I am *not* searching for a certain blue-eyed girl.

Determined to enjoy this moment, finally getting on the podium a State, I push Hannah from my mind. She could have been here, if she wanted to be. It's time to move on, she obviously has.

I just wish my stupid heart would get the message.

DECEMBER

"...*Y*OOOOOOUUUUUUU!" MAGS can't quite compete with Mariah Carey, but who can, right? Bopping her shoulders to the jingling of bells in the familiar song, I can't help joining her when the lyrics start.

This is the first Christmas I've ever truly related to the words. I don't need anything for Christmas, because the one thing I want, I can't have.

Singing along, I push Hannah to the back of my mind and attempt to be happy in the moment. I haven't seen much of Mags in the last week—she's been busy with rehearsals for the

Nutcracker while I've been buried in college applications and studying for finals.

I've also been avoiding all talk of ballet. For obvious reasons.

But Dad has a doctor's appointment and Mom needed to be there for this one so I'm stuck with driving Maggie to rehearsal, a chore I've managed to avoid by driving her to her regular ballet classes instead. I don't want to risk running into Hannah, and I know that's a very distinct possibility since Maggie hasn't stopped talking about how cool it is that Hannah was cast as one of the parents in the party scene, the same scene that my sister is in as one of the party guests.

Yes, you heard that right.

My little sister has spent weeks rehearsing with the love of my life while I haven't gotten more than the occasional selfie on Instagram. What I did in another life to deserve this torture I'll never know. And torture is exactly what it has been.

While I was busting my ass at cross country practice, she was starting her new classes at PSB. When I posted pictures of me and Derek at our first meet of the season, she posted a picture of her and Martin decorating their apartment. The day she was allowed to dance again was the day I bested my 10k time by a full fifteen seconds.

Every one of those moments, all I wanted to do was tell her, for her to want to tell me.

"Are you going to walk me to the door?" Maggie's voice echos against the concrete as I park in the structure adjacent to the theater downtown. She pulls her dance bag over her head, struggling against her heavy coat. A cold December wind blows through the city, a hint of snow in the air. We haven't had any yet, just lots of rain, lots and lots of cold rain. Climbing out of the car

I shove my arms through my coat sleeves, pulling the beanie I stuffed in the pocket out.

"Of course, Mags. Mom would kill me if I didn't," I add, grinning at her from under the beanie I've pulled down over my ears.

"But what if..." Mags trails off, glancing sideways at me.

"But what if what?"

Mags walks a few steps before answering me, the wheels in her head turning from the expressions flitting across her face. "Why haven't you called Hannah?"

Why haven't I?

I could say because she asked me to give her space and I'm respecting that decision. Or I could say it's because I've been busy with meets and all the pressure of senior year.

But deep down, it's because I'm afraid she's discovered she can live without me far easier than I can live without her. For all her worries about being able to handle moving up here, all the adult decisions being asked of her, if her Instagram is anything to go by, she's thriving.

I shove my frozen fingers deep into my coat pockets instead of throttling my sister, much as I'm tempted. "I haven't called her because the last thing she asked of me was to give her space. So that's what I'm doing. Giving her space."

Maggie huffs, her breath smoking in the air. "I think it's dumb. She misses you."

What? "And how the hell would you know that?"

"Language." Mags smirks at me. "I heard her talking about you during rehearsal to one of the other girls."

My steps slow as I take this news in. "First of all, you shouldn't be eavesdropping on other people's conversations." I clear my throat. "Secondly, how do you know she was talking about me?"

I hope Maggie can't tell how hard my heart is beating right now. It's thumping and galloping in my chest. I think I might be sick.

"*I* was standing *exactly* where I was *supposed* to be standing. I can't help it if she didn't keep her voice down." Maggie grins before shrugging and darting out onto the sidewalk. I jog a few steps to catch up.

Thank god my legs are longer than hers. I catch up in a few steps and hook my arm around her shoulders, dragging her back to walk next to me. To anyone passing by we look like a loving brother and sister, taking a stroll. They wouldn't be able to feel the tight grip I have on Maggie's shoulder, stopping her from running ahead. Evil child.

"And how do you know she was talking about me?" I grind out between my clenched teeth.

"Oh, that's easy." Maggie wiggles out from under my hand and dances ahead before turning and walking backwards, taunting me. "She said she'd been looking at this guy's pictures from the weekend and how he'd medaled at a big meet. It was the same weekend you got second at State." How she doesn't trip and fall walking backwards like that I don't know, especially when I'm tripping over my own feet at her words.

Hannah was talking about me? She knew about when I went to state?

"Quit being a wimp and just text her already." The little huff and flounce Maggie adds to the end of her sentence would be adorable if it wasn't my own little sister calling me on my shit. "You've been the worst for the last few months. Like, worse than when Dad was..." she doesn't finish her sentence, I don't need her to. I am well aware I've been a grumpy, miserable bastard for the last couple of months.

Matt and Derek both lost patience with me on Halloween, going so far as to steal my phone when I wouldn't stop scrolling through pictures of us at Matt's party. I dressed up as the Teen Titans with my family, I even helped my dad with his epic Cyborg costume, but my heart wasn't in it. Not even when they let me be Robin. Why? Because Hannah and Martin hosted a Halloween party at their house and dressed up as Beast Boy and Starfire. I couldn't believe she'd remembered—we'd talked about dressing up as Starfire and Robin over the summer, her red hair perfect for the part. How do I know this? Because I've been following Martin as obsessively as I've been following her, hoping for a glimpse of her.

I spent most of Thanksgiving debating if I should send her a text, just a "happy Thanksgiving" kind of thing. But I talked myself out of it since her parents were in town for the first time since September. How do I know? From Martin's numerous posts about his first American Thanksgiving. The picture he posted of Hannah and her mom showing off the turkey she cooked tore my heart in two. Not even Uncle Tom's famous cornbread stuffing, usually my favorite, got a smile out of me. Tyler gave me shit about it all weekend when they were visiting.

"Trevor. Just text her." I trail behind Maggie as we come up to the crosswalk in front of McCaw Hall. A crowd of dancers are already standing there waiting. Maggie darts ahead, spotting some of her friends. Her push between bodies reveals Hannah chatting to the dancer next to her, her red hair tucked inside a green beanie, the kind with an enormous pom-pom on top.

My heart freezes in my chest and time slows. Maggie glances to the side, sees Hannah and Martin standing there and pauses. Grinning, she cups her hands around her mouth and yells, "Come on, Trevor! Hurry up!"

The sadistic little…I'm going to kill her. Hannah turns, those blue eyes of hers wide, her perfect pink lips hanging open. Hungry for the sight, I keep my eyes trained on her as I take the last few steps between me and the group of dancers. "Hi," I say, wincing when my voice cracks on the single syllable.

"Hi." Hannah's reply is just a breath of a word, barely audible.

Before I can get another word out, the light changes and the crowd starts moving across the street, taking Hannah with them. Martin drags her across by the arm, some girl I don't recognize follows, giggling and looking back over her shoulder at me.

"Bye Trevor! I'm fine! Don't worry about me!" Maggie jumps up and waves from the middle of the crowd. Obnoxious brat. "I'll see you at nine thirty when you come pick me up!" Okay, maybe she's not the *absolute* worst.

My feet frozen to the ground, the crowd walks away, leaving me alone on this side of the street. Hannah keeps turning to look over her shoulder at me, but the crowd pulls her along. She looks just as beautiful as I remember, maybe a little thinner if that's possible. Better, actually, since there's no boot on her foot or pain etched in her eyes. The dark circles are still there under her eyes, but I'm sure that doesn't have anything to do with me.

I don't move until they disappear inside the theater. Once again, Hannah walked away from me. She's slipping through my fingers like dust at the end of "Infinity War," leaving me as broken-hearted as ever.

I spin on my heel and walk back to the car, fists clenching inside my coat pockets to stop them from tugging at my hair. Gripping my phone, there's no missing the buzz of an incoming message.

I don't know why, but I refuse to look until I'm sitting in the car. Maybe I just don't want to have my heart ripped out when it's not a text from the one person I want. No matter the reason, I pick up the pace and quick-walk to the van, sliding into the seat as I slip my phone out of my pocket.

> **AGENT CARTER:** I'll meet you at the stage door at 9:30. Text her loser, I'll know if you don't.

That was not the text I was hoping for. Disappointed, I toss my phone in the cupholder and start the engine, flipping on the heater before I buckle up. It rattles with the buzz of another incoming message. I ignore it while I pull my seatbelt on. I am not going to be Maggie's puppet today, thanks.

The second and third buzzes can't be ignored though. Little brat, I'll make her wait, just to piss her off. Glancing at the phone, it's not another sassy text from Mags that catches my eye.

> **LISA:** I don't know what just happened, but I just had a weird text from Hannah. Are you okay? Is she okay?

Huh. That's the first I've heard from Lisa since the night I came home. Why is she texting me now? What's different now from three months ago when Hannah broke my heart the first time? I never thought Lisa and I were friends, but I won't deny I was hurt I never heard anything from her after that night.

> **ME:** We just ran into each other for the first time since she moved up here. I'm not particularly okay. I have no idea how she is, she still isn't talking to me.

I flip to the other message that came in while I wait for Lisa to answer. It's not a text, so I tap over to Instagram to respond to the message.

> **@NZMARTINDANCES:** I'm assuming you know who this is. I know this is random, and I probably should have reached out before. She misses you. A lot. She's going home to CA for NYE. We finish performances on Dec 24, she flies home that night. Shoot your shot.

What is happening? This is seriously all it took to get her friends on my side? I should have tried harder to "run into" her earlier—not that today was on purpose.

> **@MARVELOUSSTANLEY:** Yeah, I know who this is. Um, thanks? I think?
> **@NZMARTINDANCES:** Shit, she's asking who I'm messaging. Just talk to her.
> **@MARVELOUSSTANLEY:** I'm not the one who asked for space. She broke up with me, not the other way around.

Taking a deep breath and dropping my phone back into the cupholder, I start driving so I won't be tempted to look. Nothing good is going to come from this conversation, I know it. The anger I've kept tamped down since August comes boiling up to the surface.

Everyone seems to have forgotten that I was the one who pursued her for months. I was the one who kept trying to find reasons to talk to her, despite how much shit Tyler gave me at first, despite Derek and Matt's endless teasing about my "fake girlfriend." Even my dad gave me a hard time about flying off to California to win back my girl, only for her to move a thousand miles closer and *still* not be with me. More importantly, they don't seem to remember that she's the one who walked away from me. Twice. I've done my best to be there, to help her, to be the person she can depend on and she's found a reason to be angry and walked away. And now everyone expects me to be the one to grovel and beg for her to take me back? How is that fair?

I want her back so desperately, but I'm not going to beg. Not this time.

Not that I want her to beg. I just want her to want me.

I slam my hand on the steering wheel, needing to release some of the pent up emotion coursing through me. Why is she making this so difficult? It doesn't have to be. We could just be together. It's not that hard. The Christmas music Mags left playing in the van is not helping my mood. I don't want to hear about being snuggled up with anyone right now, sleigh ride or not.

At the next red light, I snatch my phone up and find Radiohead's *Creep*. That's better. Cranking up the volume, I ignore the cars around me, drumming my hands on the steering wheel and sing, shout, whatever, as loud as I can. There's something cathartic about declaring myself a weirdo at the top of my lungs, not caring if anyone else can hear me.

Pulling into the driveway and throwing the van in park, I dash into the house. Loki bounds up to me, his wet nose cold against my thigh as I change from my jeans into a pair of running tights before pulling a pair of shorts over them. I'm angry, sad, and frustrated, but that doesn't mean I want to freeze my balls while I run my anger off. Finals are next week and I should study, but there's no way I could concentrate right now. Loki keeps dancing in my way as I tie my shoes, his nails tap dancing on the floor in his excitement.

Not bothering to do any of the warm-ups or stretches I should, I clip Loki's leash on his collar and lock the front door behind me. My earbuds blasting an angry mix of music in my ears, Loki and I take off down the street. The stinging cold air needling against my cheeks is a good excuse for the tears that occasionally leak from my eyes, right? It's just the wind making my eyes water. Definitely not remembering the glassy look in Hannah's big blue eyes as she looked up at me. Or maybe that's just the drizzle in the air accumulating on my face.

My lungs heave, my feeble, stupid heart trying to thump in my chest as I run the slowest, hardest three-mile loop in years. The mix of sadness and anger flowing through me is unfortunately familiar. Is it worse when it's over a girl or over a parent? I don't know. Does it even matter? Between the freezing cold air around me and the heat in my belly burning through my skin, I imagine the neighbors can see the steam rising off me as I flash past. Are my cheeks the same pink as Hannah's? That adorable beanie pulled down over her ears almost meeting the scarf wrapped around her neck, perfectly framing the face I love, is burned into my mind.

Even though it's just after five, it's already dark, so Loki and I stick to the well-lit streets we know. I'm upset and crushed but that doesn't mean I want to risk a sprained ankle. I almost did that the last time I was this upset, and the last thing we need is me adding to my mom's stress. Rounding the corner onto my street, Loki tugs at the leash, eager to get inside. I let him pull me towards the front door, my leaden legs slowing to a walk. Sucking oxygen in through my mouth, I'm doubly glad no one is around to hear the audible sob that escapes me as I pull the garage door open. I make Loki wait in the entry while I towel his muddy feet off, before heading straight to the bathroom to shower, biting my lips to swallow down the utter devastation seeing Hannah again wreaked in my soul.

Now that I'm inside, the cold seeps into my bones, my skin turning icy while I wait for the shower to heat up. Why won't she just let us be together? I know I've made mistakes, too. But is being protective and wanting to help so terrible? Anger and sadness continue the never-ending battle they've been fighting in my heart since September. The influx of texts from her friends now making it worse. Why aren't they on my side in this? For three months they've been silent. Not a peep. Now I get messages? What did I do that was so wrong—that deserved being ignored—and now having to be the one to apologize? Again.

By the time I'm out of the shower and can feel my fingers and toes again, I'm determined that this time Hannah is the one who needs to apologize to me. Right?

No way will I crumble and beg her to take me back the second I see her. Not a chance.

CHAPTER FOURTEEN

Hannah

"GIRL, YOU look like you've seen a ghost," Sloane, one of the few girls I've befriended here, whispers in my ear as we stand on the side of the stage, clapping to the music. I plaster a smile on my face, making eye contact with my fake husband on my left. James grins back, raising his clapping hands in acknowledgment of my own, a silent, practiced conversation while the kids on stage dance.

"It's nothing," I whisper back through clenched teeth. "Just having a bad day." The party girls and boys dance in the center of the stage while the rest of us playing their parents stand around clapping and miming what a wonderful Christmas party this is. Playing a party parent wouldn't be my first choice for a debut performance with the Pacific Sound Ballet, but I have to start somewhere, right?

Besides, since I was only allowed to start taking full classes at the end of September, after casting had been decided, I couldn't fault Marco Bethelo for putting me in a role that didn't require much dancing and freeing up one of the real corps de ballet ladies for a different role. I tried hard to be mad about it, but I would have done the same thing in his shoes.

That doesn't stop me from wishing I got to be one of the girls doing Waltz of the Flowers or Snowflakes.

James steps out in front of me, offering his hand, while Sloane's partner does the same on my right. Taking it, James leads me galloping across the stage in the line of couples, our pretend children scatter to the sides of the stage as the parents take a turn to dance. My hooped petticoat, the only part of our costume the ladies and girls are wearing tonight, bounces and swishes as we move. Tonight's rehearsal is for spacing the kids on stage and for the lighting designer to get everything set. Tomorrow's dress rehearsal for Cast A will be the first time everyone is dancing in costume, but we're wearing the hoop skirts now, so we know how much space they'll take up.

The rest of the rehearsal creeps by. Thank god I don't get any notes because I'm absolutely distracted by seeing Trevor earlier. Was his face thinner than the last time I saw him? His hair is definitely longer. I hadn't noticed anything from the pictures he's posted on Instagram, not that he's posted very much, unlike me. Every picture I post I wonder if he'll see it, what he thinks of it.

"Ready to go?" Martin sticks his head in the door of the dressing room I'm sharing with all the other female students and apprentices. His floppy brown hair is damp with sweat from his part in the Spanish dance. Glancing at my phone to check the time, indecision fills my gut. Martin must see it on my face.

"It's nine thirty-five. If you want to see him, we should go now. Or you could just text him like a normal person."

Do I want to see him?

"If you don't want him, can I have him?" Sloane teases from across the room. "We're talking about the guy who was at the crosswalk, right? He's cute! Skinny, but cute."

"He's not skinny, he's a runner." The objection is out of my mouth before I know what I'm saying. Martin and Sloane share a smirk at my words before making a show of leaving without me. In a panic, I rush to catch up. Sloane is the closest thing I have to a friend here, but I don't trust her not to flirt with Trevor. I've watched her do it at every opportunity and a little thing like Trevor being my ex isn't going to stop her. Snatching up my bag and coat I hurry after them, catching up just as they hit the big glass doors leading out to the street.

"Martin, Sloane, don't you dare…" I choke on my words at the sight of Trevor standing there, a little girl I can't pretend I don't recognize hanging off his arm. The smile he gives her is the same smile he used to give me. The one that lights up his eyes and made me feel like I was the most important person in his whole world.

I ache for that smile.

The second Trevor sees me and the smile drops off his face, my heart aches even more. A shiver runs down my spine at the guarded look in his eye. I open and close my mouth, searching for words, desperately hoping to find the ones that will bring that smile back.

I'm pretty sure they start with *I'm sorry*, and end with, *I'm such an idiot*.

But with everyone staring at me the words won't come. Someone bumps into my back, knocking me sideways. Trevor takes a quick step towards me, hand outstretched like he's going to catch me. My stuffed dance bag swings into a trash can, stopping me from falling as pointe shoes and my beanie fall out onto the wet cement.

"I got it!" The little girl with Trevor dives to the ground, scrambling to pick up my shoes. Trevor leans down and snatches my beanie off the ground while I try to control the pounding of my heart. Why am I so useless right now?

"Here you go. I don't think they got too wet. You can save them, right?" The little girl shoves my shoes into my hands. "I'm Maggie, by the way," she adds, rocking back on her heels and smiling at me.

"I know," I say, my voice quiet. I recognize her from pictures Trevor showed me over the summer. I've been rehearsing with her for weeks and haven't had the courage to talk to her. Yes, I am one hundred percent intimidated by Trevor's little sister.

"Are your shoes going to be okay?" Maggie asks again. "None of them are too damaged to wear anymore?" I catch the hopeful note in her voice.

"They're fine. Thank you for grabbing them so quickly. I'm sure they'll be dead by the end of the last dress rehearsal. If you wanted one," I add, praying I don't sound as stupid as I feel.

"That would be so cool, thank you." Maggie says, bouncing on her toes. Looking at Trevor is too hard, so I keep my eyes trained on the ground, checking that nothing else fell out of my bag.

Gentle hands pull the beanie down over my head while I look down—the only hint to their owner a pair of dirty Vans I know well. When a finger touches the underside of my chin, tenderly lifting my face, I can't stop my sharp gasp. "I like the hat, it's cute." He clears his throat and flicks a finger at the pom pom on top of my head before speaking again. "It's good to see you, Hannah." The indifferent words don't match the tightness of his voice, like he's fighting to get the words out.

"You too," I manage to say. Swallowing, I grasp at whatever words come to me first. "Are you coming to any of the shows?"

"Wouldn't miss it for the world." I swear he's about to say something more but instead we just stand there, like two idiots, staring at each other. I take in his face. The warm brown eyes have a new sadness to them I don't recognize. He looks leaner than I remember, would it feel the same to wrap my arms around his waist like I used to? If he held me against his chest like before, would his heart still have that solid thump? Would I feel as safe and calm as before?

Before I can get my fill of his face, Trevor steps back, rubbing a hand against his chest. "I need to get Maggie home." Before I can say a word, he's gripping her arm and tugging her away. Maggie looks back at me over her shoulder, grinning and giving me a big thumbs up before the light changes and he drags her across the street. I don't move, afraid I'll miss it if he looks back. I've almost given up hope, resigning myself to the fact that he must hate me now, when they reach the entrance to the parking structure. Just before they disappear inside Trevor pauses, looking back. He doesn't smile, he doesn't frown, he just looks.

If he was angry, if he yelled at me like I deserve, my heart might not be racing so hard. The world goes out of focus as tears blur my vision before arms wrap around me, pulling me into a warm chest. The tears I can't stop spill over as I sob into Martin's embrace. "Shhh, shhh. I got you." Martin's accent thickens as he rubs a hand on my back. "Come on, let's go home, I'm frozen stiff. I'll cook up some grub, yeah?"

Nodding, I untangle myself from his arms, wiping my face with frozen fingers as I step back. Sloane hooks an arm through Martin's. "I'm inviting myself over for dinner. I'll stop and grab some reinforcements on the way. Is this an ice cream or cake kind of broken heart?"

Sniffling and laughing, I dig in my dance bag for a tissue while we wait for the light to change. "Ice cream. Definitely ice cream." Martin and I follow Sloane across the street to my car. Do I keep glancing around, hoping to see Trevor's red minivan? Of course. But we make it to the car without any further incidents.

Sliding inside, I have the engine running and am backing out of my parking spot before Martin speaks up. "So, you want to talk about that?"

"We're not waiting for Sloane?"

"Well, since she doesn't know the whole story, I wasn't sure how much you wanted to share, yeah?"

He does have a point. "I don't know that I want to tell her *everything*. Sloane..." I fumble for the word. "I don't want everyone else to know about it before tomorrow. There's nothing for them to know." I shrug, looking down the street before pulling out of the structure.

"You know they would eat up any story about you. The infamously quiet Hannah O'Brian, who showed up in a boot and never talks to anyone, has ex-boyfriend drama? And a cute ex at that? They'll eat it up."

"Exactly." After having a target painted on my back all summer, all I wanted was to blend in, keep my head down and dance. "I don't want to be part of the gossip. I really, really don't." I've been keeping as low a profile as possible, something that's been much easier since the end of September when I was allowed to take full classes again and could stop showing up to class juggling my yoga mat and ball. My weekly check-ins with Dr. Lee have slowed to every couple of weeks.

Living with Martin, social butterfly and class star, is the only reason anyone pays attention to me these days, which is just fine. After my experience with Becky and her friends in the summer, I've been wary of getting close to the girls in my class.

"Talk to me, Han," Martin says, not letting me get away with silence.

"He hates me." I sigh. "There's no way he doesn't hate me."

"That was not the look of a guy who hates you."

"He *should* hate me. I broke up with him—twice—when he was just trying to help. I asked him to give me space and then… then never spoke to him again."

Martin reaches across the car to flick me on the ear. "Well, when you put it like that. Maybe he should, but I don't think he does. We talked about this months ago, you did the right thing. You needed space to make your own choices when you got here." We drive in silence for a few miles, the wet roads glistening under the streetlights. "I've been dying to ask, though. Why'd you ghost him?" Martin asks, stilling the nervous tapping of my thumbs on the steering wheel.

Silent, I shrug. I don't have a good reason other than being ashamed and scared of the way I'd treated Trevor the first time. Not knowing what to say, I said nothing. And the longer I went without talking to him, the harder it became to start the conversation.

"Hannah."

"The same reason you haven't spoken to Sammy. I don't know what to say and I'm terrified I'll say the wrong thing."

Pulling into our parking space, I propel myself out of the car and up the stairs, dance bag swinging against my hip. I've unlocked the front door and dumped my bag in the entryway before Martin can catch up. "I'm taking a shower. You're cooking dinner, right?"

"*I* THINK I'M going to be sick." Flopping sideways onto the couch, I lean back to stretch out my bloated stomach, my feet in Martin's lap. Sloane just left after all three of us ate way too much ice cream and I spent way too long telling them how great Trevor is.

"It was worth it though." Martin patted his stomach. "American ice cream is so good, even if your chocolate is terrible."

My laugh turns into a groan as my stomach grumbles. "Totally worth it. We had chicken and salad for dinner, even Alyssa would say it was a balanced meal."

Grinning, Martin tosses one of the pillows at my face which I grab and tuck behind my back. "I'm pretty sure your nutritionist would not approve of that meal, but you can continue to tell yourself that lie." He eyes me for a moment. "Are you feeling better?"

Sighing, I lean my head back against the arm of the couch and close my eyes. "Kind of?" When Martin doesn't say anything, I keep talking. "I miss him. I miss him so much. And part of me is glad that I've had to do all this," I wave my hand around at our little apartment, "on my own. I am. I needed to know I could do it."

I open my eyes and look at my friend, my friend who's been with me through all the good and bad days of the last three months. He knows how many nights I shut myself in my room, he heard me crying myself to sleep even if he never said anything. "But part of me wishes I'd had him with me the whole time. Some of this would have been so much easier with him around. But…the last time we were together he was so determined to be helpful that I couldn't speak up for myself. I knew he would offer to do everything for me, and I would let him. Because that would be so much easier for me and it would make him happy."

I shrug, meeting Martin's eyes. "It would have been easier, but would it have been better? I don't know. All I know is that right now I miss him so much it hurts."

"I get that." Martin pokes at my legs, so I lift them to let him stand up. "What happened, happened. You can't take it back. What you do from here is up to you. Just, don't do nothing." Reaching down, he takes my hand and pulls me up off the couch. "Let's go sleep off the food. Night, Han."

"Night." With a peck on my cheek, Martin heads down the hall to his room. I follow to my own room, flipping off the lights in our *clean*—take that Mom—apartment and slip into my room. Sliding under the covers, enjoying their weight and warmth, I stretch my body out, from the tips of my fingers to the ends of my toes, making space in my belly for all the food I ate.

Determined to torture myself, I pull out my phone and flip through all the photos of Trevor and I from the summer, including the screenshots of some of our conversations. I stop on my favorite, a silly little back and forth we'd shared while surrounded by our friends at the summer intensive. Our own secret conversation, even though in the end I'd been blushing so hard Gloria called me out on it. I might as well make it my phone wallpaper I read it so often.

TREVOR: What magic do you use on your skin? It's so soft.

ME: Ummm, lotion?

TREVOR: Nope, pretty sure there's some kind of magic in there because I can't seem to stop touching you. You're addictive.

ME: I don't mind. You can keep touching. I like it when you touch my skin.

TREVOR: You're killing me here TT.

ME: Um, yeah, I didn't think about how that sounded before I sent it. Sorry?

TREVOR: Don't be sorry. You're adorable. And have magical soft skin. I think I'll keep you.

ME: You can keep me forever.

TREVOR: I'm holding you to that.

Not that I'd kept up my end of the deal. I hadn't kept him forever. I hadn't even kept him for another week after that. Because I'm the worst. He's never going to forgive me, it doesn't matter what Martin thinks.

Flipping over to Instagram, I pull up his account, scrolling through the photos he's posted in the last few months. I can picture the extra photos that would be there if I hadn't been so stupid and broke up with him. A photo of us dressed as Robin and Starfire together. Yes, I secretly binge watched all of the Teen Titans cartoons and I knew exactly what I was doing when I suggested that's what Martin and I dress up as for his Halloween party. Not because I wanted to make Trevor jealous, but somehow I hoped he would know I was thinking about him.

Would we have had Thanksgiving together? I can imagine my parents, Martin and me having Thanksgiving with his family.

His sister Maggie is a riot, even if every time I've seen her in rehearsal it breaks my heart. I've known who she is since the first rehearsal, but I have no idea if she knew who I was. She's never tried to talk to me before today.

As I'm scrolling through his pictures a new one pops up. It's a picture of Loki sprawled out on his bed looking up at him with sad eyes, with the caption: Same buddy, same.

Tears fill my eyes. This is all my fault. I broke him. I broke myself. I broke us.

And why?

So I could claim I did it on my own? To feel independent? Grown up? I don't know if it was worth it. My life consists of waking up early to do Pilates, staring at my computer for a couple hours in my classes, then dancing. I don't talk to anyone except Martin and sometimes Sloane. Being able to dance again soothed a wound in my soul, sure, but it's not the same as it used to be. Physically, it feels just as good as before, maybe even better. The exhaustion, the challenge, the exactness of it—being here is refining my technique exponentially. But in my heart, it's different. I can't visualize the scenes around me anymore, I can't find the place in my mind where the magic lives.

I forgot how to dance with joy.

Maybe because I haven't felt it myself in so long.

And then it happens. My thumb, of its own volition, double taps the photo.

No. No. What have I done? I've been so careful to keep my distance, to not hurt him anymore and then I have to go and like *that* picture? Of all the ones to do it on. And it's new, he's going to know it was me, there's no hiding it. He probably already knows. What is he thinking? Have I lost my mind? Can I claim temporary insanity? Do I need to send him a message? I need to send him a message, right? But if I tell him it was an accident isn't that going to hurt his feelings even more? What do I do?

"Martin!" I shriek, dropping my phone in my lap. I need help.

Footsteps pound in the hallway before my door flies open. "What? What's wrong?" Martin asks, his words marked by the heaving of his chest. "Christ, you gave me a fright."

"I accidentally liked Trevor's photo. What do I do?" I hold the phone out to him, like a bomb about to explode.

Martin doesn't take it from me, just stares at me, one eyebrow raised. "That's what you're shrieking about? Lord, what am I going to do with you?"

I thrust it out at him. "Help me. Please?" I try adding some big eyes to help my case, although I don't think Martin can see much in the dark of my room.

"Nope, not my problem. Maybe you should just text him already. Or invite him over to talk. Do something. Anything."

"I don't appreciate your reasonableness right now," I complain, slumping back against my pillows. "He just posted about being sad. And I liked it. He's going to hate me."

"Oh, for fuck's sake." Martin holds his hand out, snatching my phone out of my hand when I don't hand it over quick enough. "Give it here." He types out a message and holds it out to me to approve.

@HANNAHBANANABALLERINA: I didn't want you to think I like that you're feeling sad tonight. I am too. Any chance I can see you again? On purpose this time?

"Yes or no?" He pulls it out of my reach when I go to grab it. I can't send that message. It's too honest, too real. My stomach bottoms out at the thought of Trevor reading those words. "Yes or no?" Martin asks again. "I'm not letting you change it. You either send it like this or not at all."

I can't say nothing. I can't.

"Yes."

CHAPTER FIFTEEN

Trevor

@HANNAHBANANABALLERINA: I didn't want you to think I like that you're feeling sad tonight. I am too. Any chance I can see you again sometime? On purpose this time?

I'VE BEEN staring at Hannah's message, not knowing how to answer. I can't tell if she had someone else write it for her, or if she's nervous, but it doesn't sound like my Hannah. I'm tempted to tease her about it, but there's too much between us now to risk it.

@MARVELOUSSTANLEY: I don't want you to be sad. I don't want either of us to be sad.

Her reply is almost instantaneous.

@HANNAHBANANABALLERINA: I have so many things I want to tell you, but I don't know where to start…

I know the feeling.

> **@MARVELOUSSTANLEY:** I know you're probably super busy with Nutcracker, but is there any chance of seeing you this weekend?

This time her reply takes longer to arrive. Loki is the winner tonight since I distract myself from Hannah's silence by giving him head scratches.

> **@HANNAHBANANABALLERINA:** Martin is having people over tomorrow for a post-dress rehearsal celebration. Do you want to come?

A second message arrives before I can think of a response.

> **@HANNAHBANANABALLERINA:** I understand if you don't want to see me again with a bunch of strangers, but I'd really like to show you our place. I know it's not what you wanted for me, but I think you'll like it once you see it.

How can I say no to that?

> **@MARVELOUSSTANLEY:** Text me the address.

Oh god, what if she blocked my number and that's why she's messaging me instead of sending a text? But my fear proves unfounded a second later when a text from Hannah arrives with an address and a time.

ME: See you there
HANNAH: See you. Goodnight.
ME: Goodnight.

I stop myself before I say something stupid like *sweet dreams*.

Waking up Saturday morning, the only thing I can think of to pass the time is a long run. Since the summer I haven't been running super long distances, Coach didn't want me to burn my legs out during the season. But today, ten miles seems like the only way to stop myself from obsessing over what tonight is going to be like.

Questions crowd my brain as my feet hit the pavement. Not even the familiar droning of Jim Dale and the Battle of Hogwarts drown out the noise.

Will she pretend I'm just a friend? What about Martin? He knows the whole story, what will he do? Do they have new friends I need to win over? Why am I the one who has to put on a performance anyway? Hannah is the one who owes me the apology, right?

Even though I was the one who tried to railroad her into doing things my way. Living with my family. Going to my school. Don't I owe her an apology for that? No matter how good my reasons, I should have realized she needed space to live her own dream. Her dreams are bigger than just me, it's one of the things I love about her, so why am I holding it against her?

There are so many things to talk about, things I never told her, words I need to say.

I'm exhausted and sweaty by the time I get home. "Hey, Dad." I say, passing him on my way into the kitchen to empty out the rest of my water bottle and toss out the bits of trash from the energy gels I took with me.

"Hey Trev, had a good run?" He pats the empty couch seat next to him, the college football game he's watching muted.

Instead of sitting, I lean on the arm of the couch, toeing off my shoes before going into the stretching sequence I learned over the summer, starting with my calves. "It was okay. Haven't run that long in a while, wasn't sure I was going to make it home." I slide one leg back into a deep lunge, stretching my hip flexor with a groan.

"You could have called me for a pick-up." Dad gives me a hard look.

"I know. I would have if I needed it." I direct my words to the floor, rather than my Dad's face. I look around, the rest of the house is quiet. "Where are Mom and Mags?"

"They went to Costco and to buy some dance stuff for Mags, I don't remember what," Dad says, turning back to the game. "I'm fine, you know that."

I wince, regretting hurting his feelings. Driving is difficult for my dad now, I hate asking him to drive if he doesn't have to. I hang out with Dad, finishing up the stretches while we watch the game.

"Have you finished your applications yet?" Dad asks on the next commercial break. "Running out of time to apply to UCLA you know."

How do I tell him I don't want to go to UCLA without him thinking it's because of him? It *is* because of him. Well, him and Hannah, but still. "I'm working on it, Dad. I promise, I'll get it done in time."

He eyes me from across the couch. "Listen Trev, I know you want to stay close to help your mom, and probably because of that girl you're still stuck on, right?"

I don't bother to lie this time. "I've thought about it."

"You gotta make the best decisions for *you* right now, son. We'll be okay. I took care of your mom for a long time before you started helping, no matter how things are now. She's going to be okay. We're going to be okay. And Hannah? She may have had the right idea, not making her plans revolve around you. Now go shower, you stink."

Passing the afternoon watching the game with Dad, helping Mom unload the car, napping on the couch, and dropping Maggie off at the theater get me through the rest of the day. I don't see Hannah when I drop Mags off. As disappointed as I am, I'm glad. There is a limit to how cool I can be in a day and I'm trying to save it up for tonight when I meet Martin and her new friends. At her apartment.

That sounds so weird.

"**H**EY MAN, glad you made it. Seriously, I'm glad you're here. She's been a nervous wreck all day over this," Martin says dragging me inside their apartment a few hours later. "Listen, I know you don't care about me and the other guys here. Lemme introduce you all round real quick, and then will you please put her out of her misery?"

I laugh, blindsided by his welcome. "Uh, yeah, sure man." I stuff my hands in my pockets, only to pull them out again a second later when Martin starts introducing me to the small crowd in the room. I glance around the place as I follow Martin inside. It's small, the furniture from some kind of discount chain, but it's clean and cozy. And the neighborhood I passed on my way in looked safe enough.

Maybe she really is okay on her own. Without me.

Two guys and a girl—James, Patrick, and Sloane—are lounging on the gray couch. A decent-sized TV dominates the wall opposite them, playing some kind of Christmas music playlist. There's a couple scrunched on a matching armchair to one side and a few more people flopped on the floor. I hide my smile, I guess dancers are the same everywhere, just a bunch of overgrown cats. Maybe that musical isn't as far-fetched as I assumed.

The second Hannah steps out of the kitchen, plastic cup in hand, I forget every single name Martin just told me. Her red hair tumbles around her face, her cheeks still pink, either from her heavy makeup or from dancing, I can't tell. The dark eye makeup she's wearing makes those blue eyes of hers pop. "Hey," I say, moving slowly so I don't startle her.

She freezes, watching me walk towards her, wariness and relief in her eyes. "Hey." She takes a shaky sip from her cup. "I wasn't sure if you'd come."

"You asked. Of course, I came." The truth comes easy.

A tiny smile pulls at the corner of her lips. It takes everything in me not to lean in and kiss it. "I'm glad you're here."

"Okay you two, go away. The rest of us can't take this Hallmark moment. We're a bunch of jaded artists, you know," the girl on the couch says, shooing us away.

"Shut it Sloane," Martin grunts. "They're having a moment."

Heat creeps up my ears at the realization that all the other conversation in the room has stopped. Hannah and I are the show. Her ears are as red as mine feel as she glances around the room. Setting her cup down on the kitchen counter, Hannah grabs me by the hand. "Come on, I'll give you a tour."

I follow willingly as she pulls me down the hall, away from the sea of eyes. Holding her hand in mine, her skin as soft as I remember, fills a tiny corner of the emptiness inside me. For the first time in months, I take a full breath. "Here's Martin's room." Hannah waves to a closed door on my left. "That's some beach he loves in New Zealand. I always forget where it is." I pause to peer at the photo on the wall, the black sand intriguing. I spy the words Karekare Beach printed in the bottom corner and make a note to look it up later.

"Bathroom." Hannah sweeps past an open door to my right. I catch a glimpse of a tidy little bathroom—the bright green and yellow shower curtain the single splash of color in the otherwise white room. "And my room." We pause in front of another closed door. Hannah tucks a strand of hair behind her ear with a nervous laugh. "Did you want to, uh, see?"

"If you want to show me, absolutely. I just wanted to have a chance to talk. But if you'd rather not be alone with me, I get it." I don't admit that I'm worried about my own ability to keep it together if we're alone. I'm torn between wanting to shake some sense into her and forgetting everything in the past and just kissing her all night long. From the look on her face, I'm pretty sure that Hannah's having the same struggle.

Silent, she reaches down and opens the door. Instead of flipping on the overhead light, she lets go of my hand and crosses to her bed, turning on the small bedside lamp. I step inside, leaving the door open, and survey her room. I recognize some of the art on the walls from our many nights hanging out on Facetime—the autographed photo of Julie King, the Degas poster. The gray and white patterned comforter is new, like the laptop on the desk, buried under a pile of textbooks and notebooks. "Um, sorry it's a little messy," Hannah says, cringing.

"It's fine." I take two long steps into the room, my thighs aching from this morning's long run, and sit on the edge of her bed. "I don't even know where to start," I admit, looking up at her. I want to wipe the sadness from her eyes, but I'm determined not to be the one to apologize first.

Hannah sinks onto the bed beside me, hands clasped between her knees. We both look around the room, not ready to meet each other's eyes. An object on her bedside table catches my eye. It's the snow globe I bought her this summer, from a Pike Place gift shop. "You still have this?" I ask, my voice hushed in the dim light of her room. I pick it up, turning it over in my hand to watch the bits of snow drift and swirl around the Seattle skyline inside.

"Of course I still have it. Did you think I would just throw it away?" We watch the globe together for a moment.

"I didn't know what you would do. How was I to know how you felt about me, about us? It's been three months, Hannah. Not a word. Not a single word." I take a breath to stop the anger in my gut from rising. Don't scare her, stupid. "The only reason I knew anything about your life was by checking to see what you and Martin posted." I put the snow globe back on the table, in the same spot she had it. She must look at it every night. Why doesn't that make me feel better?

Her voice is so soft I almost miss it. "I'm so sorry." What is she sorry for though? For ghosting me? For breaking my heart? For choosing ballet over me? Again.

"I don't want to be a dick and I didn't come over to fight with you," I say as much to myself as to her. Picking her hand up in mine, I can't stop myself from playing with her fingers as I speak. "Han, I just wanted to see you, to make sure you were okay. Maybe even find out why you've been avoiding me all this time."

Out of the corner of my eye, her shrug ends with a defeated slump of her shoulders. "I'm doing good. My ankle healed and I'm finally back to dancing everything again." She glances sideways at me. "I'd forgotten what it feels like to dance without any pain."

"I'm happy to hear that." I capture one of her long, slim fingers, worrying my way down the length of it, gently squeezing and massaging the skin I can't stop touching. "That's all I wanted for you. To not be in pain."

"I know." Was the sigh that accompanied her words one of resignation? Or relief? "I guess everything is good. I don't do much, to be honest. I spend most of my day doing schoolwork before going to class and rehearsal."

I move to the next finger, eliciting another tiny sigh from Hannah's lips. "How is it living with Martin?"

"It's been great, actually. He has a job at the coffee shop down the road, so he's gone when I have classes, which is nice, but otherwise we have the same schedule. I'm glad I'm not on my own." She risks a glance up at my face. "He's been a good friend to me. Even if he is a total social butterfly. I just hide out in my room when it's too loud."

I let go of her middle finger and start on her ring finger, switching from shorter to longer, smoother strokes, reveling in the feel of her, even if it's just this. "I'm glad you guys have each other. All I ever wanted was for you to not be alone."

Hannah laughs softly. "Well, to be honest we were both so miserable back in September I don't think anyone else could have stood hanging out with us for any length of time."

This time I'm the one who risks a glance up. I turn to face her, bending my knee on the bed to look her in the eye. "Miserable? Why?"

"Sammy broke up with him right before he left for New Zealand. And I'm pretty sure you can guess why I was miserable," Hannah says. Her other hand rests on top of mine, stilling me. The warmth of her hand seeps into mine, burning away the last bit of doubt that's kept me from asking the real question. The one I'm afraid to know the answer to.

"You could have put us both out of our misery at any time, Hannah." I pull my hands away, standing up to get some space from her. "You were the one who asked for space, remember? I was respecting that, no matter how hard it was." Pacing in the small space of her room isn't satisfying, but better than grabbing her by the shoulders and shaking sense into her like I want. "I've been waiting to hear from you. Something, anything."

"I told you not to wait for me."

"And I said you didn't have to ask, I was offering. I don't know how to stop waiting for you, Hannah. Trust me, there are days I wish I could." I pull at my hair, frustrated but determined to keep my voice calm, not to scare her.

"I'm not worth it, you deserve better than me." At her words, I drop to my knees in front of her, hands on her legs to make her look at me.

"You *are* worth waiting for. You are worth everything to me. But every day I don't hear from you breaks my heart just a little more. I don't know how much longer I can take it, but my stupid heart insists on waiting for you." I search her eyes with mine, praying to find something there to keep me going. They're glassy, tears hovering. If she blinks, they'll spill over. "If you don't want me anymore, tell me. Please," I add, my voice cracking when the tears slip down her cheeks.

"I don't want to lose you, Trevor. I didn't know how to start, how to apologize. I wasn't brave enough to tell you how much I missed you, how many times a day I needed you."

Her words suck all the air from my lungs. It's all I can do to breathe out her name before gathering her up in my arms. I don't know if I've truly forgiven her, there's still a lot we need to say, but right now, I need to hold her. I need to feel her warmth against me, wrap my arms around her. My heart beats hard and fast as I bury my nose in her hair, inhaling the cherry blossom shampoo she uses. For just a minute, everything is right with the world.

"Hey! If you want food you better come now!" someone yells from the other end of the apartment, interrupting the moment. Hannah sniffs, pulling away.

"I know everything isn't okay yet, but can we just pretend it is for tonight? I just…I need my friend back." Hannah's words were not the ones I was hoping to hear, but I'm pathetic enough to take whatever I can get.

"Sure." My words fall as flat as I feel. We were so close. Once again, we aren't on the same page at the same time. "Let's go."

Just before we step through the door, Hannah leading me by the hand, she turns back to look me in the eye. "We'll talk about it later, okay? I promise."

I nod my head in agreement, but I don't trust her. I love her, I want her in my life. But right now? I don't trust her at all.

CHAPTER SIXTEEN

Hannah

"*Y*OU SUCK."

Well, that wasn't the welcome I was hoping for. "What?" Olivia and Katy glare at me while Lisa pulls me in for a hard hug. "Merry Christmas, Banana. But you suck." Olivia is the one to elaborate on the sentiment.

"Um…Merry Christmas to you too." I say, not sure where this conversation is going. "What exactly sucks about me?" They're smiling, so I'm not concerned that we're about to get in a fight, but I don't understand what Olivia is getting at. "I suck at a lot of things. Want to be specific?" I add, hoping to lighten the tone.

Katy is the one who answers this time, dragging me up the stairs to my old room. "You suck at keeping in touch and you double suck for not telling us anything about Trevor."

"And you triple suck for not telling us about getting to dance Flowers last weekend!" Lisa calls from the back of the pack.

Oh. Right.

I guess I deserved it then.

The four of us pile into my room. Can I still call it *my* room? My old comforter is still on the bed but most of my stuff is gone, decorating my apartment in Seattle. It's my room, but it's also the guest room now. Mom replaced some of it with simple decor from Target, but the odd mix of old and new has me feeling like I don't belong here anymore

Walking into the house yesterday after flying home with Mom and Dad was surreal..

"It's so weird being in here without your pictures on the walls," Katy says, looking around. "Does it feel weird to be back?"

"Yeah. It feels like home, but it doesn't feel like home." I shrug, not sure how to describe it. "But Seattle feels the same, like home but also not like home."

"I can see that," Lisa says. "I remember that feeling when we moved here. I was little so it wasn't so bad, but it took a while to feel like our house was really home. And the first trip back to see family was," she pauses searching for the right word, "disconcerting."

Hugging a pillow on the bed, I shrug. "Yeah, that sounds about right." I look around at my friends, my heart swelling in my chest. I didn't realize how much I missed them until they came piling through the door a few minutes ago. Seeing their faces, hearing their voices, it hit me how little I've kept in touch since I left in September. "Geez, I've missed you guys." I sigh, tears pricking at my eyes.

I hadn't realized how lonely I've been for the last three months until this second, surrounded by friends who know me and love me for me. Not because I'm Martin's roommate or because I'm the object of gossip. A weight I didn't know I was carrying floats away, leaving my heart lighter than it's been since I left California.

"No crying!" Olivia shrieks from her spot next to me on the bed. She wraps her arms around me and the pillow and drags me sideways, wrapping her arms and legs around me. "We came to hang out and have fun and see your stupid face, no crying allowed," she adds, as we laugh. Katy piles on top of us, adding her own hug to the mix while Lisa sits on the floor laughing at us.

The tears that were threatening, turn into tears of laughter as I'm buried under a pile of arms, legs, and love from my friends.

"Alright, enough of that. We missed you, you missed us. You're going to do better at keeping in touch with us in the future, right?" Katy is the first one to untangle herself from the pile, opting to sprawl on the floor with Lisa. "Now, tell us everything we missed."

"Ugh! I don't even know where to start." I groan and attempt to hide my face in the pillow I'm hugging.

"Well, tell us the good stuff first, save the Trevor drama for last," Olivia says.

"How do you know there's drama?"

"A—it's you and Trevor, *of course* there's drama. And B—Tyler said Trevor is a mess."

"You know, it's not fair that you have an inside scoop," Katy points out.

Olivia just shrugs. "Not my fault. You have inside scoop on the love birds here." She points at Lisa. "I'd call it fair."

Hearing the way they're talking, without me here the three of them have grown closer than I realized. Before my friendship with Olivia exploded back in February, it always felt like *I* was the one holding the group together, that the three of them were only friends because of me. But looking at them now, they would be friends with or without me.

I suppose with Olivia's boyfriend being best friends with Katy's brothers, one of whom is Lisa's boyfriend, the three of them spend a lot of time together, even without dance. I wonder if *I* would be the odd man out if I was still living here. Yes, Trevor is Tyler's cousin, but it's not like he lives here to be part of the friend group. A strange wave of loneliness washes through me at the thought. Looks like I need to put in more effort to stay in the group, if I want to keep my friends.

"You want the good stuff? Let's see." I shake off my musings and focus on catching them up on my life. "My ankle is doing great. Dr. Lee said the bone looks good in the x-ray and I've been doing my PT exercises. In fact, I'm pretty sure my ankle is stronger now than it ever was before. Or maybe it's just from all the dancing. I can tell I've improved in class—I'm finally starting to be more of a jumper." Lisa grins, jumping has always been more her strength than mine. With my long, willowy build, I've tended to be more flexible than strong my whole life, the opposite of her.

"Are you still doing Pilates and PBT?" Lisa asks. "I have. Almost every morning."

I nod. "Yup. Every morning before school. I guess that's the one real advantage of my online school, I can go straight from working out to class without having to stop and change." I should text her in the mornings and see if she wants to do them with me. I make a mental note to ask her later.

"How's online school?" Olivia asks. "Is it awful doing two years at once?

"It sucks, but I'm glad I'm getting it done. Thankfully, I had enough credits from school here that it's not too bad. Their classes feel way easier than they did here."

"Speaking of school being easy, did you hear Lisa's news?" Katy asks.

"No, what news?" I stare at Lisa, who blushes. "Tell me, please."

"Lisa's going to graduate this year too. She had all those extra credits from summer school the last few years." Lisa just ducks her head and smiles while Katy shares her news.

"Lisa! That's amazing news!" I gush. "Wait, have you already done college applications and everything? How come I didn't know any of this?" Mortification that my supposed best friend has been doing this huge thing and I was clueless rips through me. Some friend I am.

Lisa pats my leg, with a grin. "You were a little preoccupied. It's okay. You know now."

"Yeah, but it's not okay. I'm so sorry." I shake my head. "You guys are right, I do suck."

"You only suck a little. We forgive you and you're going to do better so don't get all teary over it," Olivia says from behind me on the bed. "The only people allowed to be sad about it are me and Katy since you guys are missing our senior year." Olivia's fake pout has me laughing, an expression I recognize for what it is, a ploy to change the mood. "The worst part is, we can't even be mad. You're off doing great ballet things, and Lisa's done enough work to graduate high school three times over, it's only fair she doesn't have to suffer an extra year."

"So where have you applied to college?" There's no point in asking if she's done anything else since there's no way her parents would let her *not* go to college.

"USC, UCI and Boston Conservatory are my top choices." Lisa counts them off on her fingers. "Although Boston is a stretch because I can't double major there."

"Let me guess, you're planning to double major in dance and…"
Lisa nods. "Dance and physics."

"Physics? Dang. That's intense." If anyone can pull it off it's Lisa. I can see the appeal for her, dance *is* physics after all, just without measuring things. "Let me guess, Hunter's applied to USC, UCI and…" I pause to think. "MIT?"

Lisa's grin is all I need to confirm my suspicion that they're planning to go to the same college. I hope they can, if anyone deserves to be happy it's these two.

"They're staying in California, end of story. Boston isn't allowed," Katy declares. Lisa just rolls her eyes, I guess they've had this argument before. "It's Winter Break, no more school talk allowed." Katy lays back on the ground, arms thrown over her eyes. I can't help laughing at her dramatics. I missed this.

"No more school talk other than it sucks, just like school is supposed to," I promise.

"Are the other girls at PSB catty? Is there anyone nice?" Lisa asks. She knows first-hand how catty it can get, we had our fair share of mean girl moments over the summer at the intensive.

I shake my head. "I keep to myself for the most part. Martin is the only person I hang out with. This other girl Sloane kind of adopted me, she's nice enough." Having my best friends to talk to is such a relief, I don't stop to filter my words as I keep talking. "I don't know, I haven't tried to be friends with anyone else. I felt so lame, being the girl who showed up in a boot. None of them had ever seen me dance, and here I am, getting all this special treatment because of my injury." I shrug. "You saw how it was over the summer, Lisa. Being *special* isn't necessarily a good thing in that kind of situation. I just wanted to keep my head down and avoid being the girl to beat."

"I get that. You didn't want to be treated like the star, because that's when everyone is out to get you," Olivia says.

"Exactly. I think it's worked. The teachers don't single me out in class for anything, but they don't single out anyone. I don't think I'm top of the class or anything. Especially since I've only been dancing at my best for the last month, it took that long to do all the rehab. The only reason anyone knows who I am is because of Martin."

Katy grins. "Uh yeah, he seems like a fun guy."

"Oh, he is. He's so much like Jack, always has an entourage. So, they know me because they're at our place all the time, we're one of the few people in our class who are completely on our own. But I keep to myself. I hang out on occasion, when Martin makes me, or threatens not to feed me if I don't," I add with a grin.

"Sometimes, I am so jealous of you. No curfew, no parents. No one telling you to clean your room or terrible toddlers constantly getting into your stuff."

I shake my head at Olivia's words. "No curfew because I never go anywhere. No parents to take care of things like paying the electric bill and buying groceries. It turns out Martin is a bit of a clean freak and yells at me to clean my room at least once a week." I laugh at that, who would have thought, right? "But you're right, there's definitely no toddlers at my apartment."

Olivia sits up, jostling me on the bed. "Okay, so dance is pretty good. You're holding your own in class but not the star. Martin is a decent roommate. I think we're all caught up. Now the two most important things—we need the story of how you got to dance in Waltz of the Flowers and what the hell is going on with Trevor."

"Hang on, before I tell you about dancing Flowers, I have something for you." I reach over to my suitcase and pull three programs from PSB's Nutcracker out of a brown paper sleeve. I check the names on the back and hand them out. "Merry Christmas," I add, grinning. Christmas was yesterday, but since I had to perform on Christmas Eve, my parents flew up on the twenty-third to watch my last show before we all flew home together Christmas morning. Thank goodness it's a short flight.

"Oh my god, are these signed by all the principals?" Lisa gasps.

"Well, not quite all of them, but as many as I could find without being a total dork. But I managed to snag Lila Wilkinson's when she came to visit backstage after watching one of the shows." I grin, that had been a real feat. Lila Wilkinson was *the* ballerina of the nineties, in fact, she was Ms. Parker's idol growing up, the same way Julie King has been mine. Getting her signature for my friends, and one more for Ms. Parker, hadn't been easy, but Martin and Sloane helped me out.

"So how did you get to dance Flowers?" Lisa asks, turning the pages of the program reverently.

"So, you guys know I was only cast as a party parent, since there was a question of how much I would be able to perform when casting went up." They all nod. "Once I was cleared by Dr. Lee, I asked if I could understudy any of the other student roles. Ms. Tsvetkov said I should learn whatever I could, so I did. I just hung out in the back of the studio, trying to stay out of the way. One of the girls in my class who was in Flowers got sick, some kind of food poisoning I think, and they needed someone. Ms. Tsvetkov volunteered me to do it, so I did." It's not the most exciting story, but they get it.

From the grins on their faces, my friends can guess how amazing that moment was. The nerves, the adrenaline, all fighting with my brain to get it right.

"Did you get a chance to rehearse at all?" Lisa asked.

"I got to do one run through before the show started." I nodded. "The other corps girls were nice about it. Thankfully, everyone in the corps has to be in Flowers at some point so there were plenty of people to help me. Honestly? It was amazing. The costumes are so pretty and dancing up there with them…"

"A dream come true?" Olivia asks.

"Yeah. It was. Even better that it just happened to be the show my parents were coming to. It was the first time in ages I danced and felt the magic. Everything has been so stressful, or painful, that ballet hasn't been fun in months. It was, but it wasn't. I know I'm not making any sense." I bury my face in my pillow to avoid looking at my friends. I don't want them to think I'm whining about getting to live my dream, but it hasn't all been fun.

"I think I get what you're saying," Katy says. "I imagine recovering from an injury would make taking class a little scary, right? Like you were always waiting for the pain, waiting for your body to tell you it wasn't ready. Right?"

I nod. "Yeah, that's it exactly. Most of September and October, I was still healing. I was allowed to keep going until it hurt. So, I spent all of class waiting for the pain, waiting for my ankle to tell me when to stop. It's like waiting for a punch in the face you know is coming, but not when. The first time I did an allegro exercise without any pain, I couldn't believe it. It took two weeks of no pain before I was convinced it was real."

Olivia pulls me out from under the pillows to give me a hug. "That sounds rough, Banana. But I'm glad it's okay now."

I sniff back the tears that snuck up on me. "Yeah, me too." That gets me a chuckle from everyone.

"Okay, not to make you cry again or anything. But what's going on with Trevor?" Olivia asks, poking me in the side while I can't escape her.

"What's happening is that I'm the worst and he deserves so much better than me." I pull myself free of Olivia and flop back on the bed, staring at the ceiling while I talk. "You guys saw our fight the night before he left. We never made up after that because I'm a coward. And then I got scared on the way to Seattle and told him I needed some space. Which, being the amazing person he is, he respected and didn't fight me on. And then I ghosted him."

"You *what*?" Katy's exclamation is echoed by Oliva. Lisa just groans at my stupidity.

"Hannah, how could you? That boy is so in love with you." Olivia tosses the pillow at me, hitting me in the face.

"He is not in love with me."

"He is one hundred percent in love with you," Katy answers. "Anyone could see it."

"I didn't see it," I argue. "He's never said it to me."

Lisa reaches up to smack my shoulder. "Of *course* he didn't say anything, you idiot. You keep breaking up with him. And now this? You don't deserve that boy, you're right."

Ouch. That stings.

"But what do I do now?" I tell them all about the other night when Trevor came over, how much I wished I could just tell him that I want to try again.

"But you chickened out again, didn't you?" Lisa says when I finish my story. "I bet you told him you just need a friend and that you'd talk about it later, right?"

"It's not fair that you know me so well." I toss the pillow at her. "Yes, that's exactly what I did."

"Has he texted you since then?" Olivia asks.

"Yeah, a little. Well, I texted him first. I didn't think he would initiate anything." I can't help the tiny smile that creeps across my face, remembering his response. "He responded, so that's good, right?"

"Depends on what he said. Also, I can't believe you found him in your phone, I thought I hid him pretty well." Katy holds out her hand to me.

"What?"

"Gimme your phone, we need to see these texts if we're going to help you."

"Can't I just read them to you?"

"Nope, I don't trust you not to skip things." Olivia pulls my phone out from under me. "Unlock, please."

With a groan, I press my thumb to the pad to unlock it, then bury my head under a pillow while Olivia reads the texts out loud.

"'Hannah—thank you for coming over last night, it was good to see you again.' Okay, we're off to a solid, if boring, start."

Lisa pushes at Olivia's leg hanging off the bed. "What did he say?"

Olivia clears her throat before answering in a deep voice, "'I'm glad we ran into each other. We're coming to see the Nutcracker on December twentieth, any chance I'll get to see you on stage?' This is good, Hannah! He wants to see you again, you can tell."

"Please tell me she didn't give him a lame-ass answer," Katy groans from her spot on the floor.

"'I'm a party parent and one of the background characters in Land of the Sweets that night. Not much dancing but at least I'm on stage.'" Olivia reads out. "Do you ever actually tell him you want to see him again? I stand by my words from before, you guys are the most boring love story ever."

"Hey!" I pull my head out from under the pillow long enough to protest Olivia's words. "We're lame. Not boring. You can't say we're boring at this point." Sitting up, I cross my arms over my chest, glaring at Olivia.

Lisa at least jumps to my defense. "She's right, you know. They certainly aren't boring, even if they can't seem to get it together." I don't know if I should be offended at that. She's got a point, but still. "Love you, Han, but come on—you need to make up your mind if you want to be with him or not. You can't keep changing your mind whenever it gets hard."

I sigh, flopping back on the bed. "I know. This is why I haven't said anything to him." I voice the fear that's been keeping me from committing my heart once again. "What if it's too late? What if I waited too long and he can't forgive me?"

"After what he said to you at your house? I doubt it. He's waiting for you to say something," Lisa assures me. "Are they in town for Christmas or still in Seattle?"

Olivia grins. "Oh, they're in town all right. I saw him yesterday when I went over to the Stanley's to give Tyler his Christmas present. They're here through the New Year."

"Yeah, he said they would be. But we didn't make any plans," I add. "I didn't know what kind of plans you guys would have and I wanted to see you too."

Katy, Lisa, and Olivia share a look that I can't decipher. "What?"

"We had a feeling that might be the case. Tyler asked Trevor if he had any plans and he said no. Lucky for you, your best friends are here to make sure you two spend as much time together as possible this week. Very convenient for you that Trevor is Tyler's cousin and we just *have* to include him in all of our plans, otherwise Tyler would be a bad host." Olivia finishes her little speech with an exaggerated wink.

I push myself to sitting, intrigued. "What do you have planned?"

Katy grins. "You mean besides an epic New Year's Eve party so you can kiss him at midnight? I'm so glad you asked."

CHAPTER SEVENTEEN

Trevor

ME: Your friends are sneaky.

ME: I'm not mad about it, but they're a devious bunch.

TYLER: Hunter always says beware the ballerinas, they are sneaky and smarter than they look. Don't question them dude, just smile and nod and do whatever they say. Trust me on this.

ME: So normally I would…but it's kind of cold and Hannah doesn't have a coat.

TYLER: Guess you'll just have to keep each other warm.

THE STRING of winking faces he sends to drive home the point are unnecessary. I knew what he meant.

"They have to take Lisa home before they can come back for us," Hannah says, looking up from her phone. Her shoulders are tucked up almost to her ears, her long-sleeve shirt not doing much to keep her warm. At least I have a beanie and a flannel shirt on under my hoodie.

I pull my hoodie off and offer it to her. "I can see your teeth chattering, take it."

She just shakes her head, a distant look in her eyes as she scans the parking lot.

"Hannah, they're going to be at least thirty minutes. Take the hoodie." I gather up the sides and drop it over her head. "Where's your hat?"

Her head pops through the neck as the rest of my hoodie falls down her tiny frame. She threads her arms through the sleeves but they hang past her hands by a few inches. It's the most adorable thing I've ever seen. "My hat?"

"The green one with the cute pom pom on top." I tug her closer so I can roll up one sleeve. Eyes wide, bottom lip caught between her teeth, Hannah watches me cuff first one sleeve, then the other without saying anything. It takes every ounce of my self-control not to kiss her forehead when I finish. Or gather her up in my arms. "Better?" I ask instead.

Staring at me, she nods silently. "It's so warm." Her voice is barely audible, but thunders through me. Then in a move that has my stupid heart pounding, melting, and exploding at once, she tucks her chin, cups her hands under her neck, and inhales deep, her eyes fluttering closed. "It smells like you," she whispers before opening her eyes and smiling.

I'm so gone over this girl.

Head over heels.

Want to scoop her up and put her in my pocket so nothing bad can ever happen to her, in love with her.

Still.

"You have the goosebumps." The concern in Hannah's voice brings a smile to my face. Even better is the way she lunges forward and wraps her arms around my waist, attempting to keep me warm.

The goosebumps that prickle over my skin aren't from the cold, they're from her. But if it means I get to hold her for a blessed minute I'll let her think that.

"Hey." It takes me a full second to find my voice again. "How about we go get some coffee or something while we wait?" I nod my head towards the coffee shop next to the movie theater where we'd just been with everyone else.

I take her by the hand and lead her inside. We order our drinks and find a table tucked in the corner while we wait. I'm tempted to text Tyler and tell him to take his time coming back to get us. Sitting here with Hannah, seeing her wrapped up in my hoodie, cradling the hot cup in her hands, I could drag this night out forever.

"So they really ditched us, huh?" Hannah says, grinning at me. "It was on purpose, right?"

I grin back. "It was one hundred percent on purpose. Your friends are devious. Waiting until we were both in the bathroom after the movie? That was slick."

Hannah laughs at that. "Yeah. Lisa called out something about waiting for me outside, next thing I knew it was just you and me left." She takes a sip of her drink, her lips wrapping around the edge of the cup. Yes, I am absolutely staring at them. Can you blame me? "Well, since we're stuck here until they come get us… How were finals? Are you coming to the New Year's Eve party tomorrow night? Have you finished your college applications?"

I take a sip of my own drink, stalling to give myself a chance to come back to reality. "Uh, finals were fine. And I sent in my last application last weekend. Now all I can do is wait."

The warmth and noise of the coffee shop creates a kind of cocoon around us, a place we can just talk like we used to. About anything and everything. We talk about which colleges I applied to and how her online school is going. Just normal, mundane teenage stuff. I missed this. I don't bother glancing at my phone, trusting Tyler will call when they come back. I'm in no hurry.

"I want to try to get ahead in my classes when I get back since I'll be super busy in February." Hannah sighs, glancing at her phone. She's just worried about our friends coming back to get us, not that she doesn't want to be here with me. Right?

"What's in February? Are you doing that competition again?"

"Hmm?" Dragging her eyes from the screen, I can see a message on the lock screen, but I can't read it from this angle. "No, we're not allowed to enter those competitions without permission from the director. I don't have any one-on-one coaching anymore so I wouldn't be comfortable doing that anyway. I'm auditioning for a couple of companies. I doubt I'll get offered anything, but it doesn't hurt to try. PSB arranges to have the directors of different companies come to the school and watch classes. Sometimes they hold a cattle call audition at the school. Martin and I are going to go to the ones we can."

Panic that it might be too late, she might be leaving sooner than I thought, colors my vision. "You're auditioning? Already? I thought…" I don't know what I thought. Did I think this was like college for Hannah? That she'd be here for a few years before the next big thing in her life? "Like, to be a professional? Already?"

The edges of her big blue eyes narrow, warning me I've just said something stupid. "I'm just trying. I need to know how close to being ready I am and that's the best way to find out. PSB is supposed to be for a year or two, max. It's not like

I can wait, I'm already seventeen." She states this like it's an obvious fact.

"I know you're seventeen. What does that have to do with it? You're not even an adult yet." Warning bells are going off in my brain, but I don't understand this, and something tells me I need to.

Hannah huffs out an annoyed breath. "Trevor, do you know long a ballet career lasts? Most dancers retire in their thirties or forties, if they're lucky. There are people in companies that are younger than I am now. It's not like I have four years to wait. If I want it, I need to do this now."

I'm an idiot. I kind of knew this in the back of my head, but being presented with the reality is something else. My stress over which college I'm going to feels childish compared to Hannah's need to start her professional life. Worry about our old arguments over almost the exact same thing beats at the back of my mind. The last thing I should do right now is make her think I don't support her.

"Hey, I'm sorry. I wasn't doubting you. I just didn't realize." I backtrack, trying to diffuse her annoyance with me. Hannah's eyes go wide at my words and a pink blush creeps up her cheeks and the tips of her ears.

"I didn't mean to get upset. I'm not upset," she adds, taking a deep breath. "Sorry. My mom was giving me a hard time about it earlier. I guess I'm still a little worked up."

I eye her across the table, not sure what to make of this version of Hannah. "I thought your parents were super supportive of your dancing?"

"They are." Hannah looks past me out the window. "I think my injury scared them more than I realized. My mom has been fussing over me so much. You know she calls me every day on her way to work? Every. Single. Morning." She shakes her head, the pile of hair on her head bouncing with the movement.

I reach across the table to rest my hand on hers, the warmth of her skin sending a spark up my arm. Both of us look down at our hands on the table. Her hands are so slim, like the rest of her. Looking at her, you'd imagine that one strong gust would blow her away. It's easy to forget how tough she is underneath that doll-like exterior. "They just worry about you. I get it. I worry too."

Not taking her eyes off our hands, Hannah flips hers, threading her fingers through mine. I know body language is easier for her than words, she's used to speaking without words, but I need more. I can't trust her without them yet.

"Hannah…"

"Damn, I owe you five bucks, babe." Tyler's voice booms through the coffee shop. Startled, Hannah pulls her hand away, glancing around wildly. Olivia and Tyler are standing at the edge of our table, grinning down at us.

"Told you," Olivia says, holding out her hand.

"Told him what?" Hannah asks, eyes narrowed at her friend.

"That if we waited long enough, you two would be at least holding hands by the time we got back." Olivia smirks.

The pink that had started to fade from Hannah's cheeks flares back to life. "You suck," is all she says and I can't stop the laugh that bursts from me.

"Come on." I push back from the table and stand up, holding out one hand to her while shoving Tyler towards the door with the other.

"But I was going to get a coffee!" Olivia protests.

"Too bad, you shouldn't have ditched us." Grinning, I pull Hannah towards the door. I'm not happy about their interruption when I was finally getting somewhere with Hannah, but if Olivia wants to interrupt she can deal with the consequences.

"Happy NEW Year!" Katy shouts in my face as I walk through the door in front of Tyler. The Quinn's house is more crowded than I've ever seen. Silver, gold and black streamers decorate the walls, there's a giant spread of finger foods on the table and music pumping from the tv. I don't know most of the people crowded in the space, assuming they must be friends from school.

Tyler picks Katy up in a bear hug, swinging her out of the way to make an entrance. "Yo!" He calls, the single word training all eyes on him. A chorus of cheers breaks out at his arrival. Damn.

"To answer your question, yes, it's always like this. You've never seen my house when it's a real Quinn brother gathering." Katy laughs, pointing at my stunned expression. "Don't worry, I won't introduce you to anyone, you already know the most important people."

Following Katy into the house I get a better look at the crowd. A good third of them look older than the high school age I was expecting, beer bottles and red solo cups dangling from their fingertips. "Hey Katy…" I ask, not wanting to be a total party pooper, but not sure how I feel about the situation.

"Oh. Don't freak. Cole has his friends over too. He and Henry are guarding the drinks," Katy nods her head in the direction of the table with the drinks where Cole and Henry, who I met in August, are standing by the table, keeping an eye on it. "Besides, everyone is aware that our parents are upstairs and if they break the rules they'll get banned from our house. *No one* wants to get banned from our house."

I can't quite believe that everyone here is innocently following the rules like Katy claims, but if she thinks it's good enough then I'll have to trust her.

"Is Hannah here yet?" My eyes move from clump to clump, looking for the red hair I know so well.

"Not yet. JJ is picking her up." Katy glances down at her phone. "They're on their way though. Lisa and Hunter are back there." Katy points to a loveseat pushed against a wall where Hunter and Lisa are sitting together, oblivious to the noise around them. I head that way, tapping out a quick message on my phone as I thread my way through the crowd.

> **ME:** Just warning you, there are a lot of people here. Took me by surprise. I thought you might appreciate the heads up.

Has Hannah ever even been to a party like this? My gut says no.

> **HANNAH:** Oh god, I'm walking into a true high school party, aren't I? Are there red solo cups? No one's drinking though, right?

She adds a gif of Spongebob nervously biting his nails, making me laugh.

Heart to Heart

ME: Cole's friends are, but he and Henry are guarding the alcohol. Seems safe so far. I don't think our innocence is going to be destroyed tonight.

She doesn't answer right away so I slip my phone in my pocket before perching on the arm of the loveseat. I would say hi, but Lisa and Hunter are currently tonsil deep in each other so I take a second to look around and get my bearings. The open room I'm in is dominated by the high school crowd. Closest to the food and farthest from the alcohol. The college students seem to be congregating on the other end of the house, some of them ranging up the stairs as well.

"Oh hi, Trevor," Lisa says sheepishly from beside me.

"Hi. Need a second to catch your breath?" I tease, her cheeks going pink. Hunter just laughs, pulling her into his side and kissing the top of her head.

"Just taking advantage before the girls get here." Lisa smacks Hunter's chest at his words, but grins back at me. "You want something to drink babe? Trev?" Hunter pushes up from the couch, making sure Lisa's settled before heading for the coolers parked next to the food.

"Oh stop," I laugh at Lisa's flustered fixing of her hair. "It's fine. I've seen worse, trust me." Walking in on Derek and his girlfriend in the bathroom at his Halloween party had been a thousand times worse. You know that scene in Cruel Intentions? The one with the saliva. Yeah, imagine that's your best friend. He tried to claim the excess spit was from his vampire fangs but no one was buying it.

"Hey," Lisa looks around, as if anyone can hear our conversation over the noise of the party. "I'm glad I have you alone for a second. Listen, Hannah is my best friend and I love her dearly, but she's a mess. And she owes you an apology." Whoah. I was not expecting that to be the direction this was going. "She owes you a *real* apology. With words. Don't let her get away with anything less. You both deserve better than that."

I clear my throat, my hand going to the back of my neck and rubbing it. "Okay. Wow. That was not what I was expecting."

"You were expecting me to tell you not to hurt her, right? The whole 'hurt her and I'll kill you,' speech?" Lisa laughs.

"Well, yeah."

"I think we're way past that point. I should be saying that to her." Ducking her head, the stern tone gone, Lisa's next words are a balm I didn't know I needed. "I owe you an apology too. We didn't know what happened between you two, but I shouldn't have ignored you like I did. We're friends, right?"

"I'd like to be. If it's not too weird." I stammer, flustered by her words.

Lisa nods, like she's made some kind of decision to herself. "Right. Well, then as *your* friend I'm sorry for blaming it on you. I should have known better. When Hannah gets scared she shuts down. She sticks to what she knows is safe, it's like she puts blinders on to any other option. She's stubborn like that."

I chuckle. "I've noticed."

"Anyway, we're all on your side. You're good for her, even if she can't see it." Lisa glances around again, eyeing the front door. When she speaks again it's in a hushed voice. "She knows she was wrong. She just doesn't know how to get past it. She's scared she's blown it with you forever, but I don't think that's true." Lisa eyes me.

Heart to Heart

I shake my head in response. "I'm a sucker for punishment, I guess. I'd take her back in a heartbeat, if she'd let me."

"But?"

"But I'm having a hard time trusting that she's not going to run away again the next time it gets hard or something big happens," I admit. Damn, how is Lisa getting me to tell her all this? "I know how I feel about her, but I don't know if she feels the same way." I end with a shrug, not willing to bare any more of my soul to Lisa. The rest of this conversation is one that I need to have with Hannah.

"Just know that we're all rooting for you." Lisa pats my knee as she stands, walking away to join Hunter. I move to sit on the now empty loveseat, hoping Hannah and JJ arrive soon. My wish is granted a moment later when a break in the crowd leaves me a clear view of the front door as it closes behind the one person I want to see.

Her hair is curled, the blue oversized sweater she's wearing falling off one shoulder, her milky skin highlighted by the bright red of her hair draped over it. I hardly recognize her in the ripped black jeans she's wearing instead of her usual leggings, and the boots instead of her usual Converse. I wonder if her friends had a hand in picking out her outfit. When Olivia slips in the door behind her, eyeing her with approval before meeting my eye and giving me a thumbs up, I have to work hard to contain the laugh that threatens to burst out of me.

Her friends may give her a hard time, but they obviously love her. I better not waste all the effort they've gone to. Pushing to my feet, I stalk her through the crowd as she greets Katy and a few other people I don't know. There's an Asian dude in the group she's talking to eyeing her appreciatively, which she's oblivious to. Something about him sets my teeth on edge.

Instead of poking his eyes out like I want to, I step up to Hannah's side. "Hey." I twine her fingers in mine, tugging to get her attention, praying she doesn't pull away.

"Hi." She smiles up at me and my heart thumps hard in my chest. I've missed *that* smile, the one only I've seen. It's tiny, but a little mischievous, a little shy.

Instead of leaning down to kiss her lips like I want to, I whisper in her ear. "You look gorgeous." Her tiny gasp when I follow that with a press of my lips to the spot just below her ear is another stitch in repairing my broken heart.

When I stand back up and the hot Asian dude is gone, I don't bother to hide the grin on my face. I'm no alpha male, but claiming her as mine brings a certain sense of satisfaction with it.

We spend the whole night near each other. We may be laughing and chatting with her friends but my attention is fully focused on Hannah. We're constantly touching in small ways. Her warmth snuggled up against me on the couch, my fingers tracing circles on her exposed shoulder. I have to swallow down a groan the first time her fingers tentatively stroke the back of my neck.

The closer it gets to midnight, the tighter I'm wound. The electricity building between us is going to combust any second. No matter how casual either of us is acting, I can feel how fast her heart is beating as we stand around with everyone else, waiting to countdown to midnight. Her back is to my chest, my arm wrapped around her waist, holding her close.

"Nine…eight…seven…six…"

I turn her in my arms, needing to see her face as we count down. It's a new year, it can be a new start for us, right? Everyone counts down around us but all I see is the beautiful girl in front of me, staring up at me with so much written in her eyes. An apology, hope, longing. It's all there.

Lisa told me to wait for a real apology, but I don't care. I can't care. I love this girl too much. If she walks all over my heart again I'll let her.

"Three…two…one…Happy New Year!"

Her lips are as sweet as I remember.

Soft and pliant under mine.

It's like coming home.

CHAPTER EIGHTEEN

Hannah

LISA: We have a break in 30 mins, Facetime?

KATY: We need to know if that pimple on your chin is still there.

OLIVIA: Gross, Katy. But yes, Facetime. 30 mins. Not optional. Lisa's phone, mine and Katy's are dying.

ME: Am I calling you or are you calling me?

LISA: I'll call you.

KATY: Don't be naked!

ME: I'm at the grocery store, Katy. Definitely NOT naked.

I'M STILL chuckling at Katy's text when my shopping cart taps something in front of me. "Oh! I'm so sorr—" I break off mid-sentence when I register the grinning faces standing in front of me.

"Hey Hannah," James, one of the guys in our class at PSB has his hand on the edge of the shopping cart. He must have grabbed it to stop me from running into him. Martin is already dropping the items in his arms into the cart, a Cheshire cat grin on his face.

Those aren't the faces that have my heart jack-hammering in my chest. No, the reason my heart is working overtime is the brown-haired, warm-eyed, looks like trouble, Tom Hiddleston look-alike standing between them, smiling at me.

"Hi Trevor," I squeak. Just my luck, I run into him *again*. This is the second time this week and once again I look like trash. I'm sweaty and disgusting since Martin and I just came from the gym. Martin's New Year's resolution was to work out more. Being a good friend, I've been going with him and focusing on cardio to improve my stamina.

The cart is pulled from my hands, with an "I'll catch up with you at the front in a bit," from Martin.

As soon as they leave, Trevor is by my side. "I haven't heard from you, how's your week been since I saw you?"

That's it? He's not mad I've barely texted him in the three weeks since we came home from California? After that amazing midnight kiss, and the ones that followed, I expected him to go back to blowing up my phone with texts like he used to. Instead, he only answers when I text first and most of the time I don't know what to say so I say nothing.

I miss his ten thousand texts a day.

"Um. It's been good. We had an audition for Arizona Ballet last weekend, but neither of us heard back, I don't think it's going anywhere." I add.

"Are you disappointed? Is Martin?"

How is he so casual? My stomach is clenching and flipping with butterflies at the sight of him and he's talking to me like

I'm just a random old friend? Isn't he as excited to see me as I am to see him?

"Not really. Neither of us want to move to Arizona. The gloomy skies here are growing on me." That gets me a laugh, I tuck the sound away in my heart for later. "I'm pretty sure I would have to resign myself to being permanently sunburned if I lived there." Angling for another one of his laughs, I give a dramatic shudder. I'm rewarded with a grin. So close.

It was like this on Monday as well when he ducked into the coffee shop where I was trying to get some homework done. Martin was on a vacuuming and cleaning frenzy that afternoon but I had a paper to write, so I'd escaped the noise by going down the street.

"Well I, for one, am glad that Arizona's not going to happen. Too hot for me." Trevor looks down at me, studying my face. I'm caught in his eyes as I gaze back, my brain whirling with anxious, unfinished thoughts.

Why did he say that like he would…?

Was he planning to…?

That's not one of the places he applied is it?

I can't remember if he said Arizona or not.

I'm the worst. What is wrong with me?

Trevor taps the side of my head. "I can hear you overthinking from here." Breaking eye contact, he tucks my hand in the crook of his elbow. "Come my lady, what sustenance do you have left to procure?"

Laughing, I fall into step with him. Trevor starts pulling random items off the shelf and holding them up for my approval.

"Dost thou need the sauce of a fish? Or perhaps the salty tang of the fermented soybean?" I'm giggling too hard to answer, so he leads me down the aisle, continuing the bit until we find ourselves in line with Martin at the checkout.

"And here I must leave you, fair maiden." Trevor takes my hand from his elbow and presses a kiss to my knuckles with a small bow. "I await your sweet electronic messages, delivered to my cellular device from yours."

Before I can say a word, he's gone, his long legs carrying him out the automatic doors, leaving me speechless and Martin laughing.

"Girl...he is something else." Martin chuckles as he pulls items from our shopping cart and puts them on the conveyor belt.

"He is, isn't he?"

"GOOD MORNING, sweetie. How are you?" I don't need to look at the clock, if Mom's calling it must be seven forty already. "Did you sleep okay? How's your back today?"

"Good morning Mom." I glance at the clock. Yup, seven forty-two, on her way to work. "I slept fine. My back isn't as sore as I expected," I add. "How are you? Hey, how do I make lasagna?" I've been craving my mom's lasagna all week and since Martin and I have a weekend without any auditions or extra rehearsals, this seems like the perfect time to try making it.

"Oh, I'll send you the recipe. It's not as hard as you think if you use the no-boil noodles. It just takes a lot of spaghetti sauce." I roll out of bed, pulling socks on my feet to combat the cold hardwood floor. Getting socks for Christmas this year was a treat, my parents gifted me with a huge collection of fuzzy and silly pairs of socks after I'd complained of my feet freezing all the time. In my defense, it's the end of March and it's *still* cold here. It snowed last weekend. My California tush has been cold since October.

We chat as she drives to the office and I brush my teeth and get ready for my classes, puttering around the kitchen making some coffee and a couple of scrambled eggs. One bonus of my online school is that I don't have to get dressed or put on makeup if I don't want to. I often stay in my pajamas until I get dressed to go dance.

I haven't worn a pair of jeans in weeks. It's awesome.

We hang up as she arrives at work, my phone buzzing with her text a few moments later.

> **MOM:** Here's the recipe. You might want to invite a friend or two over to share, it makes a lot.
> **ME:** Thanks. I'm sure Martin and I can find a few people to help us out.
> **MOM:** Have a good day, love you forever!
> **ME:** Love you too

Toying with the phone in my hand, I know exactly who I want to invite to come over and eat lasagna. But is it weird? Will he think it's a date? Do I want it to be a date?

Some date, having dinner with me and Martin. Okay. Not a date. But is he going to think it's weird? Knock it off Hannah, he's not going to think it's weird. Right? I type out and send the text before I can talk myself out of it.

> **ME:** I was thinking about making lasagna for dinner tonight, do you want to come help Martin and I eat it?

While I wait for his response, I settle at the coffee table, pull my laptop out and get logged into my first class. I tried logging into classes from my bed, but it was too easy to let myself get distracted. I hope Trevor answer's soon. The app locking my social media and messaging is going to turn on any second, another attempt to force myself to pay attention to my classes.

It works most of the time.

> **TREVOR:** I can't tonight, I gotta stay home with the Magster, parents are out of town until tomorrow. I would be happy to eat your leftovers though.

Oh.

Well, that's disappointing.

My phone buzzes again, I have thirty seconds to look before my phone locks and my class starts.

> **TREVOR:** I don't suppose you want to come over and hang out with Maggie and me? I can't offer homemade lasagna, but maybe pizza and a movie would be an acceptable substitute? Pizza and lasagna are pretty much the same thing, right?

Fork halfway to my mouth, I freeze. He's inviting me over? The hunger pangs in my stomach turn to butterflies.

> **ME:** I can make the lasagna tomorrow. I'd love to come hang out tonight.

His text flashes for a moment before my phone locks me out of the app.

TREVOR: Can't wait.

Me neither.

"YOU CAN'T go like that." Sloane taps her foot against the marley floor of the studio. "I refuse to sanction you going over to this boy's house looking like…" The way her lip curls as she waves a hand up and down my body has Martin nodding in agreement.

"Hannah, sweetheart, you can't go to his house looking like you crawled out of a thrift store reject bin." Martin slings his bag over his shoulder, waiting for Sloane and I to catch up. "And no, leggings and a hoodie won't do either."

I knew I shouldn't have said anything, except I kind of had to when they started discussing plans for dinner.

"I was going to change, geez. I'm not that useless." I follow them through the lobby to the front doors, shrugging my coat on before we go outside, grimacing at the way it sticks to the sweat on my skin. I argue with Martin and Sloane over what is an appropriate outfit while we walk to our cars. They seem to be convinced I need to wear "real clothes," whatever that means. I nix Sloane's suggestion of a dress. A) it's still less than fifty degrees outside and going to get colder and B) I haven't shaved my legs in over a week. When I make my argument Martin just rolls his eyes.

"You're taking a shower before you go over, that's not a real issue." He slides into the passenger seat of my car, waving to Sloane as she climbs into her car a few spots over. "Okay cupcake. Let's go. You've got a shower to take."

An hour later I'm showered, dressed to Martin's somewhat satisfaction, and following my phone's GPS to Trevor's house. I won the argument for leggings since watching a movie means lounging on the couch, but the off-the-shoulder sweater I'm wearing is nicer than I would have picked, as are the ankle-high booties. I'm pretending that I blow-dried my hair because it's too cold to wrap it up in a bun while wet, not because I wanted to look nice. Or because when it's down Trevor has a habit of playing with it.

Pulling up to his house, I take a second to appreciate how adorable it is. The front yard is lined with daffodils and other flower beds, lush green grass filling the yard visible even in the dying light. A cement ramp leads up to a cozy front porch, I was expecting stairs but what do I know? The slate blue siding is accentuated by bright white trim. This could have been my home too, if I'd let it.

Not that I regret choosing to live with Martin. I don't. It was the right choice, even if it wasn't the easiest choice.

The front door flies open before I'm halfway down the path and Maggie darts out, a grin stretched across her face. "Oh my god, you came! I thought for sure Trevor was teasing when he said you were coming over. Do you know what movie you want to watch?" There's no stopping the whirlwind of words as she tows me towards the house. "Trevor wants to watch one of the Spiderman movies but I want to watch *Kiki's Delivery Service.*

Have you ever seen it? Or maybe *Howl's Moving Castle*? Have you seen either of them? If you don't want to watch a cartoon we can watch something else. What about *The Princess Bride*? Or maybe *Ella Enchanted*? Oh! We could watch *The Princess Diaries*! Have you ever seen it? It's kind of old, but it's still pretty good."

Maggie doesn't stop to take a breath until we're inside, and a giant black and brown dog comes bounding over to us, tongue hanging out the side of his mouth. I stumble back a step as he rears up in front of me. The beast's paws land on my shoulders for a moment before Trevor is there, shoving the dog off with a stern "down, Loki," and pulling me into his side. My heart is racing—whether from the giant beast of a dog greeting me, or the way Trevor's arm is wrapped around my waist I can't tell.

"I'm sorry, he doesn't usually do that." Trevor lets go of me and I immediately wish he hadn't. "Loki, sit. Stay." Once the dog's butt hits the ground, he isn't nearly as intimidating. "Here, just hold your hand out to him for a second so he can sniff you." I reach my fist out towards the dog's nose, letting him get a good sniff. "He loves a good scratch behind the ear. If you want to win his love forever, that's the way to his heart."

"Just like you?" The flirtatious words are out before I stop to think about what I'm saying. My cheeks burn at the memory that comes with that thought. My back pressed against a stucco wall in the Quinn's backyard, Trevor's arms braced on either side of me, caging me in. His lips kissing a path across my jaw as I buried my fingers in his hair, guiding him exactly where I wanted him. He'd started kissing down the column of my neck and I'd flexed my fingers in response, scratching lightly behind

his ears. The way he'd groaned against my throat at the movement had sent a powerful need shooting through my belly. A
need for what I didn't know, but I can't deny I want to make it
happen again.

"I had stucco marks on my arms for hours after that."
Trevor's whispered words in my ear and Loki's wet tongue
licking my hand jolt me back from my thoughts. The pink
tint at the tips of Trevor's ears tell me he's remembering the
same moment as me, but he looks me straight in the eyes, not
embarrassed by it. Slow enough that he could move away if
he wanted, I reach a hand up towards his face. Brushing the
backs of my fingers along his cheek, I let them slide into the
hair at his temple, never taking my eyes from his. Fascinated,
I soak up the way his eyelids droop as I push through his
curls. They close when I crook my fingers, scratching his
scalp with my nails.

With a quiet sigh, Trevor leans into my hand. It's intoxicating,
the way he melts at my touch. The way I melt at his. Why does
everything else have to be so complicated?

"Have you seen any of these?" Trevor steps back with a
wince as I jump, Maggie's question not registering in my mind.

"What?"

She holds up a couple of DVD cases with colorful anime
drawings on the cover. "Have you seen any of these?"

I look over the cases, intrigued by the drawings. "I haven't
seen any of these." A girl with a giant red bow is flying a broom-
stick through the air, in another a little girl is standing in front
of a dark Japanese festival. But the one that catches my eye has
a white haired girl clutching a man in all black above a little boy

holding what looks like a firework in his hand. *"Howl's Moving Castle*...that one looks interesting."

"That's Trevor's favorite!" Maggie spins away, the dog following her. "Is the pizza almost here? I'm starving!"

"Is your house always this exciting?" I can't help laughing at the expression on Trevor's face. His cheeks are bright pink, as if Maggie just revealed some deep dark secret of his. I peer around him into the rest of the house. "So, this is your house, huh? Wanna take me on a tour while we wait for the pizza?"

I step away from the front door, intending to toss my keys and phone on the table I spotted next to the couch when Trevor takes my hand. I freeze, waiting to see what he's going to say. For a heartbeat we don't move, then Trevor gives a tiny shake of his head and grins at me.

"Sure, grand tour it is." He leads me around the house, Maggie on our tail. "My room, bathroom, Maggie's disaster zone."

"Hey! It's not that bad."

"Yes it is." Trevor pulls me across the living room, pointing out the couch and fireplace. "That side is my parent's room and their bathroom." Turning around, he lets go of my hand, spreading his arms. "And the kitchen. Ta-da! Our palace."

I have to laugh at this because the house isn't huge at all. I have to wonder how he thought we wouldn't get in each other's way if I lived here, even if I had a separate space.

The ringing of the doorbell interrupts any more of the tour. Maggie runs to the door to answer while Trevor turns to Loki. "Sit." The dog sits right away, gazing adoringly up at Trevor. I kind of feel the same. "Stay." He walks off to help Maggie with the door, glancing over his shoulder at me.

I don't move from where he left me while they're at the door. Looking around, the house is cute, almost like a cottage, with hardwood floors and comfortable furniture. There's not a lot of furniture, everything is very tidy, no clutter anywhere.

"I didn't mean *you* had to stay." Trevor laughs at me as he walks back in, balancing a pizza box above his head, Maggie dancing in circles around him as he takes it into the kitchen. "Come grab some."

Once we all have pizza and are settled on the couch, Maggie starts the movie. I'm squished between them, Loki laying on the ground by our feet. It's warm and cozy and far less awkward than I imagined it would be. Maggie erupts into fits of explanation as we watch, reassuring me that Turnip-Head isn't the bad guy and that Sophie isn't really the old lady she looks like before Trevor shushes her. The movie is stunning and I find myself drawn in to the story far more than I expected.

And the soundtrack? It's gorgeous.

When the movie's over Maggie begs to watch another, so Trevor puts in *Spirited Away*. Again, I'm transfixed by how visually stunning the movie is. It's only when the movie is over and I try to move that I notice Maggie has fallen asleep against my side.

"I got her, give me a second." Trevor slides out from beside me, pushing Loki out from underfoot, before leaning down next to me and scooping Maggie up in his arms, carrying her to her room. Loki turns around and rests his head on my thighs, looking up at me with a sad expression.

"I don't have anything for you, boy." I say quietly. "But you sure are cute." I scratch behind his ears with both hands, glad that the dog seems to like me. I murmur quiet nothings while I wait for Trevor to come back, Loki grinning at the attention.

Loki's feet scrabbling against the floor as he pops up to his feet is the only warning I get before Trevor reappears. "I need to take him out for a second, you want to see the backyard?"

Pushing to my feet, I snag the blanket laying on the back of the couch and wrap it around my shoulders before following him to the back door. "There's the studio apartment." Trevor points to a little building in the back corner of the yard. I guess it really is its own space.

"Did you ever get someone to rent it?"

"Yeah, I think he's a med student or something. He keeps weird hours." The building is dark right now, it doesn't look like anyone is home. "Did you get any more audition results yet?"

"I haven't gotten any offers, no. I haven't heard from Pennsylvania yet, or from Idaho, but I think it's pretty unlikely."

"Are you disappointed?"

I shrug, not that Trevor can see much in the dark. A cold wind blows across my face, whipping my hair, but at least it's dry tonight. "Yes and no. It stings to get rejected, but I didn't think I'd get any offers anyway. I'm still recovering from my injury and I knew in my gut I wasn't ready yet. Looks like you're stuck with me for at least another year." I pull the blanket tighter around me. "But I'm glad I got a chance to practice auditioning when there wasn't so much pressure."

One of Trevor's arms wraps around my shoulders, pulling me against him. "I have to admit I'm relieved. I don't think I was ready for you to move out of Seattle, not when we haven't even had a chance..."

He trails off, not needing to say the rest. Not when we haven't had a chance to truly be together yet. Everything between us has been so on and off, will they, won't they. I don't know how to break the cycle, but I know I don't regret making the choices I have. I had to prove to myself that I could do this, that I could live the life I've wanted since I was a little girl.

Needing to break the tension, I ask the question that's been at the back of my mind since our texts this morning. "Hey, where are your parents? Is it their anniversary or something?"

"They're in Arizona. They get back Sunday night." I don't understand why Trevor's voice is tight but I let it go. Loki brushes past my legs as he trots back into the house, making a beeline for the big dog bed in the corner. I turn to follow him inside, snagging Trevor's hand and pulling him after me towards the couch.

"Can we watch another movie?" I'm not ready to leave yet.

CHAPTER NINETEEN

Trevor

AN YOU die of longing? Is that a thing?

Big blue eyes stare up at me, begging to stay. I want to say yes. More than I want to take my next breath, I want to say yes. Stay. Don't ever leave me again. She tugs on my hand and I want to pull her onto the couch with me, tangle my arms and legs with hers, bury my fingers in her hair and lose myself in the sweetness of her lips. Each kiss an unspoken apology, a promise. Do I really need her to say it out loud?

I can picture it. We'd sit on the couch to watch another movie. She'd get sleepy so we'd lay down, her tiny body tucked up against mine. I'd run my hand along her arm, her side, her soft skin hypnotizing me. I wouldn't watch a single moment of the movie, too wrapped up in her. Sometime during the movie, her eyes would close, and she'd fall asleep in my arms. I wouldn't want to fall asleep either, but eventually I would. Would we wake up in the middle of the night? Or when the sun came shining in through the windows?

And I can't do it.

I want it so badly, but Lisa's words keep echoing in the back of my mind.

Don't let her get away with not giving you a proper apology. You both deserve it.

Her unspoken promises mean nothing if I can't trust her.

Pulling my hand free, I scrape it through my hair before dragging it down my chin. "I can't, Han." I have to close my eyes against the crestfallen expression on her face. "I have a long run in the morning. Besides, I…" I swallow, hating myself for what I have to say next. "If you stay…I'm going to want to kiss you. A lot. And we can't."

Hannah's eyes widen, her mouth dropping open. She clamps it shut before swallowing hard. "Oh. I thought…is it because your parents are gone?"

I should let her believe that lie, that I'm trying to be a responsible son and brother. That my parents have some kind of rule about me having girls over. They don't, because they've never needed one. Instead, I say the stupid truth. "No. I don't trust you not to break my heart again, Hannah."

Her breath catches at my confession and she steps back, putting space between us. "I…I…" I don't help her find the words. I can't. "Trevor…" Whirling, the blanket lands on the couch, her keys and phone disappear off the side table and she's out the door in seconds. I make no attempt to stop her.

Lisa's right. I need her to be better than this, better than running away from me every time it's hard. Better than too scared to say the words I need to hear.

So instead of texting to make sure she's okay, I text Derek and Matt.

> **ME:** Long run in the morning? After I drop Mags
> off at dance.

I clean up the kitchen while I wait for them to respond, making sure to put everything in its place. If my parents get home while I'm out on my run, I don't want Dad to have problems navigating the kitchen.

> **DEREK:** Sure thing. Meet you at the trail? What time
> and how long?
> **ME:** 9 a.m., 6 miles. Last one there buys bagels.
> **MATT:** Deal.

EREK BRACES his hands against a tree, stretching the back of his calf and rolling his head while Matt sprints the last few yards to join us. "Dude. What the hell? You didn't say we were speed training," Derek accuses me while Matt leans his hands on his thighs, sucking in air. Matt chimes in by throwing a middle finger above his head and in my direction.

"Sorry, I had some steam to work off." I bounce on my toes, shaking my arms out. My heart is thumping hard in my chest, my ears throbbing to the pulse of it. Better than being numb or broken.

Instead of pulling my phone out to see if Hannah's texted me, I swing my arms in circles, loosening my shoulders. Maybe I should give my phone to one of them to hold onto so I can't look at the empty screen.

"Does it have anything to do with the ballerina girl?" Matt manages to get out. Pacing in circles, he swings his arms up over head, glaring at me as he comes back around. "I don't think that was six miles you asshole, felt more like seven, if you ask me."

"Or is it something else? How's your dad?" Derek grabs his foot, stretching out his quad as he asks.

"Dad's okay. They were down at the Mayo Clinic for a follow up test, but they get back tonight." At Derek's raised eyebrow I elaborate, of all my friends, these two are only ones who know the details of Dad's accident. "He's fine, as far as I know. I think there was some new test they wanted to try." I shrug. Dad is a constant worry at the back of my mind, but most days I manage to keep it there. All the uncertainty with Hannah has been good for one thing—I've been so busy worrying about her that I haven't had the chance to get too wrapped up in worrying about my dad.

"So, then it has to be Hannah who's got you all tied up." Derek leads the way to our cars. "I thought you were done with her?"

"Are you seriously going down this road again?" Matt sneaks in a punch to my arm as he passes me. "Wait, I can't listen to this on an empty stomach. You can tell us over bagels."

By the time we've pulled up outside the bagel shop, I've talked myself down from the ledge. Normally, a run would help me work out all my anger, letting me channel it into pushing my body faster, pumping my legs harder. Not today. It was as if the ground was vibranium, every molecule of irritation I slammed down into the sidewalk just doubled and came straight back to me. Instead of the run helping me dissipate my frustration, I was wound tighter than ever, each step doubling my resentment.

For the first time in my life, going for a run made me feel worse.

We order our bagels—Matt pays since we beat him back to the trailhead fair and square—and find a table outside to sit at while we eat. More than one little old lady wrinkled her nose as we walked past so sitting outside seems like the polite thing to do, even if the sweat freezing on my skin is sucking all the warmth from my body.

"Talk, man. What's up with Hannah? Besides the pining? It's been five months, man."

I launch a balled up napkin at his face and start talking. "We still haven't talked about what went down at the end of the summer. I don't regret calling her school. I know she thinks I could have cost her place at the school, but obviously I didn't. If she'd just listened to me in the first place…maybe it wouldn't have turned into anything serious."

Derek and Matt wince in sympathy at my words. They saw everything that happened with my dad, they *get* it, why Hannah's injury being misdiagnosed was a bullet straight to my biggest fears.

"We've heard this part of the story, we get it. If that's all she's mad about why are you still such a mess over her?" Derek asks when I stop to sip my coffee.

"I don't regret trying to make her stop, but she doesn't regret hurting herself to be able to keep dancing—I don't think we'll ever agree on who's right. Then, when she was getting ready to move up here, I may have been over-enthusiastic in trying to help her make plans."

As I say the words, it dawns on me that I've never told Matt and Derek the whole story. I'm surprised they've put up with my moody ass for so long.

"That sounds like the Trev I know. Always making the plans. What'd you do? Try and convince her to move in with your family?" Matt says, cream cheese stuck to his chin.

If my face wasn't already flushed from our run, Derek would be calling me out on the heat crawling up my neck. "Something like that," I mutter, avoiding elaborating by taking a giant bite of my bagel.

"I take it, she didn't appreciate it?" Derek and Matt give each other a look before nodding at me.

I just shake my head, still chewing.

"But all this was months ago, what's the problem now? Aren't you guys done? Finished? Finito?" Matt cocks his head, waiting for me to elaborate. The heat crawling up the back of my neck spreads, my cheeks and ears burning with it. Derek must be able to see it because he lets out a belly laugh, spraying bits of food across the table.

"Shut up, man." I growl, wiping the bits of food off the table and my cheek. "Also, you're disgusting."

"What happened, Trev? Something happened, don't deny it." Matt asks while Derek wipes the table with a napkin.

"Well, you remember we went to California for Christmas? Hannah did too."

"And?"

"Her friends are convinced we need to get back together,"

"Which you're not going to argue about," Derek points out.

I shake my head. "Nope, I'll take all the help I can get. They spent the whole time setting us up, giving us chances to be alone, to see each other. I kissed her at midnight on New Year's Eve."

Matt chokes on his bite of bagel. Derek thumps him on the back and glares at me. "And when were you planning to tell us this titillating bit of news?"

"That's not even the worst part." Blowing out a frustrated breath, I blurt out the reason I'm on the verge of Hulking out. My elbows dig into the table and I lean into the bite of metal against my skin, pulling at my hair in frustration. "She came over last night." Derek makes a noise of protest but I keep talking. "Well, technically, she invited me over to her place first, but since my parents are in Arizona I couldn't. Mags caught a peek of our conversation over my shoulder and wouldn't stop begging me to invite her over."

Derek snorts. "Yeah, *Maggie* was desperate to see her."

"And..."

"And nothing. We watched a couple of movies and then I kicked her out before I did something stupid." I look up to find both of them staring at me, mouths open.

"Whoa, *you* kicked *her* out? I don't know if that's the smartest or dumbest thing you've ever done." I can't tell if Matt's awed tone is for me or because he still hasn't caught his breath.

"I have no idea where I stand with her, guys." I pick at the edges of a napkin, shredding it into pieces as I speak. "If I was going off body language alone, I'd tell you she wants to be together, but I can't get her to say the damn words. Whenever I see her, she looks at me like I'm..." I have to stop and suck in a breath, my heart squeezing all the oxygen out of my lungs. God, it feels good to talk to someone about this instead of going over and over it in my own head. "She looks at me like I'm *it*, the thing she's been looking for her whole life. It's the same way I look at her. But it's only looks, no words. And every time things get hard, she runs away. She's like a fucking scared animal and I don't know if I should just give up or keep fighting. How do I know where I stand with her? How can I trust she's not going to walk away again the next time we get in a fight?"

Derek leans back in his chair, taking a slow sip of his iced coffee. Matt stuffs his face with a second bagel, not offering up anything to help. "Dude. I had no idea it was this bad. I don't think you're going to like my advice."

"Your advice is shit and you know it." I force the teasing words out, if I can pretend to feel less maybe eventually I will. "Who convinced me to bleach my hair in eighth grade?"

That earns me another of Derek's belly laughs. "You were the one who was trying to be Thor for Halloween. We were both too stupid to know that bleach would make such a mess. God, your mom was pissed that we ruined her good towels."

"Yes, she was." A tiny smile escapes me at the memory. "Spit it out. What's this advice I'm not going to like?"

"If you can't trust her, you need to walk away."

He's right. I hate his advice. The thought of walking away from Hannah twists my stomach in a hard knot, the bagel I just ate an uncomfortable lump. "I can't."

"Yes, you can." Derek drums his hands on the table. "You're choosing not to walk away from her and it's hurting you. How long has it been? Over a year, right?"

I swallow hard. "Yeah."

"And in that year how has she treated you? First, she was oblivious to you, then you were together long distance, where conveniently she didn't have to see you face to face." Derek is just getting warmed up. He drops forward in his chair, eyes narrowed. "Then you were together during her ballet camp, right? And how much you saw each other was limited by your schedules. You managed to be alone together, what, twice? And half of that you got in a fight and she didn't talk to you for a few days. Correct me if I'm wrong."

God, when he puts it like that our relationship sounds terrible. But it wasn't. He isn't talking about all the little moments, all the shared times even when we were surrounded by her friends. That's what I was after when I was pushing for her to live in our studio apartment, more of those little moments together, because they were the best part.

"You're not wrong, but you're not right either," I mumble into my coffee.

Derek just gives me a look. "So, then she gets injured, you guys have a big fight about you calling the office. I'm on your side on that one, by the way. Hiding an injury like that was dumb. She doesn't speak to you for a week, then you go to Cali-frickin'-fornia to win her back. You get her back and then immediately lose her again when you're over-enthusiastic about helping her move here. Because you were concerned, like a good boyfriend would be."

He takes a long sip of his drink, staring me down. I don't argue because there's nothing to say. He's not wrong.

"After ghosting you for three months, suddenly she's back? Who cares if she's forgiven you for being concerned and showing it? Have *you* forgiven *her*? If she wants to start anything with you, which I still think is a bad idea, she owes you an apology. And she needs to prove to you that she's not going to do that one foot out the door shit anymore. She's either in or she's out. Her friends may think that you're good for *her*, but your friends think she's bad for *you*."

"Matt, you don't agree with him, do you?"

Matt swallows before answering. "I'm with Derek on this one Trev. I know her friends think you're good for her, but we're *your* friends first, and I don't agree that the reverse is true."

Derek and Matt's words are a bullseye to the problem. I'm the one fighting for us, and the harder I fight, the more Hannah seems to resent my effort. "I don't know if I can just walk away, man." I shake my head. "You know, her best friend said pretty much the same thing. She didn't want me to take Hannah back without getting a proper apology first. It's the reason I didn't let her stay last night."

"I like this best friend. Is she single?" Derek smirks.

I laugh at the thought of Hunter and Derek going toe to toe over Lisa. Derek is built like me, wiry like a runner. Hunter may be a runner, but he's built more like his brother Jack, broad shoulders and beefy arms. He'd squash Derek in a heartbeat. "She is most definitely *not* single, and her boyfriend might be a science nerd, but he would eat you for breakfast for looking at her wrong."

We joke about it while we finish our post-run breakfast, the subject of Hannah pushed aside for now. It keeps turning over in the back of my mind though. Maybe it's time to stop. Or at least stop fighting so damn hard. If she wants to be with me, then she needs to work for it too. Lisa, Matt, and Derek can't *all* be wrong, can they?

CHAPTER TWENTY

Hannah

I STARE DOWN at the toast on my plate. Almond butter on toast stares back at me. Boring. Predictable. Even the banana slices and honey I drizzled on top don't help. I should have made myself something better for breakfast, but since I didn't have to get up for school I took the opportunity to sleep in a little. It may be Spring Break, but my schedule at PSB doesn't change.

If I was home in California, I'd be camped out in the sunshine somewhere—not like the gloomy skies here. I'd probably spend most of the week at Katy's house, at her pool. Dancing with Ms. Parker, seeing my friends. I don't even know what they're up to this week, I haven't spoken to any of them in a couple of days.

I wallow in my apathy, pushing the toast around on my plate, when a knock on the door snaps me from my mindless scroll through my phone. I hop up, Martin must have gotten off work early. Oh, I hope he brought me a coffee and his hands are full. I roll to my feet and go to let him in.

"Ta-da!" Flinging open the front door of my apartment, I'm met with the best sight I could have imagined. Katy, Lisa, and Olivia standing on my doorstep, jazz hands quivering.

"What? How? How are you here?" I cry, attempting to throw my arms around all three of them at once. The answer to my question is closing the trunk door and following up the stairs. "Mom!"

"Best surprise ever?" Katy asks as she pushes past me into my apartment. "Hi Martin!" she calls out.

"He's at work, but he should be home in about twenty minutes." I push them ahead of me through the door. "How on earth did you convince your parents to let you come?"

"That was your mom. She's been working on them since Christmas. We didn't say anything because we weren't sure we were going to pull it off."

"Crap, I have class and rehearsal all day." The realization hits me as Olivia surveys the living room, my mom close behind her. I'm already dressed in my leotard and tights, just waiting for Martin to get home so we could head to the studio together.

"No worries, we knew that was the case, since you don't get a spring break. We'll entertain ourselves while you're busy. Maybe we'll see if Trevor wants to hang out with us." Olivia drops her purse on the floor as my mom wraps me up in a hug. Sighing, I lean into my mom's embrace.

The mention of Trevor's name sends a sharp pang through my gut, even as Mom's arms around me are a balm to my hurting heart. I haven't heard from him since last weekend when I went over to his house. After the way he didn't ask me to stay, I chickened out of inviting him over for lasagna. I'd made it anyways and eaten the leftovers all week, each bite tasting like regret for assuming we could just move forward.

"Um…sure. Yeah. I don't know what his schedule is like." I mumble from the depths of my mom's hug. "Where are you guys planning to sleep? My place is a little small for all four of you."

"I have a hotel booked for us, we just can't check in yet." Mom is the one who answers. "And don't worry, we'll work around your schedule. Besides, we have plans of our own, right girls?"

I eye my friends. "What kind of plans?"

"We have a tour of the University of Washington planned for tomorrow." Lisa pops her head out of my tiny kitchen. "That's how we convinced my parents to let us come. And we promised to go see the Boeing museum." Lisa's dad works for SpaceX, that tracks.

"Is Dad coming? How long are you guys staying?"

"Dad had a sales meeting on the East coast this week, but if we decide we want a proper tour of Boeing, not just the museum, he gave me the name of his contact there. He has a meeting up here in two weeks, you'll see him then."

Lisa walks out with a mug of steaming coffee in her hand. Guess she found the mugs and coffee pot. "No thanks, I don't actually want to be in the aerospace industry, I'll leave that to Hunter. I just needed to convince my parents to let me come."

Pulling free of Mom, I pick up my abandoned mug of coffee, taking a sip. Gross, it's gone cold. "Does anyone need anything? Coffee? Breakfast? We still have some pastries left from Martin's shift the other day."

I scramble around to make coffee and find things for my friends while they fill me in on their plans for the week. They're going to go do the tourist thing while I'm in class and rehearsal, and we'll see each other as much as we can outside of that. Their hotel is just down the street.

"You could come sleep there with us, if you want," Katy offers. "We can squish in."

"That's okay, I'd rather sleep in my own bed." I shake my head, taking another sip of the hot chocolate I'd made to replace the cold coffee. Before I can say anything else the front door opens and Martin walks in, grinning at the sight of my friends.

"You made it!"

"You knew?"

"Of course I knew. Lisa sent me a message weeks ago to make sure I didn't mind them all crashing your week off school. The more, the merrier, I say." Martin hugs everyone before heading to his room to shower and get ready for class. How he manages to get up and go to work at four in the morning five days a week is beyond me, but he makes it work.

"Are you guys sure you're going to be okay?" Why do I already feel terrible for abandoning them? I didn't even know they were coming.

"Hannah, stop. We knew you would have class and rehearsal. Yes, we want to see you, but we know you can't just take a week off without consequences." Lisa, Olivia, and Katy nod their heads in agreement with my mom's words. "We'll be fine. Just text one of us if your schedule changes and we'll work around it. We do have to leave on Wednesday afternoon, I could only get the three days off work, so keep that in mind."

Martin emerges from his room a few minutes later, cutting off our excited chatter. My mom already has a key, so we make a plan to meet up for lunch in a couple of hours.

I smack Martin's shoulder when we slide into my car. "I can't believe you didn't tell me they were coming."

"After all the moping you've done lately, keeping that secret was worth it for the smile on your face now." His grin fades. "Han, you've been an absolute bear the last week. What gives?"

"I haven't heard from Trevor all week." The smile drops from my face. When Martin doesn't offer any consolation, I risk a glance. He's turning his phone over in his hand, biting his lip. "What?"

"You're not going to like it." If he tells me the same thing he's been saying for weeks, I swear I will pull over and let him walk the last three miles to the studios. "It's your turn, babe. You're the one who fucked it up, you gotta be the one to make the first move."

Slamming the heel of my hand on the steering wheel, I seriously consider making him walk. "I made the first move already. I asked if I could stay. He said no. He didn't want me. *He* rejected *me*. Not the other way around."

"I don't think that's true. I think he still wants you as much as ever. Did he, or did he not say if you stayed, he would want to kiss you?"

"I regret telling you things now."

"Regret it all you want, it's too late now." I'm going to wipe that smug smirk off his face.

"Yes, he said that." Pulling into the parking lot, I hunt for an empty spot.

"And…"

"And then he said that he didn't trust me not to break his heart again."

"And…"

I pull into an empty spot, using it as an excuse not to answer right away. This is the worst part. The reason why I've been a complete grouch for the past week. Because the boy I love with all my stupid, scared heart looked me in the eye, told me how much he wants me and then kicked me out of his house because he doesn't trust me.

Because I broke us.

And I'm too scared to tell him how I feel, because I can't guarantee I won't do it again. How can I? My life, my future, is at the mercy of wherever the ballet world sends me next. How do I ask him to keep waiting for me? Or to deal with my crazy ballet life? What happens if he's in college here in Seattle next year and I get offered a job with a company in Alabama? Or Alaska? Or Europe? Is it even fair for me to keep him hanging on, waiting for me?

So, I wrap my anger over being rejected around me like a protective blanket. It's easier to be angry than face the truth.

I love him too much to ask him to put up with my life.

"I left, okay? I ran away. He doesn't trust me, he doesn't want to want me. I'm not going to chase after someone who hates the fact that he still wants me, no matter how much I fucking love him!"

My heart breaking, again, I follow Martin into the building. Class is a welcome distraction from the warring emotions that threaten to overwhelm me. I'm so excited my friends and Mom are here, I'm lonelier than I've admitted since I moved up here. None of the girls here are my ride-or-die friends like they are. Yes, we have the same schedule and the same teachers and can complain about the same rehearsals, the same casting, but they don't *know* me like Olivia, Lisa, and Katy do. They won't call me out when I'm stuck in my head. Martin tries, but he has his own problems, I don't want to burden him with mine.

And Trevor can't help, he's the reason I'm twisted up in knots.

"Hannah? Do you have a minute?" Trish, one of the school admins, sticks her head out of the office door as I walk past, following Sloane and the other girls to Studio Two for our pointe class.

"I'm on my way to class, but I have a minute." I hurry over to the door to see what she wants. Sloane pauses but I wave her on. "I'll catch up."

"Mr. Bethelo wants to schedule a meeting with you this week. When do you have a break?"

Mr. Bethelo wants a meeting with *me*? That doesn't sound good. "Um, I have a break after this class?"

Trish must see the tension in my face because she puts a reassuring hand on my arm. "You're not in trouble, honey. Everyone gets a meeting with him at some point over the year. Most of the girls had theirs already, but since you were still recovering from your injury, we pushed yours back." Her words and smile go a long way to relieving me. What a roller coaster this day has been. "But we do need to block off about an hour of your time. When do you have time later this week?"

"Oh. My mom and my friends just flew up from California this morning to surprise me, but they leave on Wednesday. Is Thursday or Friday too late?" I want to know what this meeting is about, but I don't know when I'll see my friends again and they came all this way to see me.

"What a lovely surprise! Do you want to be excused from classes so you can spend time with them? We excuse dancers for a day or two at least once each year to see family."

I can do that? It never occurred to me to ask, but now that I think about it, I have noticed some of my classmates taking time off. I haven't, too scared of my reputation coming in as the "injured girl" to take any days off. Fear that my classmates and teachers will see me as needy or a drama queen, or even worse, uncommitted, has kept me from missing a day.

I arrange with Trish to be excused from classes and rehearsal tomorrow and from classes Wednesday morning. We schedule my meeting with Mr. Bethelo Thursday afternoon when I have a break in my day. It's going to be a busy week, but a better one than I anticipated when I woke up this morning.

Hours later, I drive Martin and I home, my feet aching and sore from dancing all day, but my heart lighter than it's been in weeks, knowing who's waiting for me at home.

"Your mom cooked dinner." Katy's greeting as she opens the door, along with the scent of my mom's homemade falafel and naan, has a smile on my face and my stomach rumbling in appreciation.

"So, I take it you guys went shopping?" There are new throw pillows on my couch and a potted plant in the corner. "You know I'm going to kill that, right?"

Olivia grins from her place on the couch. "It's fake."

"Oh, good." I leave my bag by the front door and kick off my shoes. "Guess who has all of tomorrow off?"

"That's great, sweetie, how'd you manage that? Food's ready, by the way."

I tell them about my conversation with Trish while we eat. Martin's appreciative groans and compliments have Mom turning pink at the ears, and the rest of us laughing.

"Now you know why we stayed Hannah's friend. Her mom is the best cook," Olivia teases, patting her belly after we've all finished eating. "Come on Martin, help me clean up. Nope, Mrs. O, you relax. You cooked."

I lounge on the floor with Lisa and Katy, my mom disappearing to the bathroom once Olivia and Martin clear the plates.

"So." Lisa clears her throat, glancing to make sure my mom is gone before speaking. "I take it you haven't apologized properly, and you and Trevor haven't patched things up yet."

Instead of answering I just throw an arm over my face, my head resting against the arm of the couch behind me.

"Hannah, you gotta use your words."

"Do I?" I don't pull my arm away, content to stay here in the dark.

"Yes, you do. I told him he had to wait for you to do it right." Lisa's voice is quiet, but fierce. What? My best friend is the reason he's doubting me?

"*You* told him not to trust me?" I throw the accusing words at her, dropping my arm so I can make sure she's listening.

Lisa shakes her head. "That's not what I said, you did that yourself. I need you to listen to me right now. He loves you and you love him, right?"

"Well, I know I love him. I'm not sure if he feels the same…"

Katy smirks. "He loves you. Even if he hasn't said it yet. Which, by the way, neither have you so you can't be mad about it."

Lisa points at me, nodding in agreement. "Loving someone's not enough. Not if you're not willing to fight to stay together. Sometimes that means you have to face big, scary decisions together, sometimes that means you have to be willing to accept that you were wrong. Sometimes that means being willing to make the first move when you both keep hurting each other."

"And sometimes you have to accept that being together isn't in your best interest." Katy looks sad for a moment but hides it with a smile. "But that's not the case here. You guys are good together. He's good for you. He makes you brave, Hannah. Be brave one more time. Be really, really brave and own up to the fact that you messed up. Apologize, then do better. And quit breaking that poor boy's heart."

The bathroom door opening cuts off the conversation before I can respond. Before I can tell them that I *am* being brave. I'm being brave enough to keep Trevor at arms distance so that when the ballet world inevitably pulls us apart, I won't hurt him again. Last Saturday was a momentary lapse, a moment of weakness. It won't happen again.

"WHEN IS your GED test, Hannah?" Lisa and I are lounging on the couch while Olivia and Katy clean up dinner. My mom has abandoned us for the night and Martin is working an extra closing shift, so we have the place to ourselves. She claims she has a headache, but I'm pretty sure she just wanted to give us a chance to hang out without her here. We spent the day touring University of Washington for Lisa's sake before heading down to the piers. It was my turn to play tour guide, not that I did a very good job.

I've been so busy dancing that I haven't explored much of Seattle. I kept waiting to do it with Trevor, now I don't know if I ever will.

"End of May, I think. You're not taking it though, right? You had all those extra credits." Lisa's parents would never let her get away with just taking her GED test to get out of high school. "Have you and Hunter heard back from any schools yet?"

"No, not yet. It's so weird thinking that we're going to be done with high school in a few months." Lisa slumps back against the couch. "Going to college sounds so grown up. I don't think I'm ready for it."

I shrug. "I felt the same way, but you get used to it once you get started. The worst was last month when I had a cold. I just wanted my mom to come take care of me. No one brings you soup and toast in bed when you're on your own." I laugh, slumping next to Lisa.

"Why would someone bring you soup in bed?" Olivia asks, plopping onto the floor across from us. "Is this when you were sick last month? You know what's weird?"

"Your face?" Katy throws herself across the couch behind Lisa and I. Olivia sticks her tongue out at her.

"No. We won't get to do any of those end-of-school, graduation rites of passage things together. Take prom. Not that you guys would have gone anyway, but I'm pretty sure I could have convinced you to at least come to your senior prom. And now, Hannah's already gone and grown up, having never gone to a single high school dance or sporting event in her entire life. And Lisa's graduating this year, so her junior prom is going to be her senior prom. JJ, Jack, and Hunter are graduating too. Katy and I are going to be the only ones left. Just us and Tyler."

Katy groans. "Please don't remind me that all the people who make school bearable are leaving me. You guys have no idea how much I hate this. *Everyone* I like, with the exception of Olivia, is leaving me at the end of the year. You're lucky I'm too proud of you to be mad at you."

I forgot that JJ is a senior. "Is JJ going away for college?"

Katy hangs her head over my shoulder. "No, thank god. She's going to the local community college for a year or two first. It's the only reason I haven't begged my parents to let me take my GED too and avoid senior year all together."

"Don't rush it. You have no idea how many times I've wished I was just a normal teenager this year. Especially when I'm so tired from dance and I come home and still have to cook dinner because it's not like there's anyone else to do it for me. Or when it got cold, and we didn't know we had to leave the faucets dripping so the pipes didn't freeze overnight. If our neighbor hadn't said something about it when I saw her on my way inside, who knows what would have happened?"

Eyes closed, I pinch the bridge of my nose. So many things about living on my own were a shock. Not just being responsible for all the cooking and cleaning, but little things like the pipes in winter, arguing with Martin over running the heater and forgetting to buy more eggs and milk.

"Yeah, but at least when Trevor comes over you can have privacy. Tyler and I have a hell of a time finding anywhere. Making out in the car only gets you so far."

"Do. Not. Say. Anything." Katy growls before Lisa can chime in, making us all laugh, Lisa's ears turning bright pink.

"Yeah...Trevor's been over once, that's it. And it was when Martin had a bunch of other people over. We haven't exactly been *together* together this whole time, remember?"

Olivia waves a hand. "I know. I'm talking in the *future*, dummy. Trust me, you'll appreciate having the privacy of your own place one of these days."

"Have you and Tyler..." I choke on my own question, heat creeping up the back of my neck. Do I want to know the answer? I just want to know that I'm not crazy or wrong for wanting Trevor as much as I do, that enjoying the sensation of his fingers on my skin doesn't make me a total weirdo. But the idea of doing anything more still scares me.

"Have Tyler and I…" Olivia lets the question hang in the air, like I'm going to fill in the blank. Lisa and Katy sit there mute, although I'm pretty sure that Lisa is listening intently.

"You know what I mean, Olivia," I groan. "Please don't make me say it, it's so embarrassing. Also, why am I, the only single one of us, the one asking this question?" I glare at Lisa and Katy who both duck their heads.

Olivia just laughs at all three of us, sitting in a row against the couch, well, Katy's head is stuck between ours, so it looks the same. "Why do you assume I know? Hmmm?"

Embarrassed, I stumble over my words, my cheeks burning. "Sorry, that's not what I meant, Livvy. It's just…well…you and Tyler have been together the longest of any of us. I just figured if anyone would know it would be you."

"Your faces!" Olivia rolls back on the floor, clutching her stomach as she laughs. "Oh my god. I can't breathe!" Wiping her eyes, she sucks in a breath before speaking again. "For your information, no we haven't. Kind of close, but not all the way, if you know what I mean."

I have a vague idea, but I'm too embarrassed to ask her to clarify.

Lisa opens her mouth like she's going to ask a question, but Katy slaps her hand over it, cutting her off. "I said no. I cannot have that visual of my brother in my head." Katy shudders.

Olivia pauses, giving Lisa a chance to try again but she just shakes her head, eyeing Katy, before pulling one of the throw pillows off the couch and hiding behind it. "It's more for lack of opportunity than anything else. It'll happen eventually, I'm sure. I got Martha to take me to the doctor so I could get on birth control. It was kind of fifty-fifty between dealing with my period and the *birth* aspect of the pill. You remember how brutal my cramps used to be?"

I nod, remembering the days Olivia would be curled up on the floor of the dressing room with her cramps. "Yeah. So, you got the birth control for that? Did it help?"

"Chica, my periods are so much better now. You should consider it."

"A lot of the girls here don't get their periods regularly, this one girl says she hasn't gotten one in a year. Mine have gotten kind of wonky in the last few months. It's so stressful, never knowing when it's coming." I hadn't thought about it, but now that Olivia mentioned it, it's true. I went almost two months without one in December and January.

Katy pokes me in the side of the head. "You know that's not healthy, right? Skipping your period because you're on birth control is totally fine, but not getting it because you're working out too much isn't. You could end up with weak bones and chronic stress fractures."

"What are you talking about?" I crane my head so I can see her face. "Where did you read that?"

"In my AP Bio class. And also that one account, that Australian one. She did a webinar on it, Ms. Parker and I watched it together."

"Ausdancersoverseas?" I check her account when Katy shares something from it, but I haven't spent a lot of time on it myself.

"Yeah. You should follow her, she's good. But anyway, back to Olivia and Tyler doing...stuff." Katy grins.

"There's nothing else to say. I'm not opposed, he's *definitely* not opposed." Olivia gives us an exaggerated wink. "It'll happen eventually. Why is it such a big deal?"

"Do you think you'll stay together after graduation?" My next thought comes pouring out of me, once I start I can't stop. "Even if I could untangle everything with Trevor, if he can ever forgive me. What happens when he goes away to college? What if I get a job somewhere far away? Maybe Europe? Martin and Sammy broke up because Sammy couldn't stay in the US and they didn't know when Martin would be back in New Zealand. Martin pretends he's happy, but I know he misses Sammy like crazy. I don't want to do that to Trevor. And taking things any further than we have, no matter how much I want to, seems like asking for both of our hearts to be hurt even more than they already have."

Tears gather in my eyes and I sniff hard to keep my voice steady. "Isn't it just asking for heartbreak if we start dating? When we have no idea what my life is going to look like in a year?"

"You think any of us have any idea what our lives are going to look like in a year, Hannah?" Olivia asks. Her words are harsh but her eyes are kind as she holds out the tissue box for me. "You're being an idiot. Why are you denying yourself the chance to be happy with Trevor now, over the fear of what's going to happen in the future? None of us know what's happening in the future. Hell, I'd be shocked if any of us end up with our current significant others long term." Katy huffs at Olivia's words, but she just shushes her. "You know it's true, Katy. Shit happens. But why are you afraid of trying the best parts now, in case it hurts later?"

I sniff back more tears as Olivia keeps going. "Do you know what I asked my dad the other day? If he would still marry my mom, knowing what would happen. He said he wouldn't trade one day of the happiness they had, for one less day of the pain of her leaving. I love him now, but will Tyler break my heart one day? Probably. Will Hunter, JJ, and Trevor break yours? Sure. Will we all survive? You bet your ass we will. Now pull your phone out and text Trevor. You're fixing this. Even if it's just for now, you two belong together."

Katy pulls my phone off the side table next to the couch and hands it to me. "She's right, you know. Apologize. For real. And put all of us out of our misery already."

I spend a moment looking at my phone, trying to think of what to say, before I type out a message, hitting send before I can chicken out.

CHAPTER TWENTY-ONE

Trevor

HANNAH: Can I take you out for coffee? Or dinner? I think we need to talk.

"WE NEED to talk." The four most dreaded words in the English language. I look over at the sleeping form of my dad next to me. Can I take one more piece of bad news right now?

ME: I don't know if I can this week. I have stuff going on.

I sound like such an asshole. I can't leave it like that.

ME: I'm sorry. Maybe? But my schedule is going to be super erratic for the rest of the week. I could maybe do coffee sometime tomorrow?

When she answers, her words sound as stiff and uncomfortable as mine feel. A nurse bustles around the room, hooking a bag up to the IV stand next to the bed.

> **HANNAH:** I'll do my best. My mom and the girls are here but I'm dropping them off at the airport at lunchtime. I have rehearsals from 3–6ish. Just let me know when you're free. I'll make it work.

She'll make it work? A glimmer of hope flickers to life in my chest. I shouldn't let it, I should squash it down, but I don't.

> **ME:** Sounds good. Would 2 be okay?

With a sigh, I lock my phone and tuck it in my pocket, numbing my mind with the endless home renovation shows on the channel my dad picked before he fell asleep. Hospital cable sucks.

"Hey baby." Mom kisses my cheek, startling me from my zoned out state a few hours later. "How's he doing?"

I glance down at Dad. "Same as this afternoon. The pain meds have him knocked out. They put in a new bag of antibiotics a couple of hours ago, but I can't tell if anything has changed."

Mom kisses the top of my head. "Maggie is staying over at Abby's house. Why don't you go home and get some sleep?"

I shake my head, not wanting to go home to an empty house. "I'll stay."

"Nope, not an option. You need to go home. He's going to be fine Trevor. I promise." She pulls me out of the chair I've been camped in all day while she was at work and with Maggie. "You stayed last night. And I appreciate it." She raises a hand before

I can protest, and keeps talking, pushing me towards the door. "But you need to go home. Loki needs to be fed and you need a shower and a decent night's sleep."

Before she closes the door in my face, Mom grabs my chin in her hand, pulling me down to look her in the eye. "He's going to be fine. Pick Maggie up in the morning, she said ten, and you guys can both come sit with him, okay? Maybe you'll even get to be the one to bring him home. I love you. Now go home."

With a kiss on the cheek, she releases me and closes the door, leaving me no choice but to head home.

This isn't the first time my dad's been in the hospital and it won't be the last. But every damn time it shakes me to my core. The fact that it's my fault he's here in the first place doesn't help.

Not this time, specifically. But the whole thing started because he was helping me learn how to be a proper runner. The memory of past hospital visits washes over me as I walk the sterile halls, the smell taking me right back to the first time. How were any of us to know that a tiny dog bite would change our lives in every way? What seemed like a simple skin puncture had taken ages to heal, but my dad just laughed it off, slapping a Band-Aid on it and telling us not to worry.

A week later, my mom had found him passed out on the floor in their bathroom, his calf red and puffy. Turns out the dog bite had turned septic and the infection had gone into his bone. For some reason, the doctors never seemed to be able to get the infection out again. No matter how many rounds of heavy duty antibiotics they pumped into him, it persisted. He'd spent months in and out of the hospital, the infection creeping back every time. Eventually, they'd had to amputate his leg below the knee, the only way to stop the infection from spreading any more.

That was the time Uncle Tom came to stay with us. To help my dad, his little brother, by giving him the punching bag he needed when recovery was too much. To spare my mom and I the brunt of his frustration. Fortunately, Maggie doesn't remember much, she was only six at the time. But I remember it clearly, how my dad grimaced or swore each time he hit a piece of furniture with his wheelchair or his crutches. The way he would stare at the photos from his races scattered around the house until one day I came home from school and they were gone. I stole the one of him crossing the finish line at the Olympic trials out of the trash. He never made the team, but just knowing that he was ranked in that tier of runners is an inspiration to me, I couldn't let it get thrown away.

Unlocking my car, I slide my phone out of my pocket, hoping for something to distract me.

> **HANNAH:** Let me know what works best for you and where. I'll come to you.

If only she would.

My fingers hover over the screen. We need to talk first, but I don't know if I can go home to an empty house without losing my mind. Dad's fall on Sunday afternoon scared all of us, Maggie especially. But after they got home from their trip to the Mayo Clinic where he was testing out a new prosthetic limb design, Dad got a cramp in the shower and lost his balance, bashing his head on the shower wall. The reason we're still here is that he sliced open his arm and the doctors wanted to hit him with a heavy dose of antibiotics. My mom was insistent that they keep him for observation. She's even more paranoid than I am.

Logically, I know he's fine, but logic and my brain don't always work together when it comes to my dad and hospitals.

"Screw it." My voice echoes in the silence of my van. I pull my phone out and type out a message. I don't care if this is a terrible idea.

> **ME:** I could use a friend right now. Or a distraction. Can I come over?

Her reply comes a moment later.

> **HANNAH:** How about I come to you? If that's okay?
> **ME:** I'll be home in twenty.
> **HANNAH:** See you soon.

CHAPTER TWENTY-TWO

Hannah

"I HAVE TO go." My friends turn puzzled glances my way, distracted from the Netflix show we've been binging. The dancing is decent, but the story line is way over the top. Dancers pushing each other off the roof? That doesn't happen in real life.

"To take us back to the hotel?" Lisa glances at the time on her phone. "It's only nine thirty, your mom wasn't expecting us until eleven?"

"Trevor needs me. I don't know why, but he said he needed a friend." I pull a hoodie over my tank top. His hoodie. The one I stole from him after our trip to California over New Year's. "This is my chance, right? My chance to prove that I can be brave? That he can trust me?"

Olivia grabs me by the hood as I storm past, pulling me to a stop. "Hold up Tiger. You're not wrong, but you can't go if you're not going to commit to this. It's not fair. I'm not letting you leave my sight until you swear to me you are apologizing so that you can stick it out. I will disown you if you run away from him again. Not without truly trying."

"Ditto." Katy steps behind Olivia, arms crossed over her chest. "You either apologize and commit, or we sit on you."

"Seriously?" I can't help asking. Katy just nods. Judging by her expression, she really will sit on me until I agree. "I promise. You guys are right. I've been stupid and running away for no good reason. But now we have to move. He needs me and I'm not going to let him down this time."

The three of them spend the drive to the hotel giving me advice I don't hear. I think it boils down to: say I'm sorry a million times and make him food, even if he says he's not hungry. According to my friends, boys are always hungry. I'll take their word for it.

By the time I pull up at his house, it's been more than the twenty minutes he said it would take to get home. His minivan is in the driveway, but all the lights are off. I tiptoe to the front door, glancing around for any clues that someone is home. Do I knock? But what if it makes Loki bark? If he's fallen asleep, or if his parents are asleep, I don't want to wake them up.

"Hannah?"

Whirling, my hand clutching my pounding heart, Trevor and Loki are watching me from the sidewalk. Loki's excited hop on two feet is the exact opposite of Trevor's slumped shoulders.

"Are you okay?" It's a dumb question, the answer is obviously no. Between his texts earlier and the dark circles ringing his eyes—they're so dark I can see them even under the streetlamps—Trevor is a mess.

Instead of answering, he steps past me to unlock the front door and let us both in. He unclips Loki without a word and hangs the leash up. I open my mouth to say something, but he shakes his head. Taking me by the hand, he leads me to the couch. I follow his lead, praying he'll tell me what's going on.

"Can I..." His voice breaks on the words and he takes a shuddering breath before sitting down, not letting go of my hand. "Can I just hold you for a second?"

I sink down onto the couch, collapsing against him as he pulls us both sideways so that I'm sprawled along the length of his body. His arms wrap around me, his face buried in my hair. Silent, I slip my hands under him, holding him as tight as he's holding me.

Trevor breathes in and out a few times, his fingers gripping the fabric of the hoodie I'm wearing. My body is stretched along his, our legs tangled together, my face pressed into the crook of his neck. Just the tiniest movement on my part and I could trace his jaw with my nose. I'm tempted, but I'm certain that isn't what Trevor needs from me right now. He said he needed a friend. So, a friend is what I'll be.

I'm about to open my mouth and ask what happened when I feel his Adam's apple bob as he swallows. "Did I ever tell you my dad was a runner, too?"

"No. You don't talk about your parents much," I whisper into his neck.

"He was. He even had a chance to compete at the Olympic Trials when he was in college, that's where he met my mom. He didn't make it, but he always loved it." I shift, pulling one hand out from under him and using it to prop myself up on his chest. I want to be able to see his face.

"When I was ten, my dad and I mapped out a three mile loop in the neighborhood that I was going to be allowed to run on my own. I had so much energy as a kid, Loki too, that my parents needed to be able to send us out to burn it off without having to come with me every time. But I loved running with my dad best of all."

"That sounds amazing."

Trevor's eyes are focused on the ceiling, like he's hunting for the words. I add my own thoughts, giving him time to gather his.

"My mom danced when she was a kid, that's how she and Olivia's mom met." I'm rewarded with a small smile. He brushes a strand of hair off my cheek before speaking again.

"This one day, I *begged* him to come with me on a run. I can't even remember now why it was so important that he came with me, but even though he was tired, he put on his running shoes and came. There was this one house with a dog that absolutely hated Loki. This little white thing would go nuts every time we ran past. Usually, the dog was inside the house and just barked out the window, but for some reason this day it was out in the yard. My memory is a little fuzzy now. But the dog tried to go for Loki, missed and bit my dad on the leg. Right on his shin. It was a nasty bite but the dog was small, so we didn't think too much about it. When we got home, my dad bandaged it up and I forgot about it."

Trevor tugs a strand of my hair free, twirling it around his finger. I missed him doing that.

"Long story short, the bite got infected and turned septic. The infection went into the bone and eventually they had to amputate my dad's leg from the knee down. He wears a prosthetic."

I push up on his chest, shock running through me. "What? I had no idea. How come you've never said anything before?" How could I have missed this? But thinking back, every picture I've ever seen of his parents, his dad was wearing pants. There's nothing from the outside to show that's the case. I haven't met them in person yet, so how could I know?

"I didn't mean for it to be a secret. It just never came up in conversation." Trevor shrugs.

"I guess that explains why you were so worked up about my ankle."

His chuckle is brief, rumbling under me. "You could say I'm a little paranoid about misdiagnoses. The doctor's missed the infection in my dad's leg until it was almost too late."

"I wish you'd told me." I lay my head back down on his chest. "I wouldn't have been so mad at you about the whole thing if I had known." I close my eyes, concentrating on the feel of his hand running over my hair. "What happened tonight?" There has to be more to the story than just that. Where are his parents right now? Is Maggie asleep in her room?

"My dad fell in the shower the other day. He managed to cut open his arm when he did it and bang his head hard enough to get a concussion. He's been in the hospital since Sunday night. He's fine. They just don't want to risk another infection so they're doing a course of heavy duty antibiotics and keeping an eye on him. He's supposed to come home tomorrow or maybe the next day."

"Is that where you've been all week?"

"Yeah. Mom kicked me out tonight, told me to go home. But Maggie is spending the night at a friend's, and I couldn't bear the thought of being in this big empty house by myself." He cuts himself off with a giant yawn, his arms squeezing me. He can't be comfortable with me laying on top of him like this.

Squirming to slide off him, he stops me before I can move too far. "Don't. Just... stay." I lift my head to look him in the eyes. Those warm brown eyes I love so much are begging me not to go. "Please?"

"I'm not going anywhere."

He pulls a blanket off the back of the couch, draping it over us both. It only takes a handful of deep breaths before he's asleep, the hand that was stroking my hair falling limply to the side. I guess my apology will have to wait.

Trevor's warm body beneath mine and the steady thump of his heart under my ear soothes my anxious mind. How do I keep forgetting how calm I am when he's around? With nothing better to do, I close my eyes and let the steady beat lull me into a mindless state. A few breaths later I fall asleep too.

FLYING THROUGH my front door, I almost collide with Martin. "Justine's waiting for you in the parking lot."

"I don't know whether to tease or congratulate you on your first official walk of shame." Martin calls through the door as I scramble to brush my teeth. Thank goodness I was excused from class to spend the morning with my friends before they leave this afternoon, but I'm supposed to meet them for breakfast in five minutes.

"It's not a walk of shame, nothing happened. We just fell asleep."

"I still want all the details when we get home tonight!" The click of the front door being locked echoes his words as I race around my room to get changed. My heart hasn't stopped racing since I woke up twenty minutes ago cocooned in Trevor's arms.

The alien sensation of a tongue licking my arm is what jolted me from a fitful sleep. Falling asleep on the couch had only lasted a short time. Trevor turning on his side dislodged me from my spot draped over him and woke me up. Half-asleep, he'd tucked me against him where I'd dozed until my arm was so painfully asleep I couldn't take a second more. I'd sat up, intending to drive myself home, it had been after one in the morning.

One hoarse "Don't go," from Trevor had been all it took to change my mind. Instead, he'd led me by the hand to his room where we'd crawled under the covers. His bed was a thousand times more comfortable than squishing on the couch, but my brain couldn't settle. Every twitch, every movement kept me awake until I'd fallen asleep around four in the morning. How do people share a bed with a stranger? I've never had such a terrible night's sleep.

Loki licking me had startled me awake, the time on my phone had sent me racing out the door with a hurried, "I have to go. I have to go right now," to Trevor. I don't think he'd really woken up until I was almost out the door. In my panic at staying at his house all night I almost yanked my arm free when he pulled me close. But the hug he'd pulled me into had calmed me enough to take a full breath.

"Thank you. I don't think you know how much I needed that," Trevor whispered in my ear. "I'll talk to you later?"

Looking up at his sleepy face, for an instant I wanted to crawl back into bed with him. "Yeah. I'll text you when I'm on my way home from rehearsal." I can still feel the kiss he'd dropped on my forehead before letting me go.

But I don't have time to dwell on it now. I'm late to meet everyone for breakfast at the hotel. If I don't get there soon Olivia will eat all the bacon.

Scanning the breakfast area of the hotel I spot my friends and Mom at a large table. It's hard to miss the loud laughter of Olivia and Katy. Dropping into a chair next to my mom, she squeezes me in a side hug without putting down her coffee.

"Hey, is Trevor okay?" Lisa asks once I'm settled with my own coffee and plate of breakfast.

I set my spoon down before I choke on the granola and yogurt concoction I've created. My cheeks burn before I realize there's no way any of them knows I accidentally slept over at his house. "Um, yeah. Well, I think so. His dad was in the hospital."

At my words, everyone starts talking at once, asking questions while I shove a spoonful of my breakfast parfait in my mouth. "He's okay, they think he's coming home today." I get the words out as soon as I manage to swallow. I tell them everything I know while we eat, grateful for my mom's reassuring presence next to me while I talk.

"Since there's nothing you can do for Trevor now, and we have a couple of hours to kill, we have a proposition." Katy, Lisa and Olivia share a look before Katy keeps speaking. "We're going prom dress shopping, since we won't be able to do it together later. Since you and Lisa and everyone are graduating this year, this is our only shot at a fabulous dress shopping montage!"

Five minutes later I'm being hustled out to my car, Katy towing me and Lisa through the parking lot. Olivia rides with my mom in the rental car while they follow me to the mall. I try to argue that I won't need a dress, but I'm outvoted.

"You might need one for a fancy gala or something," Katy points out.

"Yeah, you know they sometimes have students at those donor events. You can be like Jodie Sawyer and eat the leftover desserts."

"Did you get a chance to apologize to Trevor?" Lisa leans over the backseat so we can hear her question.

"No. He was so upset, we didn't talk at all. He just needed someone to be with him, so he wasn't alone in the house." Katy grins when I finish explaining the situation, but they both agree it wasn't the right time to start the conversation I need to have with Trevor. By the time I park and lead the way inside, Mom and Olivia are there.

Katy wasn't kidding when she said this was going to be a dress shopping montage. I'm reminded of the time she and Jack kidnapped me and took me shopping, but better. Olivia steers us to one of the department stores on one end of the mall where we make a beeline for the formal dress section. Arms piled high with a rainbow of dresses, we even make my mom pick out a few. And then we proceed to try on every single one. All four of us being the same size, we all try on as many of the dresses as we can.

"Hannah, I swear you've lost weight." Olivia says as I drop a metallic silver dress over my head. It's got a scandalously low back, the thin straps holding up the slinky material that rests just above the curve of my butt. There is no way I can wear this in public.

"I haven't, but I've gotten a lot more toned." I hold my hands up at Olivia's look, she and I are sharing a dressing room. "I swear. I've been keeping track."

"If you say so. You still look skinnier than I remember. Lemme take a picture of you, you look freaking hot, even if you'll never wear it in public."

Even though we only have a couple of hours before they have to leave, my heart is lighter than it's been in weeks. I missed my friends so much, I missed these chances to hang out and be silly. Trying on ridiculous dresses, gorgeous dresses and everything in between. I laugh until I cry when Lisa emerges from the dressing room in a hot pink floor-length gown with feathers sewn along the strapless neckline, blowing bits of stray fluff out of her face. Katy and Olivia both try on the same silver dress I did but where it looked scandalous on me, it looks positively indecent on them with their bigger boobs. My mom makes them delete the pictures of them in it off their phones, to mine and Lisa's amusement.

Turns out my friends had planned this ahead of time and all saved room in their bags for the dresses and brought spending money so they could buy them. Olivia found a short dress in a peach-tone fabric, the whole thing covered with silver appliqués. It sparkles and shimmers in the fluorescent lights, I can just imagine how amazing it's going to be under real lights. The short skirt of silver fringe has a definite Great Gatsby meets disco ball aesthetic. Tyler is going to die when he sees her in it.

Lisa picks out a black satin dress with a halter neck and structured high-low hem. The second she put it on and discovered it had pockets she refused to try on any other dresses, claiming it before the rest of us could try it on. Katy's dress looks like a throwback to the fifties, the poofy skirt and simple sweetheart neckline in a smooth red satin plain until she turns around and you see the open back is held together by a giant bow across her back.

I had the hardest time picking my dress, I tried on so many that I loved. There was a long white dress with delicate cherry blossoms painted all over it that made me feel like a fairy, and a crazy pastel rainbow one that made me feel like a unicorn princess, even though everyone claimed it clashed with my red hair.

But eventually we narrowed it down and my dress made its way into a garment bag and to my car. I have no idea if I'll ever have a chance to wear it, but the best part was getting to pick it out with my girls and my mom. I didn't realize this was a *normal high school experience* I wanted until I had a chance to do it.

After some tearful hugs they all pile into the rental car with my mom and their bags, ready to leave for the airport.

"Bye! You better keep us updated on Trevor!" Olivia calls from the front seat, sitting in the open window while everyone else climbs in.

"I will!" I promise.

"Don't be late to rehearsal!" Lisa calls as she slides into the back seat next to Katy. I laugh when Katy leans over her to wave at me through the window.

"Bye! Love you guys! Miss you already!"

CHAPTER TWENTY-THREE

Trevor

I LIMIT MYSELF to texting Hannah just once.

> **ME:** Thank you for last night. It meant a lot to me that you came. I hope you have a great morning before everyone goes back to CA. Just got word my dad is being discharged this afternoon. Text me when you have a chance.

I didn't expect to hear from her, and I definitely didn't expect the text I got an hour later.

> **UNKNOWN:** Just thought you'd want to see how hot she looks in this dress. She'll never buy it, but I thought you'd appreciate the view. This is Olivia, btw.

The picture that loads a few seconds later has my jaw on the floor. Hannah is looking back over her shoulder, laughing at something, her eyes glowing with joy. Her red mane is pulled in a braid over her shoulder to reveal the dangerously low back of the dress she's wearing. Silver fabric drips off her hips, pooling on the floor. The front of the dress is visible in the mirror in front of her, a deep V plunging low enough that I can tell she's not wearing a bra, the front held up by the thin straps on her shoulders. I can see why Olivia said she'll never buy it, it's a look more appropriate for a twenty-year-old than a seventeen-year-old, but damn does she look hot.

> **ME:** She looks beautiful, thank you for sending me that. Are you guys just trying them on for fun?
> **OLIVIA:** We're shopping for prom dresses. Hint. Hint.
> **ME:** Got it. Appreciate the heads up.
> **OLIVIA:** Don't tell Tyler we meddled. I promised not to. #TeamTrannah #notsorry
> **ME:** My lips are sealed.

"Hey Trev, I'm running to the store while Dad's asleep." Mom sticks her head in my door as I'm reading Olivia's texts. "I'm going to pick up Maggie on my way home. Will you keep an eye on Dad?"

"Of course. I may have to take a nap too though," I say as a yawn takes me by surprise. Mom just smiles before heading out.

Last night was the best and worst night of sleep I've ever had. Something about having Hannah there slowed the racing thoughts in my mind. Telling her about my dad was a weight off my chest I hadn't even realized was there. But as relaxed as I was by her presence, every time she twitched or moved in her sleep it woke me up, my heart racing at the thought that she might try to sneak out. I was trying so hard not to scare her off, not to touch her inappropriately, even though all I wanted to do was wrap myself around her and bury my face in her neck, breathing her in all night long.

My sheets still smell like her. It's torture and heaven all at once.

Hours later, I'm in the middle of trying to convince Dad to let me train for an ultra-marathon, when my phone buzzes. We've just finished watching the Barkley Marathon documentary on Netflix—I'm sure I could finish at least one loop, even if that race looks absolutely bonkers. Checking my phone while my dad looks for something else to watch, the message that pops up brings a smile to my face before I can stop it.

> **HANNAH:** I'm glad I was able to be there for you. Thank you for giving me the chance. I had a blast with the girls. We went shopping and hung out, just like regular high school girls on Spring Break. Who would have thought I had it in me?

A second message comes in before I have a chance to respond.

> **HANNAH:** Is your dad home yet? How is he doing? How are YOU doing?

Do I ask what they went shopping for? I'm not supposed to know about the dresses. Bless those girls for thinking ahead. With each of Hannah's questions my resolve to keep her at arm's length falters.

> **ME:** Can I take you up on that offer of coffee? I know it's too late tonight. I don't know about you, but I'm exhausted and going to bed soon. Do you have time tomorrow?

There. Technically, I didn't ask her out. I'm merely taking her up on the offer she made yesterday. And it's just coffee, it's not a date.

> **HANNAH:** Tomorrow sounds perfect. I have a break from 1:30–3. Can you meet me at the coffee shop near the studios? Then I'll have longer. If it's not too far out of the way. If you need me to come to you I can.
> **HANNAH:** I'm going to stop babbling now.

Is she...nervous? A spark of hope flairs somewhere deep inside me.

> **ME:** I can come to you. Dad's home now, doing fine. I'm doing okay too. Just tired.

"Who's got such a goofy grin on your face, huh?" Looking up from my phone, Dad's settled on a nature documentary and is waiting for me to notice. "Is it Hannah?"

"Yeah. I'm meeting her for coffee tomorrow."

My dad is the hopeless romantic in our family. Mom has so many stories of the romantic things he did while they were dating. "So, where do you stand? What are you thinking?" Documentary forgotten, Dad looks at me expectantly. Over the past few weeks I've filled him in more and more on the on and off mess Hannah and I have been tangled in.

"She asked me to meet her for coffee. I have no idea if I'm walking into a 'let's just be friends' kind of conversation or an apology and her wanting to *finally* try for real. But I'm hoping that it's the second one and she's done running away." My phone buzzes in my hand but I don't look.

Dad is silent for a moment, he likes to think over what he's going to say before he says it. Unlike me and my big mouth. "If it's not what you want, and she just wants to be friends, what are you going to do?"

"Accept the fact that we're never going to happen." I sigh, leaning back against the couch. "Even though I'll hate it and think of her as 'the one that got away' for the rest of my life."

"Every man has to have one of those." Dad grins at me "You look hopeful though. Is there something I don't know?"

The blush that creeps up the back of my neck burns. "I may have asked her to come over last night after I left the hospital. I didn't want to be alone in the house," I add, defending myself before he can say anything. "Nothing happened, I promise, but we *may* have fallen asleep on the couch. And she *may* not have left until this morning. But I swear, Dad, nothing happened. We just slept," I finish quickly.

There's a long silence and I can't meet my dad's eyes. There's never been a rule in the house about girls being over, because there's never been a need. The few girls I've dated before Hannah were so short-lived that I never had a chance for them to do more than meet my parents once or twice. Besides, my house is so small I would never invite them over here. There's nowhere to go that isn't my bedroom and I knew that wouldn't fly.

My parents are cool, but they're not that cool.

"I trust you. But don't make a habit of it." I flinch at my dad's tone, he's not messing around. When I look up to meet his eyes, he's watching me. "Sleeping together, yes just sleeping, is more intimate than you realize, Trev. Everyone feels vulnerable when they sleep, trusting someone enough to fall asleep with them is a big step. Don't take it for granted, okay?" I nod and he grins. "I bet it was a terrible night's sleep, huh?"

I can't help laughing at that. "Oh my god, Dad. It was the freaking worst! Every single time she moved I woke up."

Dad laughed right back at me. "That would explain the dark circles under your eyes. I'm glad you had someone to keep you company last night. I was worried about you."

Even though Dad keeps ribbing me about my terrible night's sleep while we watch the next documentary, especially when I keep dozing off, I file his words away in my brain. Maybe one day soon I'll be able to trust her not to sneak out on me. I glance down at Loki, snoozing on his bed in the corner. He may be the one named after the slippery trickster god, and I may be the one who looks like him, but Hannah's the one who has mastered his ability to disappear.

*H*ER RED hair glints in the shaft of sunlight peeking through the clouds. Hannah's sitting at a table by the window, staring into space while the coffee shop bustles around her. A nervous smile flits across her face when she spots me.

"Hey. Did you order yet?" I ask, draping my coat over the back of the chair.

Hannah shakes her head. "Nope, I was waiting for you." I follow her to the line, my hands stuffed into my pockets so I don't do something stupid. At least I have pockets. Hannah looks like she's wearing twenty layers of clothes and still doesn't have anywhere to put her hands, which is probably why they're twisting nervously in front of her while we stand in line.

"How was class?" I ask, to break the tension. She keeps biting her bottom lip and rocking back on her feet. Why is she so nervous?

"Class was good. We had a guest teacher from Canada today."

"Canada, huh? Any particular reason?" Please don't be moving to Canada.

Hannah studies the menu while she answers, not meeting my eyes. "You mean, like an audition? No, it wasn't an audition or anything. He's a former student of the school and happened to be in town, their company is touring and here this week. It was a good class, although I have a new blister now. I, uh, just had a meeting with the director of the school this morning."

Is this the news she needed to talk to me about? Are they kicking her out? "What kind of meeting?" I try to keep my tone neutral.

Hannah twists her fingers. She goes to tuck a strand of hair behind her ear in a nervous gesture, but since it's up in a bun she ends up dropping her hand back to her side. "Apparently he meets with everyone during the year, mine got pushed back this late because of my injury. I came straight here from meeting him."

A spark of happiness blooms in my chest, knowing that I'm the first person she's told. This, this is what I've been wanting to do for months. "What did he say?"

"He's pleased at the improvement I've made, and how I've recovered from my injury. But Mr. Bethelo thinks I need another year at the school before I'm ready to move on, which I kind of knew already. I did spend the first part of the year recovering. I *think* he hinted that he's keeping an eye on me for a possible place at PSB after that." She looks at me at that revelation, her face adorably scrunched. "At least, I think that's what he meant. He did say he was impressed by how I handled the first few weeks of the year, when I wasn't allowed to dance."

"That's great, Hannah." I want to wrap her up in my arms, but I don't. I'm still not sure what this means for us. Or if there even is an us anymore.

"Thanks. That's not really why I asked you to meet me, but it's a relief to have the meeting over with. I was so nervous!"

She turns to look at me, the worry still written on her face. I pull my hand out of my pocket and wrap it around her shoulder, squeezing her in a one-armed hug. The moment I do, some of the tension oozes out of her body. I know the words are what *I* need to hear, but I get the feeling that for her, physical touch is the most reassuring. I can't say I mind.

We order our drinks before heading back to the table to wait for them. I'm barely in my seat before Hannah's talking.

"Trevor? Can you...I just." She stops to blow out a deep breath. "I need to say something, and I need you just to listen. Okay?" She doesn't speak again until I nod, but once she gets started the words come at me like a flood. "I'm sorry. I'm so, so sorry. I don't think I can ever say sorry enough times. I let you do all the hard work, and every time it was my turn to be vulnerable, I got scared and ran away. You deserve better than that." When I shake my head at her words, Hannah gives me a small smile, but plows on. "I realize now that at the intensive you were trying to look out for me when I refused to look out for myself. After hearing about your dad, I get why you were so worried about me. I still don't think you handled it the right way, but it was unfair of me to expect you to know how the ballet world works."

I open my mouth to protest that any world where you're expected to just suck up the pain and never take the time to rest your body, especially when it's such a freaking physically demanding art, is misguided. But Hannah stops me with a shake of her head.

"I'm not done. Whether it's right or not, that's how the ballet world works. Maybe one day it will change, but I wasn't wrong when I said you could have cost me my shot at being asked to stay at the school. What I was too angry to realize—was that even if they hadn't asked me to stay, my dream wouldn't be over. And having someone who cares enough to look out for me when I don't know how to do it myself isn't something I should take for granted. So, I'm sorry for yelling at you and for walking away over that."

The barista calls out our drinks and Hannah hops up to get them, leaving me to think over her words. The little seed of hope I've been hiding away in my heart grows a few roots.

Hannah hands me my drink before sitting down opposite me. "Okay. I'm not apologizing for moving in with Martin. I needed to know that I could do this on my own, for myself. It has nothing to do with how much I l—" She cuts herself off. She what? What was she about to say? "How much I care about you. For my own sake, I needed to know that I could handle being on my own. Besides, Martin needed me after everything that happened with Sammy. But what I *am* sorry for is how I ghosted you. You don't deserve to be treated like that. It wasn't that I didn't want to see you, I just didn't know how to start the conversation. Well, I was afraid to start the conversation. I hate that I missed your birthday, that I missed dressing up with you for Halloween."

I can't help interrupting her for a second. "I saw your costume. Was that for me?"

Hannah closes her eyes for a moment before opening them and looking straight into mine. "Yeah. It was. That night…you can ask Martin. I was miserable. All I wanted was to see you. I spent the whole party scrolling through pictures of us on my phone and binge watching Teen Titans. Martin took my phone away when he caught me crying over YouTube videos." She looks up and frowns when she sees my smile. "Anyway, that's not the point. Let me apologize."

I reach across the table to tap her on the nose. "I'm listening, I promise. I was pretty miserable that night myself."

Hannah grabs my hand before I can pull it away, wrapping her hand around mine. "That's what I'm trying to apologize for. We both spent the whole fall miserable, for no good reason. I missed your whole cross-country season—I hate that I wasn't there for you at State. Even if I couldn't have been at every meet, I could have gone to some. I could have been there to celebrate with you afterwards. The day Dr. Lee said I could start taking class, you were the first person I wanted to tell. I made us both miserable and I'm so, so sorry."

Her eyes are glassy with tears as she finishes. How mad would she be if I pulled her onto my lap? My arms are aching to hold her. Comfort her. Kiss the tears away before they can fall. Instead, I squeeze her hand. "Am I allowed to talk now?" When her nod sets a few tears running down her cheeks I can't help myself, I tug on her hand, drawing her over to my side of the table. Pulling her down to sit on my lap, I wrap my arms around her, tucking her head under my chin.

"Apology accepted." Her little hiccup against my chest surprises a chuckle from me. "I'm not going to lie to you and tell you I haven't been miserable too. Missing all the same things as you. You're always the first person I want to tell things. Since we first met, I knew there was something special about you, something special about us, I just didn't know what it was yet."

Needing to steady myself, I take a sip of my drink, the hot liquid settling in my stomach and setting off a flurry of butterflies. "I'm not trying to clip your wings, T." Hannah tips her head up to look at me, a tiny smile at the use of her nickname. "I never wanted to stand in the way of your dreams. Your dreams are fucking amazing. I just want a front row seat, to be there to cheer you on, to help you get there."

Her smile is real, if a little watery. "I want that too. And I want to be there for you. I hate how much I've missed, because I was too self-absorbed to see that you needed me to be there for you just as much as I needed you to be there for me."

"No bad-mouthing my girl." I tap her on the nose. "I happen to love her just the way she is, scaredy-cat and all." Hannah freezes. I hadn't thought about the words I was saying until I finished and looked down at Hannah's face. I'm so used to thinking about how much I love her that it didn't register what I was telling her until it was over.

Hannah's stillness sends panic flooding through me. Shit, I didn't mean to say that. Now I've scared her again.

"You..." Hannah's eyes are wide, but she doesn't pull away like I was expecting. Her hands fist in my shirt but she doesn't pull away. Like the creeping signs of spring, so slow you almost can't see it, hope and happiness creep across Hannah's face. Her eyes searching mine, I watch as the tension in her eyes fades, replaced by a shy smile. The thudding of my heart slows and a sense of rightness follows it as her smile grows. "Yeah?"

"Yeah." My breath freezes in my lungs as I wait for her to say more. Silence stretches between us, even though she's smiling, the longer it goes the more the hope inside me wilts. "T? What are you thinking?" I can't take it any longer, I'm dying to know the thoughts I see flitting through her eyes.

"I was trying really hard to think of a cool Marvel reference to say back but I kept coming up empty. People don't say 'I love you' very much in those movies." Her little shrug is what cracks me up, breaking the tension between us. "All I could think of was Star Wars."

Laughing, I bury my face in her neck, inhaling her, my arms wrapping tight around her. "I think they're too busy saving the universe to bother saying it. And Star Wars is okay, but I'm pretty sure in this case you'd be Han and I'd be Leia. I'm not sure how I feel about that."

"Even *I* know Leia is a badass." Hannah pokes me in the chest to emphasize her words. "You should be so lucky."

"I am lucky." I let the subject drop, deciding that since I got the apology I needed, everything else could wait. "So, tell me more about shopping."

Hannah fills me in on the morning shopping with her friends until it's time for her to leave for rehearsal. The studios are only a block away, so I walk her to the door. My hands stuffed in my pockets, her arm looped through mine.

As we approach the main doors Hannah slows. There's a crowd of dancers standing around outside chatting.

"Hannah!" one of the girls calls to her, eyeing me.

"Hi Sloane, Jasmine." Hannah's shoulders twitch, with irritation or anxiety I can't tell.

"You good?" I tug her hand, turning her to face me. Her hair is wound up in a bun or I would play with it, the way I always do.

She looks back over her shoulder at the dancers waiting outside. "Yeah, I'm good. I should go." Pulling away, she gets half a dozen steps away before she turns back to me. With a little skip and a smile just for me, she braces a hand on my chest before rising up on her toes to kiss my cheek. "I'll text you later. Or you can text me."

"You really want to open those floodgates?" I tease.

"I can't wait. I missed your million texts." Grinning, she dances back to her friends, her feet doing a quick crossing and uncrossing step before she literally leaps into their midst. As she joins them, Martin waves a hand above the other dancers' heads. I wave back before turning to walk back to my car, smiling to myself at the ribbing I can hear her taking from the other dancers.

There's a definite possibility that I strut like Tobey Maguire in Spiderman 3 once I'm out of sight.

CHAPTER TWENTY-FOUR

Hannah

"HUH?" I snap out of my daydream to find Martin glaring at me. But it's not an angry glare, not really. The corners of his mouth are fighting not to turn up in a grin. He's one second away from twirling me in circles and tossing flower petals over my head.

"I was *saying*, we have a combined class with the company tomorrow morning. Aren't you freaking out?" Before I can answer Martin pokes at my shoulder. "Or were you too busy dreaming about a certain someone?"

"You don't have to do the air quotes, I know I'm ridiculous." I stick my tongue out at Martin. Very mature, I know.

"I knew it! You were." Martin hums to himself and does a little samba step out of the kitchen before I whack him with my wooden spoon.

Maybe I am a bit dreamy at the moment, can you blame me? It's been a month since Trevor and I made up. A month of late night phone calls, just like old times, except this time I can invite him over whenever I want. And I do. He's been coming over at least a few times a week, sometimes to do homework with me, sometimes to watch movies with me and Martin.

I even went over to his house last week for his mom's famous lasagna. I have to admit, I think it might even be better than my mom's. Not that I would ever tell her that.

I switch my wooden spoon for a pair of tongs and flip the chicken breasts in the pan, keeping an eye on the boiling potatoes. "Dinner will be ready soon," I call to Martin. We've been rehearsing non-stop for both the school's spring performance and the company's spring season. The company is doing *Romeo and Juliet* and we're both in some of the ensemble background scenes. I was not prepared for how exhausting it is to have to hop up and dance full-out after standing around in my pointe shoes for twenty minutes acting.

I do some rises while I watch the cooking food, lifting up to my highest demi-pointe before lowering to flat feet. My calves are extra sore from today's pointe class, we did so many hops on pointe I'm sure my left toenail is going to fall off, spreading my toes on the cold floor is exquisite agony.

My phone buzzing on the counter distracts me enough to lose count of how many rises I've done. A glance at the screen wipes away any irritation.

TREVOR: Hey gorgeous, what are you guys doing tonight? Any chance I can see you?

I snap a picture of the food cooking away on the stove and send it to him.

ME: Just making dinner for me and Martin. I don't have enough for you (sorry, we're both starving) but you can come hang out if you want?

The timer goes off the moment I hit send so I drop my phone on the counter and start draining and mashing the potatoes. It buzzes a few more times while I'm busy but I ignore it, too hungry to put off getting dinner ready.

"Martin!" I call out once the potatoes are mashed.

"Need a hand?" I whirl at the familiar voice, one without a New Zealand accent. "Surprise?" Trevor grins, stepping into our tiny kitchen. He's so tall he has to duck through the doorway. I'm pretty certain if he stood right in the middle he could reach the fridge, the stove and the cupboards without taking more than a single step in any direction. My perfectly average self only needs three steps to cross from one side to the other.

"That was fast." I giggle as he bends down to kiss my cheek. Instead of backing up, Trevor cups my face in his hands and kisses me again. "Hi," I breathe out when we come up for air.

"I was already in your parking lot when I texted," Trevor admits. He opens and closes a few cupboards looking for something until he spies the plates. I'm distracted by the way his shirt pulls up a smidge as he takes two plates down. "You okay?"

"Huh?" I snap myself out of the wanderings my mind had taken, seeing him in my kitchen. "Yup. Mmhmm. I'm good." Just drooling over my hot boyfriend making himself at home in my apartment. I check to make sure my mouth is closed, before shooing him out of the way.

"Thank you, now go out there, there's not enough space in here for both of us." I push him towards the door. Trevor takes the hand pushing against his chest and tugs me forward, into his arms. At the last second, I put the tongs in my other hand down on the counter. With both hands free, I wrap them around his neck, his arms snaking around my waist.

Instead of bending down to kiss me like I expect, Trevor bends his knees to pick me up, bringing me up to his face. My squeak of surprise is swallowed by his lips. He takes his time, exploring me the same way I explore him. It's a good kiss.

"That's better," he says a moment later, letting me back down to the floor. "Just needed to make sure I didn't dream the last month."

My cheeks are so hot I'm afraid my face is going to combust, a riot of butterflies dipping and diving through my stomach, and if I smile any harder I might pull a muscle in my face. "You say that every time. Not a dream," I manage to get out. "But seriously, get out of the kitchen, there's no space." I cover my embarrassment and the giddiness washing over me with a sassy shake of my head and hip bump to send him towards the doorway.

Instead of leaving altogether, Trevor leans against the doorway, watching me. "You only pulled down two plates?" I turn, looking over my shoulder at him. He must see the confusion on my face.

"I already had dinner. I wouldn't want either of you to go hungry for my sake." His chuckle at my words from earlier has goosebumps rippling along my spine.

"Hey man, how's it going?" Martin's voice from beyond the door is the splash of cold water I need to finish getting our dinner sorted out. The two of them chat while I split the chicken and mashed potatoes I made onto the plates and carry them out to the living room.

Our place is too small for a dining room, so our coffee table does double duty. "Can one of you grab the salad and cutlery?" Putting the plates down, I move a couple issues of Dance magazine out of the way, before sitting on the floor, my back resting against the couch. A shadow and the familiar scent of mint and soap envelops me as Trevor sits on the couch behind me, his long legs on either side of me.

Martin settles into his usual spot to my right, the big bowl of salad and an extra plate in his hands. "There's enough salad to share, if you want some." He offers the plate to Trevor.

Dinner is cozy and full of laughter. Martin and Trevor tease me for wearing two pairs of socks, I tease them for inhaling their food. Turning back to look at Trevor, leaning against his leg while I feed him a bite of the mashed potatoes and chicken I cooked, is familiar and new all at once. Seeing his eyes close as he takes the bite, the little hum of appreciation he makes—all of it has me giddy. I could live off that little noise, but they both insist I finish my meal. Well, I finish most of it and give Trevor the last few bites. Mostly so I can hear that hum again.

"I'll wash up," Martin offers as we finish eating. "You two are so adorable it's sickening. I'm going to go before I lose my dinner."

My outraged protest is drowned out by Trevor's laugh. He doesn't give me time to stew on it though. Instead he leans forward, wrapping his arms around my shoulders, burying his nose in the back of my neck. His deep inhale tickles before my insides melt at the sensation of his lips tracing the sensitive skin there.

Pulling my arm out from under his, I let my head loll to one side while my free arm lazily reaches back to tangle my fingers in his hair. We stay like that for a long moment, not speaking. Just his lips and nose tracing along my skin, my fingers tugging at his hair.

"Hannah..." Trevor's whisper against my neck sends a shiver down my spine.

"Mmmmm," I hum in response. Words are hard and stupid. I just want to *feel* right now.

"Hannah..." Trevor tries again, the tiny kisses he's pressing along the outside of my ear making it too hard to do anything but sit here like a rag doll. I could move if I wanted to. But I don't want to.

"Why are we talking?" I manage to murmur. Turning my face, I catch the underside of his chin with my lips, pressing my own kisses along his jaw. His Adam's apple is so close, it vibrates against my temple as he growls.

A metallic crash from the kitchen makes me jolt, slamming the bridge of my nose against his jaw. His teeth snap shut and a second later he's gasping.

"Ow, ow, ow, ow, ow." I gasp at the intense pain across my face, my eyes watering.

Trevor is lisping a series of curses under his breath, his eyes screwed shut.

"Are you okay?" I manage to get out as the pain subsides. Opening my eyes, Trevor still has his eyes shut right, his mouth open, head tilted at an odd angle.

"I bit ma ton."

It takes a moment for his words to register. "You bit your tongue?"

He nods, scrunching his face in pain. He must have bit it hard. "Let me get you some ice."

Scrambling to my feet, I hurry into the kitchen, where Martin is busy washing dishes. I lean around him to grab an ice cube out of the freezer and wrap it in a paper towel.

Handing it over, I sit next to Trevor on the couch. "Well, that wasn't exactly how I was hoping the night would go…"

"Same," Trevor says, pulling the ice cube from his mouth.

"I didn't mean to head butt you." I almost make it to the end of my sentence before bursting out in a fit of giggles.

Trevor frowns for a moment before laughing with me. "Dat was not ma pan fa tunigh."

"Oh? And what *was* your plan?" I stand up from the couch, hip cocked, daring him to do something about my taunting words.

Instead of answering, Trevor's eyes narrow, his lean body tensing. He pulls one foot back, testing his weight on it, but not standing. Yet. I take off running a second before he gives chase. Half laughing, half squealing, I dodge his arm as he reaches for me, my only advantage that he's stuck using one arm instead of two. He's proven to me more than once that in a race there is no contest between us.

I dart into my bedroom a second ahead of Trevor, expecting him to grab me around the waist at every moment. When I've taken a few steps into my room and nothing happens I whirl to face him. He's leaning against my closed bedroom door, hands braced against it, ready to pounce. The laugh on my lips dies at the look on his face. With a growl, Trevor reaches out and pulls me towards him, turning us at the last second so my back presses against my closed door.

His arms hemming me in on either side, I expect him to lean down and kiss me like he has before. Instead, he trails his lips along my jaw, his breath icy cold against my hot skin as he moves from my jaw to my neck. Bending down, his lips graze my collar bone as he moves from one side to the other, kissing back up to my ear on the other side. I'm a melted puddle of goo, the door holding me up, the pain of banging my nose forgotten.

I reach out and slide my hands under the edge of his shirt, his skin warm under my hands. "Your hands are cold," Trevor growls in my ear.

"Sorry?" I don't stop exploring the soft ridges of his abs—yes, I discovered my boyfriend has abs the other day—as he keeps pressing his lips to my face, moving from my ear to my cheek and up to my temple. Trevor slides his arms higher up on the door to lean close, my hands slipping around and up his back. Reaching for him, I pull away from the door and he drops one arm to wrap it around my waist. Sliding his other hand up my spine towards my neck, Trevor sends warmth shooting through my whole body.

Which ends in a half-choked scream as he stuffs the ice cube I'd gotten him down the back of my shirt, his hold on me trapping it against my skin. "Ah!" I push under his arm, squirming and struggling to get rid of the ice and the freezing trail of water it left down my spine. "That was so mean. Now my shirt's all wet."

"You kids okay in there?" Martin's voice comes through the door, his suppressed laughter audible.

"Fine!" Trevor calls, grinning at me. "Just getting a little payback for biting my tongue in half."

"Your tongue seems to be working just fine now." I cross my arms and glare at Trevor, fighting to keep from smiling.

Taking a long step toward me, Trevor works his jaw. "Hmmm, is it? Maybe we should test it out. Just to make sure." Catching me around my waist, Trevor knocks us onto my bed where we make a very thorough inspection.

CHAPTER TWENTY-FIVE

Hannah

EACHING MY arms as far out in front of me as I can, I strain to hold the pose until the music dies away. A bead of sweat rolls down my temple and I tip my head so it doesn't land in my eye. All the other dancers with me relax as Mr. Popov claps his hands. My partner, Michael, releases me and I come down out of the arabesque I've been holding.

"Right, ladies, gentlemen. We have been asked to perform this at the Open House next week. Ladies, next time you are responsible for bringing a rehearsal tutu. Your partners need to practice, yes?" A dozen heads nod in agreement before Mr. Popov dismisses us.

"Did anyone hear from Lu? Did she get offered that spot at Memphis?" someone is asking as I cross the room to gather my stuff.

Sloane, no surprise, has an answer. "Chloe says she got offered a trainee position and isn't sure if she's going to take it or not."

"I wouldn't." Sloane, Emily, and Hayoon look up in surprise at my answer. "A trainee position at Memphis isn't going to offer her any better training than a second year here." I shrug. "Besides, their trainees have to pay to be in the program. If I'm going to pay for training, I'd rather do it here. More opportunities."

Hayoon pulls a towel out of her bag, dabbing the sweat off her face. My face is beet red and dripping in sweat, I'd be better off sticking my head under a faucet to cool down. Bright April sunshine pours in, the city visible through the picture windows. I love this studio, we're on the third floor so our view is mostly the tops of the trees. Now that everything is blooming, the green carpet soothes my eyes.

"That's true." Sloane takes a long drink from her water bottle, lounging against the floor. We have another rehearsal in fifteen minutes, so we're taking the chance to rest while we can. "Besides, this late in April, you know they're just trying to fill spots that didn't get accepted from the first round of offers in February. It would be one thing if it was an actual company position. But a trainee position? I'm with Hannah."

"Do we know who's staying next year?" I ask Sloane. "I assume you have a running list somewhere," I add, teasing her.

"As a matter of fact, it's all in here." Sloane taps her temple. "You're staying, right?"

I nod my head. "Yup. Martin got offered an apprenticeship so he's definitely staying. I don't know if he was more excited about being offered the spot or being able to quit working at the coffee shop." We all laugh at that, knowing we'd feel the same if it was us. I was lucky that my parents had money put aside for me to be here for a couple of years, knowing that this was more likely my future than college, but Martin had to work to pay his share of the rent. Being a paid member of the company means more sleep and less stress for him.

Trainee positions are often the equivalent of an unpaid internship, dancers pay to take them and in return get extra training and opportunities to perform. It's not much more than we get here. There is the odd company that pays their trainees, but it's rare.

"Mark and Annelize are joining CBC Two, lucky bitches," Emily says. A second company, or an apprentice company, at one of the big organizations is the Holy Grail for us. Not only are they paid positions, but it's a chance to experience being in a professional company on a smaller scale, but with the advantage of being attached to a major player in the ballet world. Spend a year or two there and you might get invited into the ranks of any number of world-class ballet companies.

We spend our break discussing who else is staying or leaving next year. The majority of our class is staying, only a lucky few are moving on already. Next year is when the real pressure to get a job offer starts, since PSB's professional school is meant to be just a year or two. If you can't get a job by then, maybe you won't ever get one and it's time to rethink your future plans.

I'm being very careful not to think too hard about the future, although Marco's hints at our meeting last month simmer in the back of my mind. I'm focused on doing the best I can right now, not worrying about what happens next. If I start down that path, I'll do something stupid. I've been stupid enough already, right now I need to live in the moment and enjoy it while I can. That's what Trevor tells me at least once a week. When I inevitably have a freak out over what happens next.

Speaking of Trevor, he's waiting for me at the doors when I walk through them with Martin at the end of the day. "You ready?" He tucks my hand into his elbow and takes my bag from me. I hand my car keys over to Martin so he can go home. For once I took the time to shower and change out of my dance clothes before leaving, knowing Trevor was planning to pick me up and take me out on some mysterious date.

"Yup!" I reach up to kiss his cheek and follow him down the street. "So where are we going?"

"First, we're getting dinner. I assume you're hungry?" Grinning, he pulls open the door of the sushi place near the theater complex where I spend my days.

"You assume correctly." With a smile at the owner, who knows me well at this point, we make our way to one of the tables in the back.

Once we're settled, Trevor leans back in his chair. "So, I have some news."

Nerves squeeze my belly. "Is it good news?"

Smiling, Trevor leans forward to take my hand. "Yes, it's good news. At least, I think it's good news. Hopefully, you'll agree."

My hand shakes a little as I take a sip of my water. What am I so nervous about?

"I got acceptance letters from two places today." He grins. "University of Oregon and University of Washington."

"Really? That's amazing." I pick up my water glass and clink it against his. "Congratulations!"

Trevor takes a sip of his own water. "So, I have a question for you."

"Yeah?"

"Do you know if you're staying here another year? Or is it still up in the air?"

His eyes search mine. Is he looking to see if I'm going to run away again? Searching for any hint of fear in me?

"You know? For once in my life, deciding what to do next was easy. I'm staying here." The relief on Trevor's face at my declaration is instant. "It finally feels like I've found my groove here, I'm not ready to leave just yet. Besides, if there's even a chance they're considering me for the company after next year, I'd be stupid to leave now."

"And...if I said I was choosing to go to University of Washington, so I could stay here, that would be good news, right? It wouldn't freak you out?" He doesn't give me a chance to answer before he keeps talking. "Because I'm not choosing to go there just for you. Yes, it's partly because of you, but it's not just because of you. They have a great engineering school, and their cross-country team is really good too. They offered me a scholarship and a spot on the team. Oregon has an amazing team, but I don't think I want to be competing on that level. I'm not my dad you know? And there's my dad too. I don't want to be so far away, just in case. What if something happens and my mom needs me? Or Maggie needs me? Or you need me?"

He stops speaking to suck in a ragged breath and it hits me just how much I've damaged his trust in me. He shouldn't be scared to tell me he's choosing the college closest to me. My boyfriend, who I love, is worried that I'm going to be mad he's choosing to stay nearby. Taking a sip from his glass, he eyes me over the rim. This is my chance to prove to him that I'm in this for real this time.

"Well, considering the fact that I love you…" I've never seen Trevor's eye go so wide as he chokes on his water. "Yeah, I'd say that was a good thing." I finish with a laugh as he sputters and drips water all over the table.

"Did you—" Trevor's question is cut off by the server coming to take our order. I have no idea what I order. All I can see is the happiness shining out of Trevor's eyes, and all I hear is the thundering of my own heart. I'm not worried he doesn't feel the same way. After he accidentally told me a month ago he hasn't said it again, but I know. I know deep in my soul that he loves me.

"We'll be right back," Trevor says to the server after he orders. I wasn't paying attention, lost in the wonder of what I've said, he's said, what it all means. "Come here." Trevor is standing next to my chair, holding out a hand. I take it and he pulls me out of my seat, threading shaking fingers between mine.

I follow him through the restaurant to the little hallway that leads to a back door. We step out into an alley, the brick wall of the building next door the only thing I have a chance to see before I'm being pressed against the wall of the sushi place and Trevor's lips are on mine. His hands cup my face, his thumbs caressing my cheeks.

There's something about this kiss that's different from every other kiss we've shared. He pours himself into me and I pour myself into him in exchange. My heart and soul are being stitched to his, irrevocably tied together. It's no longer him and me, it's us. No matter what happens next, we're in it together.

Gripping his waist, I drag my hands up his back to pull myself closer. Sliding his hands into my hair, Trevor deepens the kiss, his tongue sweeping against mine. His fingers tangle in my hair as we explore every inch of each other. And even though it's not new, it is new. Knowing he loves me and I love him, that neither of us is running away, holding anything back, makes everything new.

It's still not enough, I need to be closer. Every molecule of air between us is too far. I'm pressing myself as close as I can, standing on my toes and pulling myself up by his shoulders. Suddenly, his hands are slipping under my hips and I'm being picked up. My legs wrap around him without conscious thought as I pull away from our kiss with a gasp.

"I love you," I whisper as Trevor kisses my neck.

"I love you," he murmurs into my skin.

"I love you," I breathe into his ear before pressing my lips into the soft space behind it.

"I love you," he groans, his fingers digging into my hips.

I tear myself away from him, the words bubbling up from deep in my heart. "I'm never running away again, I promise. As long as we're together, I'm not scared of anything."

Looking down at him, I study his face. Pure happiness shines back at me from his eyes. I push a stray curl out of his face, turning it into a caress. Closing his eyes, Trevor leans his cheek into my hand, before turning to press a kiss into the palm of my hand. Despite the fact that he's still carrying me like the koala I've become, all the tension leaves his body in a rush. I unwrap my legs and slither down his torso until my feet find the pavement. It's my turn to cup his face, pulling him down to rest his forehead against mine, content to do nothing more than share oxygen with him.

"It's you and me, okay? No matter what happens, we're in it together." My whispered words fill the space between us. "All the big, scary things? We'll do them together. I promise."

For once, I'm the one with all the words. Trevor breathes with me. Silent. The relief etched on his face crystalizing the promise I made to him, not to let him down, not to run away again.

Finally, he presses a kiss to my forehead and straightens. "That sounds like an excellent plan. Now let's go eat, I can hear your stomach growling from here."

After we finish eating, a dinner full of spontaneous grins and laughter, Trevor drags me outside. "Where are we going?" Hooking my arm in his, he pulls me back towards the theater where I've spent most of my day. "Why are we going back to the theater?"

"Because, we're going to a show." Trevor pulls two tickets out of his pocket and hands them to me.

"For real?" I squeal.

Trevor twirls me under his arm, spinning me with the finger hold I taught him. "Yup, we're watching *The Princess Bride* with a live orchestra."

I do a little pas de basque step in circles around him, giddy with excitement. Laughing, Trevor drags me, still dancing, towards the box office. "Before we go inside, I have one more very important question for you, Hannah O'Brian." He pulls me to stand in front of him, hands on my shoulders, looking down on me with a serious expression. "I know you don't care about the whole 'normal high school' thing, but it *is* my senior year and I care. At least a little bit. I know it's early, but I feel like I need to lock this down before something else happens…" Trevor slides his hands down my arms to slip into mine. "Will you come to prom with me?"

Thinking of the dress stowed away in a garment bag in my closet, I grin. "I would love to be your date to prom."

CHAPTER TWENTY-SIX

Trevor

"**D**AYUM, TREV. You were not kidding." Derek whistles as our dates help themselves to punch across the room.

"Eyes to yourself." I punch him on the arm, just hard enough to remind him where to keep his gaze. My shoulder pulls uncomfortably at the fabric of my rented tux.

He punches me right back, knocking my boutonniere crooked. "Hey, knock it off. It took us *ages* to get this thing pinned on."

"Is that why you were late?" Matt slaps me on the back instead then winces at the tight fit of his own tux. How do people wear these things?

I laugh at the memory. "Oh no. That was because Hannah was on a panicked Facetime call with her friends and Martin, trying to do her hair and makeup. Apparently, they're all amazing at makeup and hairdos that are meant for stage, not so great at it for something like this." I nod my head at the decor in the hotel ballroom where we're gathered. Silver, gold, and black balloons, streamers, and centerpieces glitter in the dim light. A

DJ is playing top-forty hits while half the kids dance, the other half are standing around the perimeter of the ballroom, like the three of us.

I'd passed the time waiting for her on my phone, looking back through pictures of Hannah and I over the last few months. At the movies, at the park, her red face when I'd dragged her out on a hike with me. Lots of pictures of us sitting right there on the same couch I was camped on while she finished getting ready.

But every second I'd had to wait for her, tonight and over the last year, was worth it the moment Hannah emerged from her bedroom. The floor length, peachy-pink dress was only a few shades darker than her fair skin, the flowing fabric rippling with each step she took. Silver beads and jewels dotted the front, covering her chest in a lacy pattern. But when she'd turned around, that was the moment my jaw truly dropped. The dress came no higher than her waist at the back. From her shoulders to her waist was covered in loops and rows of pure sparkle.

Punch in hand, Hannah crosses the room to us, Derek and Matt's dates trailing behind her. I can't tear my eyes off her. My girl is a goddess, dripping with diamonds, silky fabric swaying at the slightest movement. She may look like a waif, eight hours of dancing a day burns off every calorie she eats, but she walks like she owns the very oxygen in the room. All the other girls here look like newborn giraffes, wobbling in their heels, but not my girl.

"Why are we punching each other?" Hannah asks, stopping in front of me, offering me a sip from her cup.

Matt abandons us, grabbing his date and pulling her onto the dance floor.

"It doesn't matter." I wrap my arm around her waist, pulling her close so I can kiss her. Turning to Derek's date in an attempt to change the subject I ask, "So, Amanda, where are you headed next year?" When you're in a room full of high school seniors, it's a pretty safe question.

"Oh, I'm off to Texas A&M, what about you?"

"I'm going to Washington, same as Derek." I jerk my head towards my friend, there's a large number of us headed to Washington in the fall. "What are you going to major in?"

"Marine Biology. I know Derek is doing Political Science, what about you?"

"Biology and Mechanical Engineering." I trail my fingers down the back of Hannah's arm, enjoying the way her breath catches and goosebumps appear on the back of her neck.

Amanda nods her blonde head before turning to Hannah. "What about you?"

Hannah bumps her hip against mine, a warning not to distract her, and I hide my grin. "I'm going to do a class or two at the community college. I'm a student at Pacific Sound Ballet, so no college for me. At least, not now. Maybe in a few years."

Finishing up her punch, Hannah sets the cup down on the empty table behind us. "It's not Tchaikovsky, but I think I can dance to this too. Come on." Pulling me to the dance floor, Hannah turns, slipping her hands around my neck as I rest my hands on her hips. "Sorry, I just didn't want to talk about college. Is that how all your conversations go these days? What college are you going to? What's your major going to be?"

I snag her free hand, turning her to face me, picking up the beat with our feet. "Yeah, kind of. I guess that's what normal people do when your high school graduation is only two weeks away."

"Seems overrated to me." She sticks her tongue out then starts moving to the music. Her hips sway from side to side under my hands, her fingers teasing the hair at the back of my neck. Knowing she'll be lost in the music soon, I let her lead, following her movements but not caring what I do. My ballerina is going to dance her heart out no matter what I do, I'm just here to enjoy it with her.

Between dancing, kissing, and the music, we don't talk much. The way she's smiling up at me needs no other decoration. She switches as seamlessly as the DJ between hip-shaking, swing dancing, and the goofiest old-school moves I've ever seen, laughing at herself and me as we trip over each other and our own feet. I could care less what we look like, this is the most fun I've ever had with her. Matt and his date ignore us from a few feet away, but Derek and Amanda join us after a few songs, making their own moves up to mirror our ridiculous dancing.

Finally, the DJ changes it up and plays a slow song giving me a chance to pull Hannah into my arms. Pink Sweat$ "Heaven" plays around us as we sway, the lyrics echoing my thoughts. "Hey," I whisper, looking down at Hannah.

"Hey." She smiles up at me, her eyes trusting and filled with happiness.

"Have I told you yet how amazing you look?"

"Only two dozen times. But you can tell me again." A twinkle of mischief flashes in her eyes and I have to kiss her again.

"You look beautiful. And I'm so glad you came with me."

Hannah's spine straightens and she looks around the ballroom. "You know, I'm glad I came too. Maybe real high school isn't *all* bad." She relaxes back against my chest, where she fits perfectly. Where she belongs.

I have no idea what life is going to throw our way, what moves Hannah's career will make, but it doesn't matter. We'll face them together. I'm not letting her go and, finally, I know she won't either.

"I love you, Hannah."

Hannah squeezes me before answering. "I love you too, Trevor."

Trevor

6 YEARS LATER...

"YOU READY, son?" The reassuring weight of my dad's hand dropping onto my shoulder snaps me out of my stunned silence. Watching the love of your life fake die on stage will do that to you.

I pat my jacket pocket, reassuring myself it's still in there. "Yup." I stand with everyone else applauding, my palms already stinging.

Three years ago, when Hannah had been offered a soloist contract by *The* Classical Ballet Company, how could I do anything but support her going? The culmination of her dreams since she was a little girl were worth any sacrifice, even if it meant that my senior year at UW we'd be on opposite coasts. Her last year as a student at PSB and her first two years with the company there had been a whirlwind for us both, me getting settled into college life, her learning how to navigate being a professional dancer.

But I moved here to Manhattan to be with her after graduation and haven't regretted a moment since. I'm working at an amazing company designing medical devices helping people like my dad and I'll be running in the New York City marathon for the second time in a few weeks. We've made some amazing and interesting friends here. Hannah being promoted to principal this year is another dream of ours coming true. In fact, there's only one thing missing from our life together. But I can be patient.

Three years in the limbo of a soloist contract wasn't easy on Hannah. The occasional featured role in a contemporary piece led to the odd chance to step into a principal role while they were touring and someone was injured, but she'd hungered for the chance to prove herself. I'd had to talk her down from going back to the studio for extra late-night rehearsals more than once when she was convinced that was all that was standing between her and a principal contract.

But tonight is her debut as The Classical Ballet Company's newest principal. Not only that, it's her debut as Juliet—her dream role since that first walk on part as a student at PSB. Trust me, we've had innumerable late-night conversations about it.

Hannah's mom and Leslie are laughing at the teary mess they've become, not that Katy and Olivia aren't doing the same thing, wiping their eyes when they think no one is looking. I can't even see Lisa's face, it's buried in Hunter's chest, pregnancy hormones setting her off from the first step Hannah took onstage. We're all clapping and crying and laughing. Hannah's parents, Maggie, my parents, Mike and Leslie, the girls, and Hunter.

Yeah, I'm crying too. But they're happy tears. I promise.

I've learned better than to whistle or cheer for her when she comes to take a bow with her partner Sergei, but that doesn't stop me calling out a "Brava!" or two with everyone else. Despite the glow of sweat and exhaustion on her face, pure happiness lights up her eyes as my beautiful girl takes in the audience. Her eyes come to rest on me for a moment and her smile widens, just for me. For us.

For every day, every moment we've shared. The birthdays we've celebrated both together and apart. The adventures we've gone on around the world. Moving in together, moving to New York. Tonight is just one more moment to add to the lifetime of moments I'm going to spend loving this woman.

There's a ring in my pocket and a question I can't wait another moment to ask her.

Hannah

I MAY NOT have fallen at first sight like Juliet does for Romeo, but I know what it feels like to be young and in love. How overwhelming, all-encompassing, scary, and exhilarating it is. I've been channeling the feelings of those first few months with Trevor—the giddy excitement that made it hard to think straight—this whole performance. He still gives me butterflies, but after almost seven years together, growing up and tackling the world as a team, the giddiness has transformed. Now he's my rock, the safe place I turn to when I need comfort or courage, just as I am for him.

My legs and feet are aching as I lay on the platform, the booming conclusion of Prokofiev's score permeating the air around me. This is the hardest part, I'm beyond exhausted from all the dancing I've done already. When Sergei pulls me up into an embrace, playing dead and keeping my eyes closed takes every ounce of my concentration and will power. He drags my limp body across the stage, the boneless lifts and drops, carefully rehearsed so I don't hit my head on the ground, are a delicate balance of acting and technique.

Once I've been placed back on the platform, staying "dead" while my Romeo finishes his part is torture. When the music changes I twitch my fingers, the very last moments ahead of me. Poor Sergei lays limp on the floor, gritting his teeth as he tries not to breathe too hard and shatter the illusion.

I pictured him as Trevor once in rehearsal, but I ended up crying for real and was too upset to try it again. I tuck my love for Trevor away in my heart and let myself wallow in the feelings for my pretend love.

I throw myself into the ending—seeing the dead bodies, trying to wake Romeo, hunting for the vial of poison. Time moves at both lighting speed and crawls as I make each movement. My silent scream comes from the depths of my soul, taking a year but a moment to leave my body.

A real sob escapes me as I plunge the fake dagger into my stomach. The adrenaline of tonight ebbs as I crawl my way across the stage, dragging my genuinely limp body over the platform to drape myself in a last gasping reach for my Romeo's hand. I let the applause of the audience wash over me as I lay stretched out on the platform, arms dangling loose overhead. This was worth it all. This moment right here.

I've been working for this moment my whole life. Every class, every rehearsal, every correction. Every good day, every bad day. Every time I dragged my exhausted body home to fall into bed, every muscle that ached, they were for this moment.

When the curtains close, I roll to my feet, Sergei next to me. I'm in a haze from the extreme emotions I've put myself through on stage tonight. Other dancers come streaming onto the stage to take their places for our bows, the mood still somber. The curtain call is a blur. The thunder of applause mixes with the hammering of my heart in my chest and the gasping breaths I can't seem to control. I can't make out any of the audience, my eyes too blurred with tears, my cheeks aching from the relieved smile stretched across my face.

It's only when they drop the curtain and pull it back for Sergei and me to take one last bow that my vision clears enough to see them. The people I love most in the world, standing in a row, grinning, laughing, crying, and smiling up at me. Shock and giddiness join the adrenaline running through me when I spot Ms. Parker and Mike, Trevor's parents, Maggie, and my girls in the audience, clapping hard enough to bruise their hands. I knew my parents were coming, but I didn't know about the rest. When my eyes lock with Trevor's, his eyes glassy and the widest smile on his face, I can't look anywhere else. A happy, relieved sob catches me by surprise as I drop into another curtsey, my love for him and my family overwhelming everything else.

Finally, Sergei leads me back behind the curtain and the pages let it go, officially ending the ballet. My fellow dancers and ballet mistress come rushing out of the wings, swamping us with congratulations and hugs.

"Thank you," I whisper to Sergei, reaching up to hug him hard. He was promoted last year and has been a good friend to me, helping me get over my nerves before the first rehearsals.

"You were beautiful tonight. I'm so glad I got to share it with you." He kisses my hand and gives me one more hug before wandering off to find his girlfriend Katerina. Bella and Skye push their way through the crowd of dancers, the principals I've admired from afar since I was at PSB who now share a dressing room with me.

I hug everyone I can reach while I wait for my people to make their way backstage. Trevor knows how to get back here, the theater staff good friends with him by now. They should be after he rolled up his sleeves to help fix a busted hydraulic lift before a performance of Cinderella last year. One of the stage managers is running the marathon with him next month.

The enormous bouquet of flowers in my arms was sent by him. It's going to tower over all the other flowers in my dressing room sent by friends and supporters. Even the ones Martin sent me from London aren't this big. Bella plucks the flowers out of my arms declaring she's taking them to the dressing room for me. As she walks away, the click of heels and a cry of "Banana!" has me whirling, right into the arms of my girls.

"When? How? You're here!" I squeeze the best surprise I could have asked for, my three best friends here to share tonight.

Katy, Lisa, and Olivia laugh as they hug me back. Hunter waits nearby, pulling me in for a quick hug before Lisa steps back into his protective embrace. Her wedding ring glints as she pats the arm Hunter wraps around her waist, his hand resting on the bump there.

"Like there was any chance we'd miss this," Katy says, poking my side, as always.

"When did you guys fly in? How long are you staying?" I hug Katy and Olivia one more time before turning to hug Ms. Parker. "When did you get here Ms. Parker?"

Laughing, Ms. Parker gives me the eyebrow. "I'm pretty sure you can call me Leslie at this point, Hannah."

"Oh god, no." I laugh. "I don't think I can. Not even dancing in your costume will make that possible."

"You have mine?" Ms. Parker, Leslie, gasps, reaching for the back of my dress. She undoes the top hook to look at the fabric label sewn inside. *Leslie P.* is written in faded sharpie on it. *Hannah O.* written right below, in fresh ink. Tears fill her eyes when she looks back up at me.

"When I had my costume fitting, they pulled this one out and I knew I had to wear it. So you could be with me tonight, no matter what." More tears flow as we embrace, my heart overflowing with gratitude for her.

"The Quinn contingent arrived a couple of hours ago," Hunter interrupts the tear-fest, "Our flight from Houston got delayed or we would have been here earlier. Jack sends his love, by the way. And told me to tell you there are a pair of tickets for you the next time he's playing the Giants." Trevor will be excited since Jack plays for his beloved Seattle Seahawks these days. Turning from Ms. Parker to my very best friend in the whole world, I pull her away from Hunter for another hug.

"Can you stay? When is your fall season?" I ask Lisa. After they graduated from USC, Lisa was offered a position at Houston Ballet, which worked out when Hunter got a job at the Johnson Space Center. If any of us could have written the perfect life for those two that would be it. Lisa's working her way through the corps and soloist roles at Houston while Hunter does his real-life rocket scientist thing at NASA. The only shock they'd given anyone was when they came home married from a whirlwind weekend in Vegas their junior year of college. We all suspect that it had something to do with a bet they lost to Jack.

Lisa and I may still happily be with Hunter and Trevor, but Katy and JJ broke up years ago, before Katy even graduated from high school. Olivia and Tyler lasted into their freshman year at UCLA, but when Olivia got invited to tour with an up-and-coming pop star as a backup dancer, they'd decided to go their separate ways. They're still good friends though.

"I'm out for the season." Lisa pats her growing belly. "I popped faster than anyone expected."

"Jack is convinced it's twins," Katy adds, waving at one of the dancers walking by.

"Is there a bet?"

"Of course there's a bet!"

I make eye contact with Lisa, who grins. "What's the bet?" Mrs. Quinn's rule about no betting with money still stands. Bets with Jack have gotten more and more ridiculous as we've gotten older. Trevor learned his lesson his junior year at UW, when Jack's Colorado Buffaloes beat the Huskies and Trevor was forced to show up to Thanksgiving dinner in head-to-toe black and gold gear. His dad still hasn't let him live it down.

"Winner gets to pick the middle name."

"You are a brave lady." Olivia shakes her head. "I got here super early this morning, I took the red-eye from LAX last night."

"How's LA? Anything new on the horizon?" I want to know how my friends are but I'm antsy to see Trevor. He's always the first one to congratulate me after a show but he's nowhere to be seen. Where is he?

Maggie sneaks in for a hug while Olivia speaks. She's become the little sister I never had, following in my footsteps at PSB. Last summer she came to CBS's summer intensive and stayed with Trevor and me. I wrap an arm around her, mostly to keep her from hunting down Skye and Bella for autographs.

"My agency is good, I'm still happily dating every somewhat decent man Los Angeles offers up. Oh!" She lights up with whatever news she has. "Guess who just got tasked with casting the dancers for Baz Luhrmann's new movie?"

"That's amazing news, Livvy!" One of my old dressing roommates sneaks in a quick hug while Olivia and Katy give each other significant looks. Seriously, where is Trevor? "What's going on?"

"Well, I have a surprise for you..." Katy rubs her hands on her legs. Why is she nervous? "Remember how you guys had an opening for a new massage therapist?"

"The company? Yeah, poor Cedric has been swamped since Pauline left. Why?"

"Guess who got the job!" Olivia squeals, cutting Katy off.

"What? *You're* the new massage therapist everyone is talking about? Why didn't you tell me you'd applied?"

Katy shrugs, looking sheepish. "I didn't want you to be disappointed when I didn't get it. I didn't think I had a chance, I only applied on a whim."

Pulling away from Lisa, I squeeze her in a giant hug. "I can't believe this. This is going to be amazing! But what about your PT program?" Katy had gotten her degree in physical therapy and last I heard was in a Doctorate program in Texas, near Hunter and Lisa. She'd ended up getting her massage therapy license last year to help make ends meet while she was still in school. As her occasional guinea pig, I know first-hand how good she is at it.

"I'm transferring my credits to a place here. It might take me a little longer to finish, but I couldn't pass up the opportunity to work at CBC. Olivia is staying with me for the week."

"You have a place already? How did you pull that off? It took Trevor and I ages to find a place." My friends crowd around me, hemming me in.

Katy ducks her head. "Trevor helped me. We wanted to surprise you!" She holds her hands up in defense at my glare. "Don't be mad at him, I asked him to keep it a secret."

"Any more secrets or surprises?" I ask, trying to see around them to the stage door. Where is he?

With the biggest grins I've ever seen stretching across their faces, my friends step aside, revealing the one person I've been dying to see since the curtain dropped.

"Just one."

He's on one knee, holding out a black velvet box, a single diamond solitaire nestled inside.

I didn't think I could be happier than I was a minute ago, but my heart is about to burst out of my chest from pure joy. I'm crying, laughing, nodding my head, and Trevor hasn't even asked me a question yet. My mom and Mrs. Stanley are crying together with Leslie. Maggie is bouncing on her toes, sandwiched between my dad and Trevor's. Lisa, Katy, and Olivia are grinning and crying. A hush has fallen over everyone backstage while I wait for Trevor to speak. He has to clear his throat a few times before the words come.

"Hannah O'Brian. I love you more than words can say. I would give you the world if I could, make all your dreams come true. You are the most amazing person I've ever met." Trevor stops to clear his throat again, a tear rolling down his cheek before he continues. "You're my best friend and my favorite person in the whole world. Will you do the big things, the little things, the scary things, and all the amazing things the world has to offer with me? As my wife?"

Sniffing back my own tears, I pull Trevor to his feet. "You couldn't get rid of me if you tried, Trevor Stanley. That's the easiest question anyone has ever asked me. Yes. Yes. A million and one times, yes." I grab his cheeks and kiss him. It's wet, sloppy, and perfect.

"I love you. I'm never leaving you." I whisper as he slips the ring on my finger. "Who knew all my dreams could come true on the same day?"

The End

ACKNOWLEDGEMENTS

OW DO I say goodbye to these characters? These people who live in my head and are made of bits and pieces of my soul? I imagine them all living their lives after all this. Hannah and Trevor are happy in NYC, with a new dog that chews up Hannah's pointe shoes on the regular and Katy spending as many nights at their place as her own. Lisa and Hunter off in Houston, the twins (it's totally twins) causing havoc. Grandma and Grandpa Quinn come to visit regularly, Uncle Jack pops in unannounced for visits whenever he can, and Obaasan and Ojiisan have a weekly Zoom date with them. Olivia I can picture jetting off to a new location weekly, running her agency and looking out for a slew of dancers, Hannah included. In fact, I bet that Olivia snags Hannah perfume and high-end clothing endorsement deals on the regular, to Trevor's delight and Hannah's utter embarrassment whenever they see her face plastered on a subway advertisement.

When I got the idea for these books, I spent a long time worried whether they were too light, too unrealistic, too fluffy. Most books you read about ballet are full of back-stabbing, eating disorders and tragedy. I didn't want to write that. Yes it exists in the ballet world, far more than it should. But I wanted my books to present an idea of what *could* be. That teachers don't have to get the best of their students through fear and intimidation, that dancers can have a healthy relationship with food and their bodies. That back-stabbing happens but so does love and camaraderie. Most importantly, I wanted to show a place where the joy of dancing is about more than the tortured artist stereotype. That you don't have to be poor, starving and unhealthy to make great art. Great art can come from love, happiness and a place of security.

People have asked me if these characters are based on people I know in real life. The short answer is no—Hannah, Olivia, Katy and Lisa are unique. If anything, they all have a little bit of me in them. But also they are an amalgamation of my friends and students in all my years in the studio and something else entirely themselves. I could list hundreds of names and it wouldn't be enough. Just know, if you see yourself in any of these characters, I hope you feel the love that I wrote them with and know you are treasured.

How do I thank everyone who's helped me go from nothing to a completed series?

Melissa — how do I thank the woman who's been by my side my whole life? We've held each other up when life was too hard, we've celebrated when life surprised us with joy. Whether it's been a day since we've talked, or a year, it doesn't matter. We call each other out on our crap and hold each other up when we're too tired to do it ourselves. Through boys, ballet, babies and moves, you've been there for me. A piece of my heart is always with you. Everyone should have a friend who knows them inside and out like you do.

Lasairiona — how can I thank you enough? You saw something in me that I couldn't.You've held my hand through my fledgling author bumbles, dragged me kicking and screaming into the big kids pool and whenever I think I'm full of crap and no one cares, you tell me I'm not terrible while teaching me how to be better. While I would be happy to hide in the shadows, tentatively poking my nose out to offer up a few words here or there, you drag me out into the light and make me speak up. Everyone should have someone who believes in them as much as you believe in me.

My author tribe—Alina, Stella, Norma, Danielle, Robyn, Battie, Hattie and everyone else in RWR. Thank you for lifting me up when I needed a laugh or a reference check and for going through this crazy author journey with me. No one understands what it's like quite like the people in the trenches with you.

My family—When you're lucky enough to have a family as supportive as mine, it makes the journey of life so much richer. Thank you Mom and Dad for handing out copies of *Toe to Toe* to everyone you meet on your travels, sometimes whether they want it or not. Patti, I couldn't ask for a better mother-in-law, thank you for your endless support and encouragement. My siblings and siblings in law, thank you for all your support, even when you have no idea what I'm up to.

The boys and men who taught me what love is, and what it isn't—Life is about the journey and I'm so glad I walked part of it with you. You know who you are. A piece of my heart will always be with you.

My amazing daughter—thank you for being you, in all your messy, contradictory glory. I see so much of myself in you, and yet, you are so completely yourself. You are the most amazing kid I've ever had the privilege to know. The fact that I get to be your mom is a gift. I'll always be there for you, for the cuddles, the jokes, the "power ups," and the tears. Nothing could make me love you less.

I'm going to thank some people who don't know they need to be thanked, in fact, they probably don't even know these books exist (but I'm thanking them anyway). Ausdancersoverseas, The Hard Corps Podcast, Conversations on Dance, Movers Shakers Makers, Final Bow for Yellowface, The Lazy Ballerina, Twin Talks Ballet—thank you for speaking out on things in the ballet world that need to change. We all love it enough to want it to be better, don't stop pushing and questioning. If you want to listen to people who are in the trenches, working to make the ballet world a kinder, safer place, give these people a listen.

And of course (I always save him for last) —I couldn't have done any of this without the support and encouragement of my husband. He feeds me, cheers for me, forces me to leave the house on occasion, and has acquired a sixth sense for when to come home with wine and chocolate.

Hannah and her girls may have their story finished, but I'm not done writing. Look for a brand new series in Summer 2021! You won't want to miss this one!

Keep up with all my news by signing up for my newsletter, following me on TikTok, Instagram or Facebook

Heart to Heart

NEWSLETTER:

https://sendfox.com/penelopefreedbooks

TIKTOK:

https://www.tiktok.com/@penelopefreed

INSTAGRAM:

https://www.instagram.com/penelopefreedbooks/

FACEBOOK:

https://www.facebook.com/groups/enpointewithpenelope

ABOUT THE AUTHOR

Penelope Freed lives in the Pacific Northwest where you can find her learning how to drive in the rain, walking her dog and making a mess in the kitchen. Her husband and daughter think she's a little bit bonkers and really hate it when she dances embarrassingly in public.

Which she does, often.

After a lifetime in the ballet world, Penelope decided to start writing down the stories in her head instead of narrating her ballet classes with them—her former students are very thankful for this decision. Now, Penelope writes stories about dreamers, just like she is, who are willing to do whatever it takes to make those dreams come true.

Made in the USA
Middletown, DE
16 June 2024

55871843R00177